WITCHBANE

MORGAN BRICE

CONTENTS

Witchbane	v
Prologue	1
1. Seth	13
2. Sonny	22
3. Seth	31
4. Sonny	37
5. Seth	53
6. Evan	63
7. Seth	72
8. Evan	84
9. Seth	96
10. Evan	112
11. Seth	132
12. Evan	144
13. Seth	151
14. Evan	156
15. Seth	160
16. Evan	174
17. Seth	182
18. Evan	191
19. Seth	200
20. Evan	205
21. Seth	213
22. Evan	220
Epilogue	227
Acknowledgments	233
About the Author	235

WITCHBANE

By Morgan Brice

ISBN: 978-1-939704-68-9
Copyright © 2018 by Gail Z. Martin. All rights reserved.

The right of the author to be identified as the author of this work has been asserted in accordance with the Copyright, Designs and Patents Act 1988.

All rights reserved. No part of this publication may be reproduced, stored in a retrieval system, or transmitted, in any form or by any means, electronic, mechanical, photocopying, recording or otherwise, without the prior permission of the copyright owners.

This is a work of fiction. Any resemblance to actual persons (living or dead), locales and incidents are either coincidental or used fictitiously. Any trademarks used belong to their owners. No infringement is intended.

Cover art by Lou Harper.

Darkwind Press is an imprint of DreamSpinner Communications, LLC

Dedicated to my family, for their support and encouragement. And to readers, who are always looking for a new story, and thereby make it possible for writers to keep writing.

PROLOGUE
TWO YEARS AGO

"...AND THEN I SAID, 'IF YOU THINK YOU CAN HEAR COLORS, YOU'VE gotta lay off the energy drinks!'" Seth Tanner finished his punch line.

Jesse laughed hard enough to bring tears to his eyes. The one-liners had been going non-stop for most of the afternoon.

Jesse held up a hand. "Dude, give me a break. Let me catch my breath!" He flopped down on his bed with exaggerated drama, flinging his long arms out to either side for effect. Just like he used to do in the worst of his tween years, only now at twenty-two, the move was intentionally comical.

Seth threw a pillow at him, catching Jesse in the stomach. "Come on. We've gotta finish packing. This is going to be epic!"

Jesse groaned and sat up, tossing the pillow back in a half-hearted attempt to hit his brother in the face.

"Can we get a green film to put over the flashlight?" Jesse asked with a grin. "Then when we record with my phone, we can both keep saying, 'did you hear something' like those phony ghost hunters on TV. I tell you, if we do it right, we'll get a bazillion hits on YouTube and go viral. Then we can start our own channel and never have to do real work." He followed up his daydream with a cheesy grin.

"Like the time you decided to let everyone watch you play video games live online and got one follower. Who turned out to be Mom."

"Hey, don't dis my game mojo," Jesse replied with mock indignation. "And for the record, Mom was impressed."

Seth reached out and ruffled his brother's dark blond hair. For once in their lives, Jesse's was shorter than his. After six years in the army, Seth was home for good, and that included growing his hair out longer than military regulation.

God, he'd missed Jesse. No one could mistake them for anything but brothers: Same tall, broad-shouldered lanky build like their dad, same dishwater blond hair, and brown eyes, with the thin face and high cheekbones they got from their mom. Both of them stood six foot three, within a fraction of an inch of each other. With Jesse's growth spurt and the workouts he'd been doing while Seth was gone, there wasn't as big a difference in their builds as Seth expected, comparing a twenty-four-year-old former soldier to a twenty-two-year-old newly-minted college graduate.

"Come on, dweeb," Seth said as Jesse ducked away from getting his hair mussed. "We want to be out at the tunnel before dark so we can get our camp set up."

"*Tunnel* sounds so boring," Jesse mock-whined. "We're going to stake out the legendary Hell Gate of Brazil, Indiana, and record the otherworldly results for posterity!"

"I'm going to kick your posterior if you don't get it in gear," Seth threatened. He scooped a hoodie off the floor and flung it at Jesse. "Catch!"

"Bastard!" Jesse muttered as he missed and the sweatshirt hit him in the face.

Seth grabbed his bag from outside his bedroom. His mom had kept the room just like when he shipped out, contending that he'd need somewhere to get his feet under him when he got his discharge. That had touched him more than he let on.

"Hurry up! I've already got the cooler and the beer in the car," Seth paused as he passed the dining room.

"What? I thought you were in a hurry?" Jesse asked.

Seth set his duffel down and walked over to the sideboard next to the dining room table. He pulled out a drawer full of his mother's good flatware, the stuff that only got used on Christmas and Thanksgiving.

"You want to take the good dishes, too? Are we camping or glamping?" Jesse taunted.

Seth made a face. "Do I want to know how you even know that word?"

"I was flipping channels one night. Don't judge."

The old carving knife had a wicked edge on it and a sharp point. Seth wrapped it in a couple of cloth napkins and put the knife into his bag. "It's silver," he said with a shrug. "Monsters hate silver. That's what I learned from cable TV."

"Mom's gonna kill you if you bend that," Jesse warned. "It was Grandma Ruth's, and it's—"

"—real silver," they said in unison, recalling their mother's oft-used admonition. That got them laughing again as Seth zipped up his bag.

"How's Mom gonna find out unless my dweeby little brother rats on me?" he asked, shouldering his bag. "By now, Mom and Dad have the camper parked by the lake, and they're probably roasting marshmallows and having a drink, not worrying about the good silver. We'll be home before they are, so I'll put it back, and she'll never know."

Jesse gave him a wicked grin. "I promise not to tell. Until I need blackmail material."

Seth leveled a glare. "Don't even. I think I still have some of the pictures you drunk-texted me from your twenty-first birthday."

"You wouldn't."

"I might." Seth waggled his eyebrows and gave his best nefarious grin. Then he smacked Jesse in the chest. "Come on. The early bird gets the monster!"

They had packed Jesse's yellow Mustang to the gills, opting for comfort rather than traveling light. Screw that. Seth had his fill of roughing it in the army. Besides, they could park the car next to where they pitched the tent, so it wasn't like they had to pack in supplies on a miles-long hike.

Seth cast a glance back at the locked garage.

"Your pretty baby will be fine," Jesse teased, knowing Seth was reluctant about leaving his black Hayabusa cycle behind. It was the first thing he'd bought when he'd come home, a touchstone in his new civilian life and the promise of exciting times ahead.

Excitement could be hard to find in Brazil, Indiana a town with fewer than ten thousand people, not far from Terre Haute. Seth always thought it was fitting that the town's most famous native son was Orville Redenbacher, the popcorn king. That was so family-friendly, so down-home, so...Brazil. Other than being named for a foreign country with much warmer weather, Brazil was so completely small-town Midwest America that Seth sometimes wondered if it had been designed by a sit-com writer.

Except for the Hell Gate.

"You know, I've been hearing stories about this Hell Gate since I was in middle school," Jesse said as Seth climbed into the passenger seat and buckled in. Jesse's car, so Jesse drove. They had their seats forward to fit all their gear, and their knees were practically in the dash.

"Yeah, and you woke up screaming when Jimmy Nelson told scary stories about it at that Halloween party." Seth poked him in the ribs.

"C'mon. I was ten! And he did the thing with his flashlight under his chin, so he looked like the devil."

Seth gave him a look. "Not unless Satan has chubby cheeks, freckles, and hair sticking up like a hairbrush," he countered.

"Seriously, I looked the legend up online yesterday. Plenty of creepy stories out there."

"Which is why we're gonna settle this once and for all," Seth replied. "Get it all on camera, and if nothing happens, then we can say it's busted."

Jesse grinned like a little kid. "I can't believe we're finally doing this. We've been saying we were going to since forever."

"Personally, I'm in it for the beer. I figure nothing will happen; we'll get a little bro time without Mom and Dad around, just you, me and the six-packs, and check it off our bucket list."

"But wouldn't it be cool if we saw something?" Jesse said, heading out on Highway 59. The so-called Hell Gate was actually in Diamond, a speck on the map and less than a half-hour drive. "Like on TV. Orbs. Cold spots. Creepy noises. It'd make a great story!"

"So we'll fake the video and have a good laugh." Seth leaned back, resting his arm on the door and drumming his fingers. He'd been afraid that he'd come home and find that his little brother had become a different person. They'd both grown and changed and had plenty of adventures to confide, but much to his relief, they still seemed to be same Seth and Jesse. Seth had seen more than his share of dangerous situations in Iraq and Afghanistan, things he didn't want to remember, that gave him nightmares from all-too-human monsters. He'd been afraid that might have made it hard to reconnect with a brother who'd spent that time in high school and college, though he was grateful that Jesse was safe. Yet here they were; sliding back into old roles like no time had passed.

Jesse turned up the classic vinyl station, and they both sang along, gloriously off-key. They turned off the highway onto the county road, and the late afternoon sun sent long shadows across the asphalt. Halloween night, perfect for a ghost hunt.

"Hey, you remember the time we dressed up like Spider-Man and Batman for Trick-or-Treat and ended up climbing the library?" Seth chuckled at the memory.

"Shit, I haven't thought about that in ages. We were what—ten and twelve? Had to be, because you thought you were too old to go, and I talked you into it."

"It'll be fun, you said," Seth mocked playfully. "Let's be real superheroes and scale the wall."

"Have to admit, the view from the roof was pretty great."

Seth snorted. "All two-stories of elevation. And man, did we catch hell afterward."

"Only because you insisted on sending out the 'bat signal' with your flashlight, and the cops showed up."

"Isn't that what the cops are supposed to do when they see the signal?"

"I don't think Batman ever got grounded."

"See if I ever let you in my secret superhero lair," Seth retorted.

Jesse eased the Mustang down roads that narrowed and changed from pavement to gravel. Before long, Seth could see the old cement train overpass. The date at the top read *1906*. Jesse found a wide spot on the road and pulled over.

"Should we drive through it?" Jesse asked, eyeing the overpass. A freight train lumbered across the tracks, and its whistle gave a mournful howl. "The stories say that if you pull into the middle and flash your lights three times, a mysterious gatekeeper appears."

"You sure that isn't the Crypt Keeper?" Seth joked.

Jesse grinned, but now he looked a little apprehensive. "They said the walls bleed, and if you see your name written there and it glows, you're going to die."

"Yeah, and if I look in the rear-view mirror as we drive through, I can see the gates of hell close." Seth rolled his eyes. "What next? If I say 'Bloody Mary' three times while I'm looking in the mirror, she'll show up and slit my throat?"

"Don't joke about that shit," Jesse said. "Somewhere, there's gotta be something behind it. Where there's smoke, there's fire, you know?"

"Seriously?" Seth eyed his brother. "If you're really nervous, we don't have to do this."

Jesse made a face. "If it weren't a little scary, it wouldn't be fun. Hell, no. I'm in." He looked up as the end of the train passed by, and the *clickity-clack* of the wheels echoed. "One of the stories says that a train derailed and all the passengers died and went to hell."

"Pretty damn good reporting, to know where people spend the afterlife," Seth said. "I heard there was this weird satanic cult back in the Sixties and they woke up a dark spirit from some haunted mine."

"Sounds like a bunch of misunderstood D&D players." Jesse pulled back out on the road and eased the Mustang into the tunnel. Midway, he stopped and flashed his lights.

The old stone tunnel had more than its share of graffiti, but none of it glowed or bled. After a moment, Jesse backed the car up and parked. "So…no gatekeeper." He sounded relieved and a little disappointed.

"Maybe it's got to be the right time of day," Seth replied. "Or the solstice, instead of Halloween. Or maybe it's just a crock of shit."

Jesse clasped his hands over his heart and threw himself backward.

"Heresy! You wound me!" He sat up with a grin. "Come on. Let's get settled."

Seth set up the tent in front of the car while Jesse arranged the cameras. Seth went back for the sleeping bags, beer, junk food, and a Thermos of hot chocolate. A kerosene heater would help ward off the chill without getting them cross-wise with the fire department. He didn't figure they were going to get any sleep, but they could be comfortable and warm while waiting for nothing to happen.

When they were kids, he and Jesse camped and built forts more times than he could count. When they got older, their adventures ranged beyond the backyard, to neighbors' woods, and then nearby state parks. The best part was sitting up all night talking. Something about the dark made it easier to confide, and he and Jesse had a lot of catching up to do.

"How about this?" Jesse asked. Seth looked up. Jesse had his cell phone set up on a tripod at an angle that could take in the whole of the Hell Gate tunnel. He had a sports cam on his cap; and another of the light, tough action cams in another tripod across the road.

Before Seth could answer, Jesse started to record. "Hey, ghost fans! This is Jesse Tanner, and I'm here with my brother Seth, and we're gonna blow the story of the Hell Gate wide open, so stay tuned tonight!" He clicked the camera off and sauntered back to the tent with a smug grin. "I can control everything with a remote!" He held up a gadget in his hand.

"Wow. That was just kinda...um...wow-ish," Seth replied.

"Admit it. You're impressed."

"Maybe. A little."

Jesse climbed into the small tent, and they clinked beer cans. "Can you believe Dad bought that trailer?" He took a long sip of the beer.

Seth chuckled. "He's been threatening to do it for years."

Jesse gave him a look. "He's also been threatening to get a hunting dog, turn the garage into a man cave, and get a tattoo, but I don't think those are going to happen."

Seth shrugged. "Maybe the man cave. But seriously, he and Mom have talked about this for a long time—even before I went overseas. Don't you remember? Mom always picked up all those tourist brochures, and she and Dad had that book of national parks. We'll be lucky if they ever come home again."

His father had taken his retirement bonus and bought a new truck and a second-hand fifth-wheel travel trailer. Seth had been grudgingly impressed. The trailer had been well cared for and had every comfort imaginable, including a small gas fireplace and an entertainment center.

"He was so excited. Got a really good deal on it from one of the other guys at the plant. The guy's wife got sick and couldn't do much traveling. So he offered it to Dad."

"I'd say he got a bargain," Seth replied. "And the truck's pretty badass, too." The black Silverado was another dream purchase for his dad. Since his mom got to pick the options, there'd been no complaining.

They sat in comfortable silence as the sun set. "So…the new job still good?" Seth asked. Jesse had gotten a programming job with a local company right out of college, and Seth couldn't be prouder of his little brother.

"Yeah. I like the work and the people. And I work the same hours as Michelle."

"Are you two serious?"

Even in the twilight, Seth could see Jesse blush. "Yeah. Kinda. Okay—yeah. Just, we're taking things slow. Need to get our feet under us."

"When did you get grown up and sensible?" Seth jabbed Jesse with his elbow.

"You still seeing Ryan?" Jesse asked.

Seth felt his cheeks flush. "Yeah. I really like him. It's nice, being out of the army and being…out."

"As long as he makes you happy," Jesse replied. "Not like that douchebag, Colin."

Seth sighed. "Colin wasn't a douchebag. He just had different priorities."

"Ditching you to go to college wasn't a 'priority,' it was a dick move." Jesse's defense made Seth smile.

"It probably wouldn't have worked out anyhow, after I left for the service."

"You meet anyone while you were in?"

Seth shrugged. "Not really. 'Don't Ask, Don't Tell' might have been overturned, but things don't change that fast. Being out...wasn't really an option." He didn't want to tell his little brother that he'd gotten by on rushed one-night stands and hurried jerk offs behind crummy bars.

"You going to tell Mom and Dad?"

Seth's brother had known about him almost from the time Seth figured it out for himself. And while Seth would bet money his parents had caught on, he'd never actually come out to them, not even when Colin had broken his heart.

"Figured I'd do it next weekend after they get back from their big trip," Seth replied, knowing he shouldn't be nervous, and still feeling his stomach flutter.

"They'll be cool with it," Jesse said. "You know that, right?"

"Still awkward," Seth admitted, not looking at his brother. "But yeah, I hope they'll be okay. I mean, it is what it is."

After that, the conversation turned to all the movies and TV shows Seth had missed, with Jesse offering snarky recaps that had them both laughing. Seth kept Jesse chuckling with stories from his tours.

"...and then the base doc actually had the motor pool tape 'do not stick fingers in fan' signs on all the Jeeps," Seth recounted.

"Seriously? We trust you guys with nukes and missiles, and you're getting the tips of your fingers sliced up in the Jeep fan?"

"I didn't do it," Seth countered. But I knew two people who did."

Seth turned on the heater as the night grew colder, and despite their coats, hats, and scarves, before long, both men had burrowed into their sleeping bags, although they remained sitting up to watch as nothing happened at the old trestle.

"Man, we've got to have something to post, or I'll never live it down," Jesse groused. "I told Matt and everyone that we'd have this amazing Blair Witch video. They're expecting it."

Seth felt relieved that nothing had happened, but Jesse had obviously been hoping for a ghostly encounter. He was just about to suggest that they rig something up when the whistle of a train sounded, making him jump. He looked up toward the trestle and saw the dark shapes of rail cars speeding past. It took him a moment to realize that no accompanying clack of wheels could be heard.

"Jesse—"

"Yeah. I see it—and I don't hear it." Jesse clicked his remote before the last of the cars sped past, and the red lights glowed brightly in the darkness.

Seth nudged the heater out of the way and tossed a flashlight to Jesse. The full moon gave enough light to see, but deep shadows provided too much cover. Seth reached into his bag and pulled out both the silver knife and his service pistol.

Jesse's eyebrows rose. "You didn't tell me you were bringing a gun."

"Didn't think I'd need it," Seth said quietly.

"Up there," Jesse pointed. Standing atop the tunnel arch by the now-empty rails stood a man in a long coat and a broad-brimmed hat. "The Gatekeeper."

"There's no such thing as ghosts," Seth murmured. He snapped the heater off, then unzipped his sleeping bag, sliding it behind him and crouching in the doorway of the tent.

"What are you doing?"

"What I was trained to do," Seth replied. "Stay behind me. We're going to get in the car and lock the doors."

"What about the stuff?"

"We'll get it later. You have your keys?" When Jesse produced the keys from his pocket, Seth nodded. "Okay. You ready?"

"Yeah." Jesse's voice sounded less sure about their adventure than he had been a few minutes earlier.

"It's going to be okay. Probably your friends pranking us," Seth said, though a knot in his gut told him otherwise. "We'll be safe in the car. Go!"

Six feet. Just six feet to get to the car door. Seth moved in front, covering Jesse. Then it all went to hell.

Seth felt himself being picked up and thrown across the hood of the Mustang. He rolled and came up in a firing stance, but he saw nothing. Not even Jesse.

"Jesse!" He shouted, barreling around the car.

Jesse's screams echoed in the darkness. Only seconds had passed, and yet no one was in sight.

"Get your hands off my brother!" Seth ran toward the tunnel. The shadow man was gone from above the opening, but markings Seth had never seen before glowed as if they had been written in fire on the Hell Gate walls, and a dark, thick substance oozed from the stone, filling the cold air with the coppery tang of blood.

"Jesse!" He advanced with both his Beretta and the carving knife. He had no idea what the strange, fiery designs meant, but just looking at them made his skin crawl. This was real and awful, not someone's prank.

Jesse screamed louder, and Seth knew when they changed from fear to pain. "Give me back my brother!"

The temperature inside the tunnel plummeted, and sudden, complete darkness descended. The flaming letters vanished. Seth knew he was no longer alone. He heard feet scrabbling on the loose gravel, and then powerful, unseen hands hurled him against the tunnel wall, knocking the breath from him. Jesse's screams continued to echo, and Seth's heart hammered in his chest.

Something powerful and unseen slammed Seth against the opposite wall and pinned him with his feet off the ground. At six-three and two hundred twenty pounds, few people could throw Seth around like a rag doll, let alone keep him suspended in mid-air. A hand squeezed against his throat. Seth brought the Beretta up and fired, point blank, where his attacker's chest should have been. The force holding him never wavered.

Seth bucked and kicked, using everything his training had taught him about close combat, only to have each blow meet thin air.

The invisible hand on his neck let go, and Seth fell, gasping, to the ground. He lunged, slashing with the silver knife, and this time, although his blade cut through empty space as before, an unholy shriek made the hair on the back of his neck stand on end.

Nothing human made a sound like that. And as Seth continued to fight his shadow opponent, he couldn't shake the certainty that nothing natural moved or fought like this.

Again the entity threw him, and Seth landed hard on his back; his shirt ripped and his skin scraped against the rough stones. He rolled, coming up in a crouch.

Jesse's screams were thin with pain now, begging for mercy.

"Jesse! Jesse, I'm coming!" Seth fought panic, afraid that even if he got past his supernatural assailant, he might be too late.

Seth threw himself into the darkness. He collided with something cold and tangible, but not solid, and he reeled, stumbling until he could get his balance. The shadow creature hissed, and then a bruising grip pushed Seth into the wall. It grabbed both his shoulders and slammed him against the concrete.

Seth unloaded his entire clip into where the creature had to be, but the only impact he heard was the bullets hitting the other side of the tunnel. Twisting with all his strength, Seth buried the carving knife to the hilt into where he imagined the creature's rib cage had to be.

Another ear-splitting shriek tore through the darkness, filled with pain and rage. The smell of burning flesh mingled with sulfur made bile rise in Seth's throat.

The creature slammed a fist against the side of Seth's head, and Seth's vision blurred. He kept his grip on the knife hilt, twisting the blade, earning another scream from his assailant.

They had staggered to the mouth of the tunnel, nearly into the moonlight. *If I can get to the car, I can drive it through the tunnel. Jesse's got to be on the other side.*

The next blow split his lip and broke his nose. Blood poured down his face, hot against the frigid cold of the night air. A hit across the shoulders drove him to his knees.

"Jesse!"

Another punch sent him sprawling, unable to fight the darkness that enveloped him.

1

SETH

PRESENT DAY - TWO YEARS LATER

"Jesse!"

Seth sat bolt upright in the bed, wet with sweat and shaking. He rolled to the floor of the trailer, landing on his hands and knees, with just enough time to grab the waste basket before he threw up. Shirtless and freezing, he gasped for breath, trying to get himself under control as the memories replayed in his mind.

He woke up at dawn, alone on the road just beyond the maw of the Hell Gate, beaten and bloody.

The silver carving knife lay next to him, its blade charred and twisted. His Beretta was still in his hand, out of ammunition. The tent and its contents hadn't been touched, but the cameras and Jesse's phone were strewn across the road in pieces. The Mustang didn't have a scratch. Jesse's keys lay on the ground beside the door.

"Jesse!" He got to his feet and staggered through the tunnel. No burning sigils, no bleeding walls. Fresh bullet holes pockmarked the stone, holes that hadn't been there the night before, reminding him that his memories were real.

He tucked his empty gun into his waistband and kept moving, afraid of what he would find on the other side. Unwilling to head into another fight without a weapon, he grabbed a rock and a sturdy fallen branch.

A large old tree sat apart from everything on the other side of the trestle.

He was running toward the tree before his mind completely processed what he saw.

Jesse hung from a noose, suspended several feet off the ground. His torso had been shredded from the ribs down, deep gashes severing arteries. Blood pooled at his feet and soaked his clothing. Crows rose in a dark cloud as Seth ran closer, and Jesse's corpse slowly twisted in the autumn wind, pale and lifeless.

It took him a while to realize that the screams he heard were his own.

"No, no, no." Seth tightened his fists in his blond hair and brought his knees to his chest. He pushed up to sit on the bed, but he didn't expect to get back to sleep. Instead, after a few moments of deep breathing to quell his shakes, Seth padded to the kitchen for a cup of coffee.

He opened the door and sat at the top of the fifth-wheel trailer's steps, looking out at the abandoned campground. His hand still trembled, and the t-shirt clung to his back, soaked with sweat. A late October dawn blossomed above the treetops in shades of yellow and orange. The coffee warmed him but would play hell with his stomach later.

Seth didn't need dreams to remind him of the rest of the story. The cops who'd tried to pick apart his story while he was in the hospital, who made him repeat the tale although it tore him apart. They'd finally concluded the boys had stumbled upon a drug deal gone bad.

His "breakdown" when he insisted on having seen something evil and supernatural.

Their parents, distraught and shaken.

Pictures from Jesse's funeral, and the way no one had ever looked at him the same way again.

Seth finished his coffee and headed back inside for another cup. He touched the gingham hand towel that hung from a hook like it was a talisman. For him, it was. He'd been stuck in a psych ward for six weeks "under observation" until he'd wised up and told the doctors what they wanted to hear. They released him then, to face more despair.

While he was hospitalized his parents had been killed in a car wreck—hit and run—in his mom's Honda. The house burned days later under mysterious circumstances. When he got out of the hospital, his boyfriend wanted nothing to do with him.

All he had left was some money in the bank he'd inherited from his parents, his Hayabusa, and the truck and fifth-wheeler that should have been his mom and dad's ticket to retirement paradise.

Seth took his coffee to the trailer's small table and looked out the window. His finger ghosted over the scar on his chin he'd gotten from the beating the night of Jesse's death. When he shifted in his chair, newer, barely healed scars pulled at his skin—a gash on his hip from where a vengeful ghost pushed him down the stairs, a slash across his ribs from the were-cougar he had hunted last month. Those scars joined several others he'd gained from near misses when he was in the service, and some he'd earned learning the trade of killing monsters. He and Jesse had been naive, innocent about what really lurked in the shadows.

Seth had come so far since then. Now, it was time to start getting his vengeance. Jesse's vengeance.

His phone chirped, and he reached for it, knowing from the ringtone who it was. Nobody else would be calling at this ungodly hour. Then again, few other people were likely to be calling, period.

"What's up, Toby?"

"You in Richmond?"

"Just outside it. Yeah." Seth rubbed his eyes and took a long swig of coffee. "Why?"

Toby Cornell had been the first person who believed Seth when he said he saw something that wasn't normal the night Jesse died—and it sure as hell wasn't a drug deal. Cornell was a Vietnam Vet and former recon specialist with a passion for ghost hunting and legends about the occult. Mostly, he debunked rumors, but on the occasions when the facts panned out, Cornell documented and if necessary, eliminated supernatural threats. He'd taken Seth under his wing, taught him everything he knew, helped him research what happened that night by the Hell Gate. Connected him to other people who hunted things that went bump in the night. Together, they'd pieced together a more plausible explanation for what killed Jesse. Plausible, and terrifying.

"Got a little more information for you. Ready?"

Seth drained his cup and refilled it, then settled in at the table with his laptop to take notes. "On Gremory's disciple? What'cha got?"

"I confirmed what you turned up about the Malone family deaths," Toby said. "There's been a male Malone death ruled 'accidental' every twelve years since 1900. So that checks out. Firstborn for each generation from the original deputy, and if the firstborn is already dead, then the oldest surviving. In this case, Jackson E. Malone."

"I tell you, the guy is like a ghost." Seth poured cereal into a bowl, and following up with enough milk to float the corn flakes. "He's not on social media, I can't find any decent photos, and there's no address or phone listed. You got something?"

"Nothing on him. It looks like the trail's been swept clean. I can't find any arrests, either," Toby replied. "I can't personally get into any of the official databases that should have info. But I might know someone if you really get stuck. Hate to do it more than we have to—the Feds get testy about that sort of thing."

"Thanks, Toby. I'm not ready to hack into the IRS or the DMV just yet, but I'll keep the offer in mind. I found one lead—a bar in town called Tredegar's, like the old foundry. Slim. Just a mention on someone else's post. I'm going to check it out tonight. Just in case."

"Be careful," Toby warned. "Even with everything you've learned, stopping Gremory's disciple from carrying out the ritual isn't going to be easy, and he's not going to go out without a fight."

"Figured that," Seth replied. "But you've taught me well, Obi-wan."

Toby snorted. "Proof's in the pudding, as my grandma used to say. Seth—good luck. And be careful, there's still a lot we don't know."

Seth smiled. "Roger, that. How's Milo?"

Toby made a rude noise, and in the background, Seth could hear Milo make an equally impolite comment. "Still a stubborn ass, same as always."

"Glad you two are the same old lovebirds I remember."

"More like buzzards," Toby chuckled. "Stay safe now, you hear?"

"Thanks, Toby. Say 'hi' to Milo for me. I'll be in touch."

Seth finished his cereal, downed more coffee, and took his dishes to the sink. Toby was right. There was still so much they didn't know, but what he had uncovered shook him to his core.

Everyone talked about the train wreck at the Hell Gate back in Brazil, but the real deal was a hanging—a sheriff and his deputies getting the drop on a dark witch who went by the name of Rhyfel Gremory. Back in 1900, from what Seth and Toby had uncovered, Gremory and his coven of disciples had been causing problems—cattle mutilations, animal sacrifices, vagrants and hobos gone missing. No one seemed to know exactly how a small-town sheriff and his posse captured a warlock—*hexenmeister*—of such supposed power. When they hanged him out by the railroad bridge, all hell broke loose.

Those who swore they had seen things firsthand told of lightning on a clear night, green fire, and a body that burned but was not consumed by the flames. In his dying breath, Gremory cursed the sheriff and his deputies and assured his scattered coven of their immortality. If Gremory himself was immortal, it wasn't his body—which had been burned with acid, covered in lime, and—according to one source—dismembered.

Within a year, the sheriff and his deputies were dead.

One of those deputies had been a Tanner, Seth's ancestor.

Since then, so many deaths. Twelve deputies. No one knew for certain how many witch-disciples. Gremory's death apparently had imparted immortality to his followers, and Seth suspected that the ongoing sacrifices renewed the blood pact. Every year, a descendant of one of the deputies died, moving one by one through all twelve families, only to begin again. That spaced the deaths out enough so that no one noticed the pattern. Some just vanished, while others met bloody deaths blamed on farm machinery or train wrecks. Plausible, and comforting excuses. But Seth and Toby had discovered the truth.

Two years ago, it had been the Tanner family's turn for a sacrifice.

It should have been Seth. Firstborn.

It hadn't been the "where." It had been the "who."

When he'd found that out, Seth hadn't sobered up for a week. He was the older brother, the designated victim. The killers had gotten sloppy. Seth and Jesse were the same height, the same build, and everyone always said Jesse looked older than his age. They'd grabbed the wrong brother, and Jesse died. Part of Seth died, too.

Had he known, he would have gladly switched places with Jesse. Guilt just added to the pain. He couldn't change the past, but he sure as fuck intended to change the future.

The plan was simple and insane. Find the families of each unlucky deputy, and figure out who was the next sacrifice. Stop the murder. Save the victim. Destroy the witch-disciple. Avenge Jesse.

Repeat, for as long as it took to end the cycle. Seth intended to bring an end to the killings or die trying. To get justice for Jesse, and make atonement for having survived. Everyone he had loved had left him. He couldn't let that happen to anyone else.

Seth changed into sweats and running shoes. He grabbed his keys, locked the travel trailer that had become his home, and headed out to train.

The campground was closed for the season, but he'd talked his uncle who owned the place into letting him stay for a while. The hookups worked, and he had access to the social room for times when the trailer made him claustrophobic. The empty acres gave him plenty of room to run and train without prying eyes.

Seth started at a jog, then worked up to a full run, letting the rhythm of his steps clear his mind. He'd measured out several courses, so he could change up his routine and still know how far he'd gone. Seth missed his fitness tracker, but he'd ditched it when Toby pointed out the device could be hacked to track his location. Today, he started with four miles running, then switched to parkour, something he'd learned to love from the obstacle courses in the army. He vaulted fences, scaled cement block walls, walked a large supply pipe like a balance beam, and went over, under, or around the buildings, utility structures, and decorative features of the park.

By the time he finished his course for the day, sweat dripped from his forehead, and he had unzipped his jacket. Choosing a flat open space, Seth took a few minutes to prepare himself before launching into a challenging series of martial arts katas, something else he'd hung onto from his time in the service. Moving through the forms stilled his mind and calmed his body, while keeping him strong and limber.

Toward the rear of the campground, where it backed up to the forest, he had set up a shooting range. He worked through some target practice with his gun and throwing knives.

After that, it was time for magic.

Seth once again closed his eyes and breathed deep, centering himself and calming his mind, focusing on nothing but the moment. He stretched out his right hand, turned his palm upward, and pictured a tongue of flame hovering above his skin. Seth spoke the incantation, willed the energy outward from the core of his being, and felt a shift as power answered his call.

When he opened his eyes, a thin flame danced above his palm without burning the skin beneath. He kept his focus and made the flame grow and shrink. So far, so good.

He spoke a few more arcane words and made a gesture with his hand like a sudden, hard push. The flame leaped from his hand in a stream of fire…and then winked out before it had gone more than a few feet.

He tried again. This time, the fire might have gained another foot of reach, but it hardly qualified as a badass force to be reckoned with.

Seth felt a headache starting behind his temples, and ignored it, for now. He bent down and picked up a rock about the size of a chicken nugget, then tossed it into the air and spoke a different incantation. The rock hovered at chest height, no longer falling. Seth smiled, spoke another word, and pushed outward with both hands. The stone flew across the clearing, hard enough to leave a small dent in the side of a metal shed. He varied the size of the stone and the direction of the push, pleased at his results.

He walked to the shed and put a hand on the padlock, then murmured the words he had memorized, picturing the lock snapping open, willing the energy to flow through him and work his will. A few seconds later, the lock dropped to the gravel at his feet.

The discomfort in his head became a pounding he couldn't disregard, and Seth knew it was time to quit for the day before pain escalated to nosebleeds or worse. He looked at the dent in the shed wall again. Progress. Magic was one more weapon to be mastered. Even the headaches were fading, not as bad as they used to be.

It had taken him more than a year to learn a handful of basic spells.

Burn.

Unlock.

Throw.

Locate.

Summon.

Translate.

Ward.

Each had required days of practice and pain. Magic did not come easily. For some gifted people, harnessing power came instinctively. He imagined that for those folks it was like when someone could play any song by ear without written music. Seth figured he was like the determined kid who had no musical talent but practiced for hours until his fingers bled so he could play a few songs perfectly. "Rote magic" some called it, meaning the spells were memorized like multiplication tables, instead of calling up power and improvising. He'd take every advantage he could get.

Toby's connections in the occult and paranormal community yielded all kinds of useful information. One was an introduction to Sebastian Kincaid, a history professor with an extracurricular interest in the history and documentation of magic and shamanism. Kincaid had been almost as helpful as Toby, helping find grimoires and lore books, translating from ancient texts, and most importantly, teaching Seth about the power of rituals and relics so he could hope to go up against Gremory's disciples and have a chance of winning.

He'd sparred with Toby and learned from Kincaid, even though Kincaid was an academic, not a witch himself. Witches would not have anything to do with Seth once Gremory's name came up, out of fear and self-preservation. Toby hooked Seth up with some hunters who went looking for creatures that lurked in the shadows, and he'd put his new skills—magic and martial—to use on ghouls, were-animals, wendigoes, and other monsters. He'd learned the hard way, one scar at a time. Now it was ready to put those lessons to use.

Seth headed back to the trailer, shucked his sweaty clothes and took a hot shower, debating what to wear. He didn't often go out unless he was researching or meeting a contact. Admittedly, his people skills were rusty, and he hadn't gone looking for company—even a quick anonymous fuck—in longer than he could remember.

Seth had checked out Treddy's the previous night. He had barely gone inside, just enough to get an idea of the crowd and the dress code so he wouldn't stick out. Although he was only inside for a few minutes, that had been long enough to notice the good-looking man behind the bar. And while Seth told himself he needed to stay focused on finding Jackson Malone, he'd have been lying if he hadn't admitted that the hot bartender made him look forward to making a longer visit.

I've got five days to find Malone and stop the witch-disciple. This is no time for a hook-up.

Still, he thought as he toweled off and dried his hair, he needed to look presentable if he expected people to talk to a stranger about Malone. Seth trimmed his scruff to look more hipster than hermit, and dug into the better clothing he rarely wore, selecting a russet button-down shirt that would set off his brown eyes and a newer pair of jeans as well as his least-scuffed pair of boots.

Easy there. It's just going to a bar, not heading into battle. For some reason, his gut couldn't tell the difference. He grabbed his motorcycle helmet, locked up the trailer, and roared off on his Hayabusa.

2

SONNY

"Hey, Sonny! Did we get the new shipment of Jack?"

"Yeah, I haven't unpacked it yet." Sonny looked up from behind the bar at Tredegar's—Treddy's to regulars. "You need me to get you a bottle?"

"Nah. Just checking to see if it came in." Liam, the bar manager, stood at the end of the counter. "Didn't want to pay for it if it hadn't arrived." Muscular, red-haired and with a thousand watt smile, Liam was the reason so many singles in Richmond—gay and straight—found their way to Treddy's.

"I'll check it out. Need to restock, and I'll put the rest away."

Treddy's took up three stories of what had once been an old tobacco warehouse. The unfinished brick walls and exposed wooden beams gave the place history and authenticity missing in newer buildings. Sometimes, Sonny swore he could smell tobacco, and when he looked up, it wasn't difficult to imagine bundles of broadleaf hanging from the rafters to dry.

The first floor had the main bar and restaurant. The second floor boasted a dance floor and a DJ, and the third floor was mostly for catering and events. Sonny held court at the first-floor bar, a job he'd held since he came back to Richmond two years ago. Just one more stop on his long journey to shed his past, his family, and his stalker. Sonny hoped this time would last. He'd been bouncing around for seven years since he graduated from high school.

"It's a bar, not a mirror," Liam joked, as Sonny polished the heavily varnished wood. The counter and backbar had come out of a swanky club from the late 1800s. Rumor had it the chandeliers used to hang in ritzy Paris townhomes before Liam got them from a New Orleans antique store. The wood of the mantle over the fireplace had the maker's chisel marks and was once part of a hundred-year-old barn. Put them together, and Treddy's felt comfortably lived in, welcoming and warm.

"Hey, Sonny. You're on early today." Jackie, one of the servers, came by to pick up drinks for her table. Her Jersey accent stood out in the crowd of Richmonders, as did her Bettie Page black bob and bright red lipstick. She had always gone out of her way to make Sonny feel welcome and was one of the few people he counted as a friend.

"Been working a lot of nights. Needed to change it up a bit," Sonny answered as he poured refills for the crowd at the bar.

"Tips are better at night," Jackie replied with a shrug. She was a VCU student and one of the staffers who'd take any shift that came open to help pay for tuition.

"Nice to see some new faces. Keeps it fresh." He didn't want to get into what he'd told Liam, that he'd seen someone who looked like Mike, his stalker, and freaked out. *It wasn't Mike,* he told himself. Mike belonged back in Oklahoma. But that hadn't stopped him from showing up in Missouri and Ohio, popping up like a bad rash every time Sonny moved.

He rubbed his left forearm, over the spot where Mike had broken it. The injury didn't leave a visible scar, but Sonny swore it ached on rainy days. Worse, it hurt like a motherfucker in his dreams. *Three years later, and it's still not over in my head. Maybe it never will be.*

The police had taken his complaints, given him forms to fill out, and he filed a restraining order. Sonny had changed addresses, phone numbers, and jobs, deleted everything from social media, begged any sites with his photo on it to take down the information, started using a nickname at work.

Lately, he'd gotten up the courage to go on a few dates. Nothing serious, just some fun times and casual sex, which felt like an enormous step after leaving Mike's crazy jealousy and unpredictable rages behind.

And then, that guy showed up. *Not Mike*, Sonny told himself, hating the way just thinking about it made his hands shake. He'd come up with an excuse to get close enough to see for himself that the guy wasn't Mike. Yeah, there was a resemblance from a distance, but too many details were wrong to be Mike, even with a couple more years under his belt. Still, Sonny hated how it brought up old memories, dented his newly minted self-confidence. And the worst part was, stalker-Mike still wasn't as bad as his first boyfriend, Trey, whose tearful repentance over being gay betrayed Sonny's trust and got him kicked out of his house, his church, and their tight-knit small town. So he'd finally come back to Richmond, the city his parents had left when he was a kid, and hoped for a fresh start.

"Hey, over here!" A patron hailed him, and Sonny pulled himself out of his thoughts, hurrying to refresh the guy's martini before his hair caught on fire.

Jackie was right about nights being better for tips, but Sonny had enough put by that he could do without, for a few shifts at least. Give him time to clear his head, get some sleep. Treddy's did pretty well for a day crowd. Started at brunch and went on to the wee hours of the morning. The lunch crowd was split between corporate types and the "ladies who lunch" in their twinsets and pearls. Dinner picked up more mid-level executives plus the young professionals who liked the martini list and the atmosphere. Late night, the action shifted to the second floor, where the DJ made Treddy's a good place for a hot hookup, while the first floor took care of those looking for a tasty meal, fine whiskey, and a nice place to take a date.

Sonny lost himself in the rhythm of the work, swaying to the music from the sound system, watching for signals from the barflies for another round, hauling ass on orders, so the servers got credit for quick response. Although he'd never been much for the "shoulder to cry on" bartender stereotype, he knew his regulars and noticed when they were off their game.

"You doin' okay, Pete?" He asked, leaving it up for interpretation whether that meant in life or needing another drink.

"Just a shitty day at work," Pete replied. He had loosened his tie and turned up his shirtsleeves. "What else is new?"

"Sucks, man," Sonny empathized. "But it beats a pink slip."

Pete knocked back his scotch. "Not always sure about that. Maybe."

Sonny gave him a commiserating smile. "Hey, you want to get something to eat with that?"

"Sure," Pete said. "Fries and wings. The usual."

Sonny put in the order, picked up food from the kitchen for the customers who were waiting, and scanned for who needed another drink. A glance out over the dining area told him they'd reached wait-list capacity, not bad considering it wasn't six yet. The early crowd drew a mix, young and older, professional and hipster. Treddy's had even found a new fan in a tired-looking off-duty cop who'd shown up a couple of times in the past few weeks. Something about the place just put folks in a good mood.

"What'll you have?" He said without looking up as he saw a newcomer pull up a seat.

"Jack and Coke, please."

The "please" made Sonny look up. Most people, even the polite ones, just put in their order, mumbling "thanks" if they weren't too deep in conversation or their own thoughts. "Please" stood out. On second thought, so did the newcomer.

Well, well. That's a fresh face. Um-hmm. Sonny took in the new guy without being too obvious. Tall—maybe a few inches over his own six-foot-one frame, a nice height to fit together. Broad shoulders, and the way the button-down clung in all the right places, Sonny bet on a toned chest underneath. Dishwater blond hair short on the sides and a little longer on top, fashionable without being trendy. Broad hands and long fingers. *Bet he's proportional.*

"Coming right up," Sonny said with a smile, meeting the blond's eyes with a hint of a wink, surprised to find them brown instead of blue. He came back with the drink and slid it toward the newcomer.

"Taste it and see if it's what you like," he said, with a smile suggesting ideas of other things worth tasting.

If he'd had any doubts about whether the guy played for his team, the look that lasted a bit too long and the slight flush that came to the man's cheeks answered the question. Sonny watched as the newcomer sipped, then licked his lips.

"Just right," he said with a hint of a smile in return.

Shit. He's cute. And alone. Sonny knew the two patrons on either side of the blond had been there before he came, and it didn't appear the man intended to retrieve a drink and retreat to a table.

"First time at Treddy's?" Sonny asked as the regulars on both sides of the man continued their conversations.

"Heard it was good." He looked around. "Looks like it's got some history. That's…nice."

"It's the kind of place people keep coming back to," Sonny said with a shrug. "Makes people feel at home."

"Hey, Sonny—need you down here!" Izzy, a petite server with a pink pixie cut, looked ready to chew nails.

"What can I do for you, darlin'?"

"Don't darlin' me," Izzy said. "Table five is giving me an ulcer, but if you mix their drinks strong, maybe they'll ease up."

"You got it," Sonny said with a grin. Izzy had a temper, but for all her epic bitching, he'd seen her out back feeding scraps to the stray cats.

By the time he got back down the bar, he was afraid the blond would have moved on, but instead, the man nursed his drink as if he were in no hurry. "You want some food to go with that?" Sonny asked.

The man shrugged, and Sonny thought he seemed a bit uncomfortable in the press and hustle. "What's good here?"

"Everything on the menu, and a few things that aren't," Sonny replied, with a flirtatious tone. *Seriously? When's the last time I flirted with a customer? Shit, I must really need to get laid.*

"Any recommendations?" This time, there was no mistaking the way the blond held Sonny's gaze, shifting a little closer to the bar. Sonny felt a tingle go straight to his groin.

"I've got a couple of favorites," Sonny said, leaning in. "By the way, I'm Sonny."

"Seth."

"Nice to meet you, Seth. New in town?"

"Just visiting. I like what I've seen so far."

That absolutely wasn't in my imagination, Sonny thought. The new guy was definitely interested, but not overly slick. Either Seth was a master pick-up artist or his edge of self-consciousness was genuine—and very sexy.

"So here's what I order," Sonny said, bending closer to share the menu with Seth, just brushing his fingers for a second. He pointed to two or three choices, sure to please because everything was good. "What sounds good? And is that for here or to go?"

"For here," Seth replied, pointing to his choice. "Maybe I'll be up for some to-go later."

Oooookay. Definitely on the same wavelength. This could be interesting. "Let me know, and I'll go over the options with you," Sonny replied, making direct eye contact. Seth didn't blink or turn away, confirming that Sonny hadn't lost his touch with reading signals.

"Be back in a few," he promised, going to type the order into the system. Jackie came up to pick up more drinks.

"Since when are you in the game?" She asked just loudly enough for him to hear. "I've never seen you hit on a customer."

"Technically, he's hitting on me," Sonny replied. "I'm just responding. It's polite."

"Sure it is."

Sonny mixed her drinks and fiddled a few seconds longer down at the end of the bar. What was he doing? Not that Liam would care if he took a customer home with him. Wouldn't be the first time one of the wait staff—or Liam himself—had hooked up with someone. But that wasn't usually Sonny's thing. Then again, he'd been gun shy since Mike, practically a monk—if you didn't count the hurried hand jobs, porn, and jacking off in the shower. Pretty sure monks at least jacked off.

Maybe it was time to get out of his shell. Take the guy home, have a nice roll in the hay, and shake off the ghosts of the past. No strings, no complications. After all, Seth was just visiting, so no worries about him wanting more than Sonny was ready to give.

He set Seth's order down in front of him. "Watch out; it's hot."

Seth smiled. "I like it hot."

Sonny swallowed. Somehow, that didn't sound totally cheesy coming from Seth.

"If you'd like, I could show you around when I get off at seven," Sonny said. "Since you're new and all."

"That would be great," Seth replied, and a bit of pink colored his cheeks.

Damn. Maybe it's been a while for him, too. This could be a great evening. Sonny whistled as the next hour flew by. Even Izzy's gripes about cheap tippers didn't get him down. He had a date with a cute stranger. Okay, maybe a hook-up more than a date, but still, more company than he'd had in a while. This was just what he needed.

Seth took his time with dinner, nursing his drink and ordering fries and a Coke to give him an excuse to dawdle. That earned him points in Sonny's book. By the time Sonny was ready to clock out most of the customers in the dining room had turned over from the early dinner crowd. Even the cop had moved on.

"I need to cash out my drawer and hand off to Eddie, and then we can go," Sonny said, slipping Seth's bill to him. Seth reached for his wallet and paid in cash. Sonny held his breath, wondering how the tip would go. Too little was an insult. Too much felt like paying for his company, given their plans. To his relief, Seth came in at twenty percent, appropriate for good service, not trying to buy favors.

"Tell us all about it tomorrow, you sly dog," Jackie murmured as he passed her on the way to get his coat.

"I want pictures," Izzy added with a rare smirk.

"In your dreams," Sonny replied and found himself grinning. Fuck, what had gotten into him? This was hardly his first rodeo, and that thought led to wondering who might be riding whom. *It might not even get that far,* he warned himself, then tried to remember how well he was stocked for lube and condoms. *More than enough for one night. Even if he's...energetic.*

He met Seth at the door, and they headed out. The October wind was cold for Richmond, but Seth didn't seem to mind. "Not sure what you're used to or where you're from, but Richmond isn't exactly New York when it comes to nightlife," Sonny said. "Don't get me wrong; it's a great city. Plenty of history, close to the beach. And there are some good clubs. But it's not a big party kind of place."

"That's fine," Seth replied. "I'm not much for clubs."

That made two of them, although Sonny had tried hard to fake it to keep up with Mike before everything went to shit between them.

"How about I give you the five-cent tour, and then see what you want to do next."

"Sounds good to me."

Sonny pointed out a few landmarks like the Iron-front building and the park by the Capitol, as well as rattling off some local trivia he'd picked up from the last time he'd helped out on game night. Seth seemed comfortable, but a little guarded, and Sonny found himself wondering what the sexy blond's story was. Not that it mattered; they'd have a nice night together, and that would be the end of it. But still, something about Seth intrigued Sonny. Not to mention the fact that he had a great ass.

Sonny thought about what highlights to share from his newly adopted town. Richmond was a city torn between its past and its future. Glittering new office towers lined the waterfront, growing universities sprawled through the downtown, and well-groomed parks provided a great view of the James River. The Virginia Museum of Fine Art hosted world-class traveling exhibits, the State Capitol building and its fountain were photogenic, and tourists and locals flocked to the beautiful grounds at Maymont and the Louis Ginter Botanical Gardens. Downtown boasted a growing number of trendy shops, bars, and restaurants.

And yet, Richmond had a darker side, in the whispers suggesting that no matter how many years passed, the Civil War would never be over. At the Museum of the Confederacy and the Confederate White House, docents told a tale of the "martyrs of the Lost Cause" that could have come right out of *Gone With The Wind*. Monument Avenue's statues were popular with history buffs, but the men they memorialized had long ago ceased to be defensible, except to those who even now refused to surrender. Richmond, like Charleston, New Orleans, and Savannah, was a beautiful city built on rivers of blood, and that past might never completely release its grip.

"Richmond has plenty of interesting stuff, depending on what you're into," Sonny said. "Museums galore, concerts, and NASCAR. Plenty of ghost tours. It seems like everything's haunted—restaurants, hotels, churches, even an old collapsed train tunnel. Something for everyone."

As a bartender, Sonny had plenty of chances to watch people, and he counted himself pretty observant. One of his favorite ways to amuse himself on slow nights was to make up a whole history for a stranger at the bar, and then see if he could tease out enough conversation to validate his guesses. He was right—or close enough—more often than not, at least on the parts he could customers to 'fess up to.

Hmm. He's alert, even when he's trying to be relaxed. Cop? Maybe ex-military? He considered the haircut and figured on the latter. *So who's he visiting?* "Family" didn't feel like the right answer, and he'd shown up solo and willing to take Sonny up on his offer, so not here to meet up with a boyfriend. Somehow, Seth didn't strike him as the tourist type. *Maybe business, but not something he wants to discuss? Could be.*

They bumped shoulders as they walked, too close to be just friends. Sonny was pretty sure he'd seen Seth sneak a look at his ass. He liked Seth's long-limbed stride, and how confidently he moved, despite his height. Not graceful like a dancer, more the kind of smooth, seamless motion Sonny had learned in Tae Kwon Do before switching over to mixed martial arts. That would figure for ex-military.

Sonny had been gone from the heartland for a long time, but he thought he recognized a bit of Midwestern twang in Seth's voice as they chatted, and a little small town vibe around the edges. He wondered if Seth had left his family and home for the same kind of reasons that had forced him out. Although he hoped not, it was more common than anyone liked to admit.

Quit overthinking. Take what's been offered and don't make too much of it. It's just one night. Not like it's gonna change anything.

3

SETH

How the hell did I end up on a date with a cute bartender? Seth walked beside Sonny as they meandered around downtown Richmond. Still, being with Sonny felt comfortable, in a way Seth hadn't felt with anyone in a long time. Maybe it wouldn't be so bad to get to know one of the locals, blow off a little steam, and make a friend who might be able to help him find the elusive Jackson Malone.

Seth had spent all evening watching Sonny tend bar. Sonny was good at his job, helpful to the servers, and made the customers feel at home. He was also damn good looking, and his worn jeans pulled just right across his toned ass. So when Sonny started throwing signals, Seth responded, and suddenly the evening had taken an unexpected turn.

"What do you do for fun?" Sonny asked, making conversation as they walked. Seth knew that behind the casual questions, Sonny was trying to figure out whether taking Seth home was a good idea. Seth found himself wanting to make a good impression.

"I read," Seth said, sticking as close to the truth as he could. "Watch movies. Action flicks, superheroes, that kind of thing. Play video games, when I have the time. When I got out of the service, I thought

I'd take a little time off to see the country, so I'm finally taking the road trip I promised myself."

"By yourself?" Sonny sounded torn between being impressed and concerned.

Seth shrugged. "I've got friends scattered around, from the army and before. So I drop in and catch up. But yeah, mostly by myself. Clears my mind, you know?"

I should just ask him about Malone, Seth thought. *The clock's ticking. If Malone is a regular, Sonny'll know.* Then again, asking the guy he might be hooking up with about another dude was awkward, to say the least. *It's not like I can say, "I need to protect this guy I don't know from a dark warlock. Do you have his number?"*

"You want to go get some coffee?" Sonny asked after they had walked for a while. "This place I know has really good desserts, and it's a nice place to just sit and chill for a while."

It had been so long since Seth had been on anything resembling a date that he wasn't quite sure what to expect. "Sure," he said, less because he wanted dessert than because he didn't want his time with Sonny to end yet.

Maybe he'd misread the signals. He'd thought Sonny was interested in him. Like, *interested*. Not that Seth wanted to have a quickie in the alley behind the bar, but he hadn't expected Sonny to want to invest time getting to know him. After all, Sonny knew Seth was just passing through. It's not like there might be a relationship to build.

And yet, as Sonny led him to a cool little indie coffee shop with an Edgar Allen Poe theme, Seth discovered that he felt all right with taking it slow. He liked that Sonny wasn't rushing things, focused just on getting into Seth's pants. It had been a long time since Seth had spent time with an attractive guy just talking...and flirting. God, he was rusty. But Sonny made it seem easy. Somehow, just sitting and chatting seemed natural, unforced. And for the first time in a long while, Seth felt himself relax.

"If you want to talk sports, you're out of luck," Sonny admitted as they found a cozy alcove with two plump leather chairs angled for conversation. "I know the scores for the latest games because the TV plays in the bar, but I don't follow any teams."

"Thank God," Seth replied, settling into his chair. "I'm better on cars and motorcycles if that's your thing."

"I'm not a true gearhead, but I had an uncle who ran a garage and I used to help out in the summers." Sonny paused to drink his coffee. They'd each paid for their own, but Seth had overheard Sonny's order. Chai latte. Fancy, but hardly flamboyant. Seth splurged and added cream to his regular coffee. It tasted as good as it smelled.

"I learned to do some basic repairs, more out of necessity than anything else," Seth admitted. "I've got a long way to go before I can strip a car down to the axles and rebuild it...although I think it's cool to watch someone who can."

The conversation turned to video games, a passion they both indulged, and Seth enjoyed the chance to talk in detail about his favorites with someone else who had played them through. "We should so do a campaign together," Seth said and wrote down his username on a napkin for the big multiplayer game they both enjoyed. On impulse, he added his phone number. His heartbeat spiked when he slid the napkin to Sonny, afraid he'd been too forward. But when Sonny tore off a part of the napkin and returned the favor—including the phone number—Seth relaxed again.

"It'll be fun to campaign with someone I've actually met," Sonny replied. "So many of the guys out there are total douchebags."

Seth was about to agree when Sonny's phone rang. "Sorry, it's work. Gotta take this." Sonny frowned at the distraction. He listened for a moment, and his expression morphed from annoyance to resignation. "Okay. Give me twenty. Thanks."

He shoved his phone back into his pocket and looked up at Seth. "I'm really sorry. Eddie, the guy who was supposed to work the night shift, got really sick and had to leave. Liam can't handle both bars himself. So...I need to go in."

"That's okay." Seth tried to ignore his disappointment. Even if they didn't end up in bed, he'd been enjoying the company. "This was fun." Had Sonny set it up for a co-worker to call him with an out if the evening didn't shape up the way he wanted? Maybe Sonny had been waiting for Seth to make the first move, and decided things weren't moving along fast enough? *Shit, how can I fuck up a date?*

Sonny leaned over and put his hand on Seth's arm. "I had a great time," he said, making a point of meeting Seth's gaze. "And if you're still in town, I get off at seven tomorrow, too. If Eddie's still sick I'll make sure Liam has a different replacement. So come by if you want to try this again. Maybe go back to my place afterward, you know, Netflix and chill?"

"I'd like that," Seth said, surprised at how warm Sonny's hand felt on his arm. "Can I walk you back to Treddy's?" Since he figured that they had both parked behind the bar, it only seemed right.

"Sounds like a plan," Sonny agreed. They finished their coffees and headed out into the night. The walk back passed quickly, and Seth discovered he didn't have to stretch to make small talk. Chatting with Sonny came naturally, and Seth felt a little sad to find them in front of Treddy's so quickly.

"See you tomorrow?" Sonny dared to stretch up to brush a quick kiss over Seth's lips. He had pulled away before Seth collected his wits enough to think about kissing back.

"Definitely," Seth replied, hoping he didn't sound twitterpated after the surprise of the kiss. Sonny shot him a wink and disappeared inside, and it took Seth another minute to realize he needed to move away from the door.

Sonny's kiss went through him like a bolt of lightning right to his balls. Seth turned away from the doorway and tried to subtly adjust himself. The Hayabusa sat right where he had parked it, but Seth paused to think about his grocery list and what was in his laundry basket so that he didn't have to ride home with a hard-on.

Back at the campground, Seth let himself into the trailer, surprised at how disappointed he felt. When he'd gone to Treddy's, he'd expected to have a beer, chat up the bartender and some regulars about Malone, and make an early night of it. Now he felt a little cheated—and frustrated. Seth fished a beer out of the fridge and sat at his laptop.

His phone chirped as he waited for the laptop to power up, and for a moment, he found himself hoping Sonny had decided to text him. He'd already added Sonny to his contacts. Instead, "Luis" came up, and Seth resigned himself to talking shop.

"Hey, Luis. What's up?"

"Hey, yourself. I couldn't turn up anything on that warlock in Richmond you're chasing, but I did get some hits on the one in Pittsburgh. Noah and I were over that way last week chasing a pack of shifters, and I had the chance to dig around while we were there."

"Thanks," Seth replied, trying to get his head back into the game. "Your hunt go all right?"

"We're alive, and the shifters aren't, so I guess that's a win. Normally, I'd be 'live and let live,' you know? But this pack had gone gangland, and they'd already killed three cops. So Noah and I took care of it." He paused. "I got banged around plenty, but Noah got clawed in the leg, so we're holed up until that heals."

"That sucks, man. But I'm glad you're mostly okay." Luis and Noah were friends of Toby's, some of the first hunters Seth had met. Since then, he'd gotten to know several other teams, either people he happened upon in the field or friends of friends. He hadn't found it unusual that many hunters worked in teams, but the number of those teams that were more than just work partners did give him pause. Then again, hunting was a lonely job, and "civilians" didn't understand. Some of the hunters he'd heard about had a home base and kept to a radius. Many of them traveled like he did, from job to job. Seth supposed that hunting solo was the perfect gig for natural loners. If he were honest with himself, Seth had to admit he was a little jealous of guys like Luis and Toby, who'd found partners in every sense of the word.

"You get any leads on the Richmond warlock?" Luis asked. "Noah and I aren't too far away—if you want back-up."

Seth knew Toby's opinion of him going after Gremory's disciple by himself. His mentor had waxed obscenely creative in telling him just how foolhardy he thought it was for Seth to go up against the warlock solo. But Seth also knew that neither Luis nor Noah had any magic of their own, and so he didn't want to be responsible for getting anyone else hurt.

"Thanks, but I think I'll be okay. I appreciate it, though. And if I can help you out, just call."

"We're near Cleveland if you change your mind. Got a line on a couple of vengeful ghosts to put down once Noah's healed up. But we could be in Richmond overnight if we hauled ass."

"Go gank those ghosts," Seth replied. "I've got this. Thanks for the intel. Anything you turn up on the witch-disciples, shoot my way. And let me know how to return the favor."

"Sure thing," Luis replied. "Watch your back."

Seth hung up, and somehow the trailer felt emptier than usual. He turned on some music and pulled out a file on Corson Valac, Gremory's disciple who had made Richmond his home. But as he slogged through the information, he found his focus had gone to shit. His mind wandered, wondering how Sonny's evening was going.

Did Sonny make a habit of picking up dates at the bar? Seth wanted to think their connection had been special, but a guy who looked like Sonny would have his pick of partners, and Treddy's probably turned into a meat market late night. He hoped that Sonny had been telling the truth about meeting up with him tomorrow.

But was he going back tomorrow? After all, he only had four days until Halloween, when Valac was likely to make a move against Malone, and Seth still didn't know what either Malone or Valac looked like, or where to find them. Maybe the whole thing with Sonny was a bad idea, a diversion he couldn't afford when Malone's life was on the line.

Then again, Sonny might be a good ally, someone who could lead him to Malone and who knew the area. And if he spent the day chasing down leads, trying to uncover Valac's current identity and getting his bearings, surely he could spare a few hours in the evening? *Does it count as interrogating a witness if I'm giving him a hand job while I ask the questions?*

By one a.m., Seth finally gave up on research, pitched the beer bottle, and headed for bed. And if he jacked himself off to thoughts about a certain dark-haired bartender, Seth figured that was his dirty little secret.

4

SONNY

"Your boyfriend's back."

Izzy's words sent a chill down Sonny's back, and he turned quickly, scanning the crowd for stalker-Mike. "Where?"

"Chill," Izzy said, laying a hand on his arm. "I meant, the cute guy from last night." Her eyes narrowed. "Or did he turn out to be trouble? Just say the word, and I can spill hot sauce in his food."

Sonny's heart slowed when he realized Izzy meant Seth, then sped up again for an entirely different reason. "He's here?" This time he didn't turn, hoping he could hang on to some dignity instead of looking like a besotted schoolboy.

"You like him," Izzy teased in a sing-song voice.

"What's not to like?" Sonny replied, trying for off-handed.

Izzy grinned. "If he came back for a second round, he's totally into you."

Sonny rolled his eyes. "We never got to round one," he admitted. "Eddie called off sick, remember?"

Izzy gave him a look. "You were gone for more than half an hour. That's more than enough for most guys."

"TMI, Iz." Sonny resisted the urge to comb a hand through his hair, which would only get him more teasing from Izzy. "Hey, what's put a bug up Jackie's ass tonight? Someone stiff her on tips?"

Izzy shrugged. "Don't know. She got a phone call right after she came in, and that put her into a snit." She leaned forward. "And if she says anything to you...don't let her spoil the mood. I think she must have just broken up with someone. She grumbled about you hooking up until Liam called you back in."

Sonny raised an eyebrow. "She does know I'm gay, right?"

"It wasn't like she wanted you, more like she was jealous anyone was getting some, and she wasn't."

"Not my problem," Sonny said, "I'm planning to have a very good night."

Izzy thumped him with a backhand to the chest. "Now who's TMI? Go get him, Tiger."

Sonny took a deep breath, hoped he didn't look too excited, and walked over to where Seth had taken a seat. "Can I get something for you?" he asked, trying to gauge Seth's intentions. He'd been afraid Seth might not come back, that maybe Seth had either wanted a quick hook-up or might be busy with other plans. Sonny couldn't stop himself from grinning and felt warm all over when Seth smiled back.

"I'm looking forward to that beer you mentioned," Seth drawled. His gaze met Sonny's, and he shifted on his barstool like he needed to adjust himself.

"Glad to get you one for now, and we can decide where to go later," Sonny replied, pitching his voice so only Seth could hear him.

"I already know where I want to go," Seth answered, still making eye contact. If he'd dropped his gaze to Sonny's package, it would have sounded cheesy, but when he didn't look away, it was fucking hot.

"Coming right up," Sonny managed, finding himself unusually tongue-tied. He brought the beer, and Seth gave him a slow smile that lit up his eyes. Sonny hoped no one would notice he'd just popped a boner behind the bar.

The night got busy after that, giving Sonny little time to flirt. Jackie's mood only got worse, but Sonny and Izzy managed to keep the customers happy. Finally, seven o'clock rolled around, and Seth was still loitering over a plate of cold fries at the end of the bar. Sonny rang out, hung up his apron, and told Cole, the replacement bartender, to lose his number tonight, no matter who called off or didn't show.

"Ready?" Sonny asked after they left Treddy's. He definitely hoped that before the night was done, he'd get to see Seth's lean, muscular body in bed, but he wasn't really in the mood for a fast fuck. It was still early. They could go home, fool around, fool around some more, and maybe get down to business, make an evening of it. For the first time in a long while, that really appealed to Sonny, and since Seth hadn't tried to drag him into any dark alleys for a sloppy blow job, he hoped they were on the same page.

"Did you drive? You'll want to follow me. My place is too far to walk."

"I parked behind Treddy's," Seth replied, and when they went back to reclaim their vehicles, Sonny let out a whistle at the sleek motorcycle.

"That's yours? Sweet. Had her long?" Sonny couldn't resist running a hand along the Hayabusa's curves, and Seth gave him a proud grin.

"Couple of years. She's fast and maneuverable." Seth grabbed his helmet and strapped it in place, then swung a leg over the bike. Sonny felt himself get hard just looking at those long legs straddling the seat.

"I've got the Camaro," he said with a nod toward the older black sports car.

"Nice," Seth replied. "I bet she's a good ride," he added with a suggestive smile.

Holy shit, he's got a mouth on him. Maybe this won't go slowly after all. He looked at Seth's lips, pink and full, and pictured them around his cock. *Thank fuck its cold outside, or I'd be getting a hard-on in the parking lot. It's past time to get home and get this show on the road.*

"Follow me. It's not far, and you can park beside the building," Sonny said, with the feeling that Seth was giving him an appreciative once-over, too.

Sonny rented an apartment in a converted old house in the district known as The Fan. It wasn't as fancy and luxurious as the newly built complexes, but it felt comfortable and lived in, something the ritzy modern apartments lacked.

The three-story house had been split into three large apartments, one on each floor, and the main stairway reconfigured to provide a common outside door and private interior entrances. The tenant in the second-floor apartment worked nights, and the woman on the third floor had been on vacation for a couple of weeks, so they had the whole building to themselves. Sonny parked in his spot on the small gravel lot for residents behind the house and noticed that Seth pushed his bike against the wall behind the bedroom window.

"We can go in the back," Sonny said, opening the door to the kitchen and leading the way inside, glad he had tidied up that morning. He headed into the living room. What had once been a dining room was now his office, and the bedroom lay behind the living room. "The house is seventy-five years old, and they upgraded the mechanical systems when they split it into apartments, but they left as many of the original details as they could. So, yeah, plaster walls, hardwood floors, nice fireplaces. It's not as fancy—"

"It's really nice," Seth said, carefully taking off his leather jacket and draping it over the back of a living room chair. "Feels…homey."

Sonny tilted his head, trying to get a read on whether Seth was mocking him, but the voice and expression looked sincere. "That's what I liked about it," he said with a shrug, walking back to the kitchen to get two beers from the fridge. "Quiet and not in the thick of things."

What did the apartment say about the man who lived in it? Sonny wondered. He hadn't brought anyone home in a long time. A bookcase held the sci-fi and fantasy books he had accumulated over the years, mostly from yard sales and used book stores, plus his collection of DVDs from the same sources. Here and there were framed snapshots of him with friends kayaking, backpacking, and swimming, and a few from his martial arts competitions. He had nothing from his childhood, no soccer trophies or graduation photos, and even if he did have pictures of his family, he wouldn't display them. He was dead to them.

Sonny had sunk most of his money into his computer, camera, stereo, TV, and gaming systems. His couch was overstuffed, comfortable, and long enough for him to lie down. A worn leather recliner and a battered oak coffee table made up the rest of the room's furnishings. A few framed photographs on the walls were shots he had taken and blown up of local landmarks. Sonny spoke a command to the app on his phone, and the lights got brighter, the TV turned on, and music began to play.

Seth raised an eyebrow. "Nice," he said.

Sonny felt awkward. After last night, he figured this wasn't going to be a hard fast fuck up against the wall, although he wouldn't be opposed to trying that later on. That made it more of a date than a hook-up, and Sonny was out of practice. *When in doubt, improvise.*

"You want to pick something on Netflix?" Sonny offered, taking a seat on the couch with plenty of room for Seth to join him. Seth smiled and dropped beside him, close enough for their knees to touch.

"I'm pretty easy to please," Seth said. "I like any movie where lots of shit blows up."

"Our tastes run in the same direction." Sonny pulled up an old Bruce Willis movie and getting a pleased nod in response.

"So...you do a lot of outdoors stuff?" Seth asked, glancing at the photos.

Sonny shrugged. "The weather's good here most of the year, and its cheap entertainment. How about you?"

"I camp a lot," Seth replied. "Did you take those pictures?" he asked, with a nod toward the framed landscapes.

Sonny grinned. "Yeah. I'm still practicing, but photography's my hobby. Obsession, maybe. I do some graphic design work on the side. Maybe it'll turn into something someday."

Sonny took a pull from his beer. Seth was giving off all the right signals, but not making any moves. Was he waiting for Sonny to set the pace? Sonny shifted, so their legs touched hip to thigh. Seth leaned back, stretching his arms over his head and arching his back. His shirt rode up, exposing a strip of tanned skin and a flat belly. Sonny's cock was rock hard, and from the bulge in Seth's jeans, he wasn't the only one.

Taking a chance, Sonny shifted and brushed a kiss against Seth's jaw. Seth turned toward him, meeting his lips and bringing a hand up behind Sonny's head, tangling his fingers in Sonny's dark hair.

Never breaking contact, Sonny pivoted and straddled Seth, his knees on either side of Seth's hips. "This okay?" He murmured between kisses.

Seth nodded, and drew Sonny back to him, tasting Sonny's lips with the tip of his tongue. Sonny opened to him, and Seth's tongue slipped inside, exploring and tasting. Sonny ground against him, their cocks sliding against each other beneath the denim, and Seth's breath hitched.

"Like that?"

Seth murmured his assent, and Sonny brought his hands up to Seth's chest, slowly opening the buttons on his shirt and pulling it loose from his jeans. He slid his hands across the smooth, hard muscle, as Seth let his hands explore Sonny's back, then settled with a firm grip on Sonny's ass and pulled him even closer.

Sonny rutted against him, and Seth raised his hips, bucking up into him. "We keep this up, I'm gonna come just like this," Sonny murmured breathlessly. "I've got a better idea."

He gave Seth a last, sweet kiss and slid down until he was on his knees between Seth's legs. He met Seth's gaze, looking for consent, and Seth threaded his fingers through Sonny's hair, spreading his legs wider. Sonny worked Seth's belt free, then the zipper, and pulled them away far enough to eye the thick, hard bulge in Seth's boxer briefs. He leaned forward, mouthing along the cotton, and Seth gasped and pushed forward.

Maybe it's been a while for both of us.

Seth's swollen cock was leaking pre-come, and Sonny got a taste of bitter, salty fluid that made his own erection ache. He pulled Seth's jeans down farther, and then his briefs, freeing Seth's dick and letting it stand up full and proud out of a nest of blond curls. Sonny palmed his own hard-on to keep himself from coming in his pants like a teenager as he stretched out his tongue to lick a stripe up Seth's prick, taking his time, working his way up to the round knob, letting the tip of his tongue sample the bead of fluid at the slit. Seth groaned, and his fingers tightened with urgency in Sonny's hair, not painful but eager.

His other hand grabbed a fistful of cushion, and he threw his head back as Sonny opened his mouth and took Seth's long cock all the way down to the root.

"Jesus. Fuck, Sonny," Seth gasped.

Sonny hummed in acknowledgment, and Seth writhed at the vibration. Sonny pulled him all the way in until the tip of Seth's cock bumped against the back of his throat, inhaling to lose himself in the smell of soap and musk that was distinctly Seth. He smelled like campfire and fresh air, and the combination had Sonny squeezed himself again to stave off his building climax.

Neither of them were going to take long at this rate. Sonny bobbed and sucked, letting his tongue lave against the veins on the tender underside of Seth's cock, sweeping over the head and teasing at the slit.

"Fuck, I'm close. Sonny—"

Instead of pulling off, Sonny went down on him all the way, burying his nose in those wiry blond curls, and Seth arched up with a cry, spilling his release down Sonny's throat. Sonny swallowed it all; licking an errant drop from his lips when he was sure Seth was looking.

"Stand up." Seth's pupils were blown so wide only thin rings of brown remained, and his flushed face and mussed hair were the picture of desire. "Right there," he said as Sonny got to his feet. Seth's eyes took on a predatory glint as he pushed up Sonny's t-shirt and leaned forward, letting his tongue trace the trail of dark hair to his waistband.

A look between them asked and answered, and then Seth worked the buttons of Sonny's 501s urgently, clumsy with desire. He pushed down both jeans and briefs at once, eying Sonny's straining erection like a meal to be devoured. Seth reached out, grasping Sonny's ass with both hands. *God, those long fingers.* Sonny wasn't a small man, not at six-one and one-eighty, but Seth's hands covered his ass cheeks, giving them a squeeze that made Sonny's breath hitch and pulled him closer.

Seth licked his way up Sonny's rock-hard cock and brought one hand around and between his legs to fondle Sonny's balls, as the other still grasped his ass. Seth shifted forward, bracing Sonny's knees with his own, keeping him upright as he began to tease the blood-red prick in front of him, lapping up the sticky trail of pre-come and then swirling his tongue against the sensitive head, caressing the stiff length with sinfully soft, plump lips made for sucking.

It was Sonny's turn to moan, and he bowed forward, silently begging Seth to take him in. He reached out, one hand on Seth's strong shoulder, feeling the muscles there, and the other hand in Seth's soft hair, long enough on top for him to tangle around his fingers.

"Oh, fuck. So good. Don't stop. Please—"

Seth swallowed him down, taking his whole swollen length until Sonny felt Seth's throat close around him.

"Shit. Damn. Fuck, Seth, I'm not gonna last."

Seth pulled back, then went down again, as his hand rolled Sonny's balls, gently tugging and stroking them. Sonny trembled with the strain of keeping himself on his feet as Seth devoured his cock with that hot, wet mouth, plush lips sliding up and down his length, sucking and swirling. Fingers slid back from Sonny's balls, sliding against his taint, and farther stroking and teasing but not breaching his hole.

Sonny lost it, and his orgasm roared through him, stealing his breath and whiting out his vision. His heart thundered in his ears, and he couldn't catch his breath as Seth slid down on him over and over, then sucked as he released, swallowing down his come, finally pulling off with an obscene "pop."

Sonny swayed, and Seth caught him, easing Sonny down beside him on the couch. "That was…" Sonny gasped, trying to find both breath and words.

"Yeah. You were," Seth replied, a warmth in his voice Sonny hadn't noticed before. He shifted, and Seth kissed him. He could taste himself on Seth's lips, and that sent a spark right down to his cock, arguing for another round. Sonny kissed him back and felt the same hunger as their tongues slid against each other and teeth clashed.

Sonny surprised himself how soon he was hard again, and when he reached toward Seth, he found a stiff cock waiting for attention. He curled his hand around Seth's length as Seth did the same for him, and they fell sideways on the couch together, jacking each other and kissing, a tangle of legs and half-shed clothing. Seth pushed Sonny's t-shirt up and helped him strip it off one-handed, exposing Sonny's smooth, toned chest, a smattering of dark hairs and brown nipples. Sonny pushed back Seth's shirt, loving the ridged muscle under his palm, tweaking his pink nipples to hard buds.

He felt Seth's urgency, and strength enough to easily hold Sonny against him. Sonny had wondered what Seth would be like, soft or demanding, aggressive or yielding. If this encounter was anything to go by, Seth was an intriguing mixture. Hungry, but gentle, not pushing for more than Sonny offered. Holding back, willing to let Sonny set the pace, but beneath that, Sonny suspected Seth would have no problem being in control. That thought went straight to his cock, and he jacked Seth faster, letting the slick from his tip ease the delicious friction.

This time, they spilled almost at the same time, Seth just a stroke or two behind him, and collapsed together, with Sonny's head on Seth's shoulder, and Seth's arms around him. He reached over their heads to grab a box of tissues from the end table and cleaned up the come that streaked their bare chests.

"That was...amazing," Seth said, brushing a kiss across Sonny's lips. "But it's going to take a bit to be ready for a third go."

"Do you want a third go?" Sonny murmured, pushing up on one elbow to look at Seth up close. God, he was beautiful. High cheekbones, reddish scruff, and brown eyes the color of milk chocolate. Sonny traced a scar along Seth's jaw, and Seth's eyes darkened enough Sonny knew not to ask where it came from.

"I do if you do," Seth said. "I'd say I was up for it, but, as you can see, I'm clearly not just yet."

"Since we've worked up an appetite, how about we bake the pizza I've got in my fridge, have another beer, watch the end of the movie, and then you fuck me," Sonny said.

Seth's eyes widened as if he hadn't quite expected that. "You sure?"

"Unless you'd rather it the other way around."

"I'd like to fuck you," Seth said, lifting a hand to cup Sonny's face. "I think I'd like that very much."

Sonny dipped down for a quick kiss, then extricated himself from

Seth's arms with regret. He tucked himself back in as Seth did the same, then headed for the kitchen and pulled out a frozen pizza. "This okay? I can order in if you'd rather."

"Fine with me. I like that brand." Seth fetched two more beers from the fridge and leaned against the counter as Sonny turned on the oven and dug out a bag of chips from a cabinet and a jar of salsa from the fridge.

While the pizza baked, Seth asked about Sonny's hobbies, and they compared notes on movies and TV shows that they hadn't covered the night before. Sonny enjoyed the conversation and the fact that they had a lot in common, but it didn't escape him that Seth aptly deflected any questions about himself, or answered in the most general terms.

Sonny didn't push, knowing that it didn't matter, not if Seth was just passing through and this was a one-night-only pairing. That thought made him unexpectedly pensive. It had been a long while since he'd met someone he'd felt such a strong attraction to so quickly, and who shared a lot of the same interests, and it didn't seem fair that they didn't even have the option of seeing where things went.

"That smells so good," Seth said as Sonny brought the pizza out of the oven.

"My secret recipe," Sonny said with a chuckle. "I add red pepper flakes and a dash of garlic powder." They took their plates and beer into the living room and sprawled on the couch to eat, sitting close. They cheered for Bruce Willis, fist-pumped the air when large buildings exploded, and mocked the villain, both of them knowing the lines by heart.

By the time they had devoured the pizza and chips, a second movie was nearly done. They were full and comfortable, with Sonny turned to lean against Seth's chest and Seth's arm slipped around his shoulders, his hand splayed across Sonny's belly.

No one would mistake Sonny for being petite in any way, but next to Seth, he felt small. He had carded Seth at the bar, so he knew they were close in age, with Seth just two years older. Not only was Seth taller by a couple of inches, he probably had Sonny by at least thirty pounds of muscle. None of Sonny's prior boyfriends had been bigger than he was, and the contrast, the feeling of being secure and safe, was a surprising turn-on. Something about Seth felt solid, and Sonny hadn't realized how much he wanted that from a partner until right now.

He's not a partner. He's not a lover. He's a one-night stand. Geez, get a grip. You don't need to come off pathetic, he warned himself.

On the other hand, Seth seemed to be enjoying the evening as much as Sonny, even if they talked about nothing important. When the movie wrapped up, Seth realized it was nearly midnight.

"About that third round," he murmured, turning and stretching up to nip at Seth's neck. Seth bent down and kissed him.

"Yes?"

"Still interested?"

Seth took Sonny's hand and pressed it against the hard length of his cock beneath his jeans. "What do you think?"

"Let me take the dishes to the kitchen and lock up," Sonny said, then hesitated. "I...I don't mean to assume. Would you like to stay the night? Morning sex is one of my specialties, and I make great pancakes."

Seth hesitated, and Sonny feared he had pushed too far, but then Seth smiled. "Sure. Do you have to work early?" He stood and helped gather up the plates, heading toward the dishwasher as Sonny double-checked the deadbolt and slid the chain, then turned off the TV and the lights.

"Nope. Not until around ten. I switched to early shifts for a while."

"My lucky night," Seth said. He threw his jacket over his arm and paused outside the kitchen, and Sonny realized he was waiting to be led to the bedroom. What might have been uncomfortable didn't seem awkward at all, and Sonny cursed fate again for teasing him with someone he liked and couldn't keep.

Maybe I'll get lucky, and he'll come back to visit again. Stranger things have happened.

Sonny took his hand and headed through the door into the bedroom. The king-sized bed had been one of his few non-electronic splurges, that and good sheets. The bed took up most of the room, along with a nightstand and bookshelf filled with more second-hand treasures, as well as some of the boxed tabletop role-playing games he sometimes brought to staff parties at Treddy's. Seth hung his jacket over the back of a chair and toed out of his shoes.

"Bathroom's that way," Sonny said. "I've got extra toothbrushes in the closet, on the shelf below the towels. This place also has decent water pressure, so the shower's something to look forward to in the morning."

Seth poked his head into the bathroom and grinned wickedly. "Big enough for two. Saving water and all."

Sonny'd never been a morning person, but that offer might make him reconsider. Right now, he focused on getting ready to enjoy the rest of the evening. Just the thought of prepping for Seth to fuck him made Sonny throb.

"Going somewhere?" Seth asked, noting a small packed duffel back to one side. He stepped around it, looking out the window, checking on his bike, which was parked just below.

"Some friends and I are going down to Virginia Beach this weekend just to get away. It's off-season, so the rooms are cheap." He found himself wishing Seth could go with them. It might be too cold to go in the ocean, but he'd pay money to see Seth come out of the indoor pool in a pair of wet board shorts.

Seth squatted to see the titles on the bookshelf, and Sonny liked the way Seth's jeans pulled tight over his perfect ass. He wondered if they'd be up to a fourth go in the morning. Seth hadn't flinched when Sonny questioned who'd bottom, suggesting Seth might be willing to switch. As much as he ached to have Seth's thick length buried deep in his ass, the thought of pounding into Seth's tight channel nearly made him spill just thinking about it.

"I've played all of these. Especially this one," he said, pointing to one of Sonny's favorites. "You've got good taste."

"You have a regular group?" Sonny asked as Seth rose.

"No, not since I got back. We played a lot when I was in the army. Something to do when they weren't shooting at us for real."

Sonny had so many questions, but he didn't want to make Seth pull away. If they only had one night, he intended to make it a great memory. "I had some other games in mind tonight," Sonny said, slipping up behind Seth and sliding his arms around Seth's waist. Seth turned to face him, and Sonny reached up, meeting Seth's gaze as he pushed his open shirt over his shoulders and let it fall to the ground.

Fuck, he was ripped. Sonny felt his mouth water as he got a good look at those washboard abs and the V of his Adonis belt that led Sonny's gaze to the bulge beneath Seth's button-downs. Several scars marked Seth's skin, pink or white against his tan. More than one must have been serious. That just added to the delicious mystery. But damn, that body. Sonny was in good form, he worked out, and he trained at the dojo, but he wasn't in *that* kind of shape. He felt a pang of insecurity as Seth pulled him close.

"Look at you," Seth murmured, and Sonny had never before thought that the phrase "devoured with his eyes" was a real thing, but he felt like a steak in front of a hungry man. "So beautiful." He reached out to trace Sonny's jawline, stroking his cheek with the back of his fingers and running the pad of his thumb over Sonny's lips. Sonny let Seth draw him close, chest to chest, and tilted his head back for a kiss. He'd never had to stand on his toes before to reach a lover, and that sent a bolt of lust right to his dick.

"I want you to fuck me, Seth," Sonny said, pulling back from the kiss far enough to look up at Seth from under his lashes. "Don't make me wait."

Seth kept his arms around Sonny, walking him backward toward the bed until Sonny's calves hit the mattress and he let himself fall backward. Seth gave him a sinful look and reached out to unbutton Sonny's jeans, then yanked them and his briefs down in one pull.

"Oh, God," Seth groaned and swallowed hard. "Look at you."

Sonny pushed himself up on his elbows, bent one knee and spread his legs a little wider. He reached down to take himself in hand, keeping eye contact with Seth the whole time as he jacked himself. Being naked and spread wide for Seth's view while his partner was still partly clothed made him unbearably hard.

"Fuck."

"That's the idea, but it's kinda lonely here," Sonny teased. "Don't want to be dancing with myself."

He could have sworn Seth growled, shucking off his jeans and boxers and crawling over Sonny as Sonny moved up on the bed to make room. Holy hell, up close Seth seemed even larger, looming over him on his hands and knees, his erection bobbing against his tight abs, leaking a stream of pre-come.

"The lube and the condoms are in the drawer," Sonny said, amazed his voice didn't tremble at the predatory look Seth leveled at him.

"We'll get to that. No hurry," Seth said with a dirty smile. He sank down, catching Sonny's swollen cock in his mouth, wrapping his lips around Sonny's girth and swallowing him down.

"Fuuuck," Sonny breathed, trying not to come before they'd even gotten started. Seth chuckled and pulled off, then turned to leave a trail of kisses and light nips down Sonny's sensitive inner thigh on one side, repeating the sweet torture on the other as Sonny grabbed fistfuls of the sheets and writhed.

Sonny felt Seth shift, then gently take his sac in his mouth, licking and sucking, rolling the sensitive orbs between his tongue and cheek.

"Roll over," Seth said quietly, and Sonny obliged, grabbing a pillow to put beneath his hips. Sonny opened the drawer and took out a tube and one of the foil packets.

"Just so you know...I'm negative," Sonny managed to say. "In case it breaks or something."

"So am I," Seth said, and the sound of the packet tearing and then his hand slicking up his wrapped cock nearly undid Sonny.

Seth leaned over Sonny, keeping his weight on his arms but pressing himself against Seth's back, licking and kissing his way down Sonny's spine until Sonny didn't think he could take any more stimulation. Seth gave a playful bite to one ass cheek, then spread him wide and licked a stripe down his cleft and over his hole.

Sonny couldn't figure out if Seth had a lot of experience, a good imagination, or had watched a lot of porn, but wherever his ideas came from, Sonny was totally on board. Seth rimmed his pucker with the tip of his tongue before slipping a slick finger inside, and Sonny couldn't put his thoughts together enough to swear. All he could do was hang on to the sheets, trying to imagine it feeling even better with Seth inside him.

"Fuck yourself on my fingers," Seth murmured, letting a drizzle of lube slither down Sonny's crack. "I don't want to hurt you." A second

Witchbane

finger joined the first, scissoring to stretch Sonny open, and Sonny pushed back, riding the stretch and burn, knowing that even three fingers wouldn't completely open him up for Seth's thick cock.

"Come on," Sonny urged. "Fuck me already."

Seth angled his fingers, brushing over Sonny's prostate, nearly sending him off the bed. He pulled his fingers out, and put his hands on Sonny's hips, lining himself up with his partner's hole.

Sonny gritted his teeth as Seth pushed in, knowing the burn would give way to pleasure. Shit, it had been a long time since he'd gone this far with anyone. He had to trust someone to let them fuck him, and he preferred to like someone to go farther than rubbing each other off or a quick blowjob. Seth made trusting easy.

"Come on, come on," Sonny urged, even as he appreciated Seth giving him a chance to adjust. Seth was big, maybe the same length as Sonny but thicker, and Sonny knew he would feel the sweet intrusion tomorrow.

He turned his head to glimpse Seth on his knees behind him, beginning to rock back and forth, and Sonny had to grab himself and squeeze to keep it from all being over too soon. Seth bottomed out, balls slapping against Sonny's ass, and gripped his hips tightly.

"Hang on," he murmured, drawing back and thrusting forward. Before they'd gone half a dozen strokes, Sonny was pushing back to meet Seth, finding a rhythm. Seth tried to make it last, but neither of them could wait. Sonny didn't expect it when Seth wrapped one arm around his chest and drew him up onto his knees, changing the angle and going deeper. The other hand came around to stroke Sonny, pumping his leaking cock.

"Come for me. I'm not going to last much longer," Seth whispered in his ear. Sonny groaned and shot, coating Seth's hand and painting his chest. A few more thrusts and Seth lost his rhythm, his movements stuttering as he chased his release.

"Good?" He murmured, easing Sonny back down to the mattress. He pulled out gently, slipped out of the condom and tied it off, dropping it in the waste can by the bed.

"That was...pretty amazing," Sonny said, still in a post-orgasmic haze. Seth reached for tissues and cleaned them both up. He hesitated, and for a moment, Sonny feared Seth might have had second thoughts about staying. He didn't want to pressure Seth, but he also really didn't want this night to be over sooner than it had to be.

"Something wrong?" Sonny asked.

"You mind if I leave a light on in the other room?" Seth asked, giving him a self-conscious smile. "I don't like to wake up in the dark someplace new. It's an army thing."

"Turn the light on over the sink in the kitchen," Sonny said, too boneless to move. Damn, but he was going to be sore tomorrow, although it was worth every twinge. "It'll light the living room but won't be too bright from here."

Seth padded out, checked the locks on the door, switched on the light and came back. Sonny was already beneath the blanket. He lifted one side, inviting Seth to join him.

"I had an amazing evening," Sonny said, taking the opportunity to lay his head on Seth's chest while he could. "Thank you."

"I had a pretty amazing evening myself," Seth said with a chuckle. "So thank you. It wasn't what I had in mind when I first went to Treddy's, but I'm happy it ended up the way it did."

Sonny thought of a million things he wanted to say, none of them reasonable. He knew what Seth was able to give him when they left the bar together. That didn't stop him from wishing he could have a lot more. But giving voice to any of those thoughts would just spoil a perfect night, so he pushed up to brush Seth's lips, and then settled into the crook of his shoulder. "Good night. I promise that fourth round bright and early."

Seth smoothed a hand over Sonny's hair, twisting a strand around his ear. "Then 'sweet dreams' is more like it," he said. "Something to look forward to."

5
SETH

SETH WOKE, UNSURE FOR A MOMENT WHERE HE WAS. THEN IT ALL CAME back—Treddy's, Sonny, and amazing sex. The lean, warm body that pressed up against him felt good. Yet a knot in his gut warned of danger. He heard sounds beyond the living room. *Noisy neighbors.* Then he remembered no one else was supposed to be in the building.

The outside door splintered with a crash.

"Jackson Malone!" A man's voice shouted.

Seth sat bolt upright. Sonny barely stirred. Running footsteps headed toward the bedroom, and in the light from the kitchen, Seth glimpsed several armed men.

Seth reacted. He grabbed Sonny with one arm, pulling him off the bed and onto the floor. In the next move, he drew his Beretta from his jacket pocket, dodging a bullet that struck the wall behind him, and returning fire to wound the shooter in the shoulder. Seth kicked the door shut and slid the dresser in front of it.

"What the hell?" Sonny looked disoriented, jolted out of a deep sleep.

"Someone broke in. They're shooting at us. Get dressed, grab your wallet and your bag. We're getting out of here." Seth snapped, going into combat mode. The dresser wouldn't hold long, and a shot ripped into the door knob and flimsy lock.

"Shit. My phone's in the kitchen."

"Leave it."

Seth didn't bother lacing his boots. He pulled up his jeans and threw a coat from the closet at Sonny, then his pack. "Come on!" He hissed as the thud of bodies battering against the door grew louder. Seth flung open the window and crawled out, pulling Sonny with him. "Get on," he said, climbing onto his Hayabusa. "And hold tight."

They roared away, and Seth expected to hear shots behind them, feel bullets tearing into them. The cold wind whipped through his hair and sliced against his skin.

The shooter had shouted for Jackson Malone as if he expected him to be there.

Fuck. Jack*son*. Sonny.

Shit. He'd just slept with the guy he'd come to town to protect.

Sonny's arms were tight around Seth's waist; his body pressed up against Seth's back. If they hadn't just been shot at, it would have made Seth hard. Fuck, this had gotten completely out of control.

Seth had intended to ask Sonny about "Jackson" over breakfast. He'd found him all right. Bonus for saving him from a bunch of thugs.

Explaining was going to be a real bitch.

After Seth felt certain they'd gotten free, no trace of a tag, he headed for the campground. Since it was closed for the season, neither the sign nor the entrance lane were lit. They roared down the dark road, pulling in next to where Seth's fifth-wheeler sat detached from the truck, across from the campground canteen building.

Seth waited for Sonny—Jackson—to dismount before parking the bike beside the trailer.

"What the hell just happened?" Sonny demanded

"Someone broke in and started shooting."

"Why the fuck would anyone do that?" Sonny paced back and forth, eyes wide with panic.

"I have a pretty good idea why they were after you. Just—let me explain."

"This is where you live?" Sonny asked, eyeing the camper suspiciously.

"Told you I did a lot of camping."

Sonny's dark hair was a wind-blown tangle. The cold wind stung his cheeks, and fear widened his eyes. It hit Seth that Sonny's fear included being afraid of him.

"Come in, please. I can explain."

He thought Sonny would refuse; then it must have occurred to him that at the moment, he had nowhere to go. Sonny slumped and followed Seth into the trailer. Seth turned on the lights and the gas fireplace, then went to get a kettle boiling for tea. Just for background, he flipped on the flat screen TV and muted the sound.

"What the fuck happened back there?" Sonny exploded. "Who were those guys? Why were they after me—with guns?"

"I can explain, just—"

"And why the fuck did you shoot one of them?"

"Listen—"

"Did you know they were going to show up? Is that why you had the gun?" Sonny looked wild, anger covering terror.

"*You're* Jackson Malone," Seth returned, still stunned at the unexpected turn of events.

"Oh, shit. Those guys yelled my name. I heard them. Shit, fuck, damn." Sonny turned away and ran his hands through hair. "What the fuck is going on?"

"If you're Jackson, why did you tell me your name was Sonny?"

Sonny looked at him incredulously. "Does it matter?"

"Yes. Fuck. It matters!"

"No one calls me Jackson. My friends and family call me Evan—my middle name. And I go by Sonny at the bar because I had a stalker, and that way it's harder for anyone to find me." He stared at Seth. "Who are you?"

"I'm exactly who I said I was. And I came to Richmond to save your life because in the next three days, people are going to try to kill you."

Sonny's expression made it clear he thought Seth was insane. "No. That kind of thing happens in movies. It does not happen to me. I'm a bartender. A fucking bartender. There is no reason for anyone except my crazy ex- to want to kill me."

"Do you owe gambling debts? Cheat with some jealous guy's boyfriend? Skip out on paying a dealer?"

"Hell, no!"

"Then why do you think those guys broke into your apartment shouting your name at three in the goddamn morning?" Seth argued. "They sure as fuck didn't come to wish you Merry Christmas."

Sonny dropped onto the leather couch and leaned forward, putting his head in his hands. "None of this makes sense. Why would you come here to save my life? How did you even know who I was?" He looked up, and this time his eyes filled with hurt more than fear. "Is that why you went home with me? Why you slept with me?"

Seth started shaking his head before Sonny even stopped talking. "No. No. That…I didn't plan on that. I…made a mistake."

"A *mistake*?"

Shit. Could he be any more stupid? "I didn't mean it that way," Seth said, holding up both hands in appeasement. "Sleeping with 'Sonny the cute bartender' wasn't a mistake. Letting down my guard when I should have been protecting Jackson—Evan—that was where I screwed up."

"Hello? I'm all the same person."

"Yeah? Well I didn't know that when we met. I was in town looking for you—Jackson."

"I guess you found me."

Fuck, he was screwing this up royally. Not only was his opportunity to get…Evan…to believe him slipping away, he was also completely blowing any chance he might have with the great guy he had really enjoyed spending an evening with, never mind the awesome sex.

"Okay…shit. I'm not even sure what to call you. Sonny? Or Evan?"

"Evan."

"All right then. Evan—will you at least let me explain?" Seth went to pour hot water for tea and returned with a steaming mug, which Evan accepted gratefully. Seth poured himself a cup as well and started a pot of coffee. It was going to be a long night.

"I'm listening."

Shit. There was no way this was going to go well. Seth rubbed his neck. "Two years ago, my brother was murdered. The police blamed it on interrupting a drug deal, but that's not what happened."

"How do you know?"

Seth met his gaze, letting Evan see the pain and guilt. "Because I was with him. They beat me, knocked me out. When I came to, Jesse was dead. Mutilated."

"Jesus," Evan swore under his breath.

"The police stopped looking into it. I didn't. I've found evidence that the man who killed Jesse was a member of a violent cult. Their hero was hanged for his crimes a long time ago, and ever since, the cult members have been hunting down the families of the deputies who killed their leader." Seth said, trying not to freak Evan out by bringing witches and magic into it. Not yet, anyhow.

"Twelve deputies. Each year, one of the members kills the firstborn or oldest of the next generation of the deputies' descendants. Did a man in your family die unexpectedly twelve years ago? An accident? Disappeared?"

Evan paled. "Uncle Vince. Farm machinery accident. It was…bad."

"It wasn't an accident. He was your father's older brother?"

"How did you—"

"It fits the pattern. I've spent nearly two years researching, piecing it together, finding the descendants, tracking them—"

"You stalked me," Evan gasped. "Shit. That's how you found me."

"Except there aren't any pictures online."

"So you didn't recognize me…"

"I didn't 'stalk' you," Seth said, trying to keep the conversation from becoming a complete clusterfuck. "It's called 'protective surveillance.'"

"This is crazy." Evan stood and paced. "You're crazy. This is what happens when I bring a stranger home."

"And if you hadn't brought me home … what would have happened then?"

"This…can't be happening to me."

"You're in danger, Evan," Seth said. "Those guys who broke down your door—"

"Maybe they were just there to rob me," Evan said. "Maybe you've got it wrong. Maybe—"

"Because robbers always yell out your name, and bring along a SWAT team?"

"You shot somebody!"

"He shot first! And I winged him," Seth retorted. "He sure as hell wasn't shooting to wound."

Seth expected Evan to respond, only to see him standing still and pale, staring at the TV. "Turn it up," Evan said in a strangled voice.

"...house fire in The Fan tonight. Neighbors say this house in the 700 block of North Lombardy Street erupted into flames just after three this morning. Firefighters turned out to fight the blaze, but could not save the building. Luckily, no one was home at the time. In other news, a local nightspot is out of commission after a gas leak exploded at Tredegar's in Shockoe Bottom. Police are still on the scene, and sources say that the building was empty since the explosion happened after hours..."

"My car," Evan groaned, and Seth looked at the screen. He could just make the crushed back end of Evan's car beneath debris where a wall had collapsed on it.

"My apartment," Evan croaked, swallowing hard. "Treddy's. They're gone." He sat back down, hard. "Oh my God. I'm homeless. And my job is gone. Oh, God." Evan's breath came short and fast.

Seth knelt in front of him and reached for his hand. He winced when Evan flinched away. "Don't," Evan warned breathlessly. "None of this makes sense. You don't make sense. Why would anyone want to kill me because of someone who got hanged a long time ago?"

"According to legend, the man who was hanged back then was said to be a powerful warlock, a man named Rhyfel Gremory. The cultists were his...disciples. When he died, they believed his power went to them, making them immortal. They swore vengeance on the sheriff and deputies who killed him, and Gremory's curse lets them keep their immortality so long as they sacrifice one descendent a year," Seth explained, knowing that it sounded insane, even to his ears. So much for trying to keep the magic out of his explanation. Maybe he could still, somehow, get Evan to believe him. "Each disciple…hunts…a particular family, coming back every twelve years for another sacrifice to remain immortal."

Evan stared at him, incredulous. "You're insane. You want me to believe that I'm supposed to be some kind of sick offering to the ghost of a dead warlock? Have you been watching too much TV? That…that doesn't happen. There's no such thing as magic."

"I didn't believe in it either until Jesse died. I swore on his grave I'd keep others from the same fate, that I'd shut down Gremory's disciples for good. I wasn't ready for the fight last year. Richard Pearson is dead because I wasn't up to speed yet. I have to live with that," Seth said, hoping Evan could see the truth in his eyes. "I'm not going to let anything happen to you."

"Not going to let—fuck! I've been shot at, dragged out a window, brought to an abandoned campground by some guy I just met, my apartment burned down, and my bar blew up. Buddy, fuck-all has already 'happened' to me."

Evan stood. "I've got to get out of here." He headed toward the door. Seth was quick to block his path. "Get out of my way."

"Where do you think you're going to go?" Seth asked quietly.

"Are you kidnapping me?"

"No one's kidnapping you. But seriously, it's almost five a.m. The guys who tried to shoot us two hours ago are still out there, looking for you. You're safer here with me."

"Safe? Safe?" Evan looked as if he was headed for an aneurysm.

"At least wait a few more hours," Seth bargained. "Please."

Seth could see that Evan wanted to argue, wanted to storm out the door. He could almost watch the internal argument pro and con and knew which side won the fight when Evan sighed. "All right. I'll wait until it's light. Then I'm leaving."

"What about the guys who shot up your place and set it on fire?"

"I'll go to the cops. One of them is a regular at Treddy's. Officer Clark. He'll help me."

Seth shook his head. "They won't believe you. Or they'll say it was a burglary gone wrong. And meanwhile, Gremory's goons are going to be looking for you."

"Assuming you're not just crazy. After all, you're the one who tracked me here. I've only got your word for the rest of it."

"Fair enough," Seth said. After the fight and the wild ride, his adrenaline had crashed, leaving him exhausted and making his head pound. "Look, you can sleep in the bedroom if you want. I'll stay out here."

"To keep me from escaping?"

"To guard the door."

They stared each other down for a moment, neither willing to budge. Shit. Sonny—no, Evan—was beautiful. Tired, terrified and still feisty, the way Evan braced himself for a fight went right to Seth's cock. Which was just stupid, he told himself. *Even if he didn't think I might be a crazed stalker serial killer, this is doomed before it starts. I'm just the bodyguard. When this is over, he'll go back to his life, and I'll go after the next disciple. He'll leave. Jesse, mom, dad, Colin, Ryan—they all leave.*

"All right," Evan finally conceded, but the stubborn set to his jaw told Seth it wasn't over. He sighed. "I'm not saying I believe any of what you've told me."

"I understand."

"I'm not sure I trust you."

"Can't blame you."

"But...thanks for getting me away from those goons." Evan looked around the trailer as if just now seeing it. "This is nice."

"It was my parents'. They were going to go see all the national parks when my dad retired."

"Were?"

"They died. Car accident."

"I'm sorry."

"So am I."

Evan walked up the steps toward the bedroom. "Bathroom's on the left," Seth called after him. Evan went into the bedroom and closed the door. Seth heard the *snick* of the lock.

Fuck-all. Seth walked back into the living room, knowing he wasn't likely to get much, if any, sleep. He put Evan's empty cup in the sink and sank down on the couch. The TV news ran a never-ending loop of Evan's apartment building in flames, followed by Treddy's with its windows blown out and smoke billowing from its interior.

How did it go so wrong so fast? And how the hell did I end up sleeping with the one guy I shouldn't be fucking? Shit. He really wanted a stiff drink, but he needed his wits sharp. He leaned back against the leather, rubbing his eyes.

Evan didn't believe him. Worse, Evan thought he was a stalker, and that just triggered all kinds of history. Not to mention that normal people didn't believe in things like magic and warlocks, or curses and immortal witch-disciple serial killers. Keeping him safe was going to be a real bitch if Evan fought Seth at every step of the way. He didn't know what he was going to do when Evan wanted to leave, but letting him walk out and get himself killed was out of the question. Then again, so was keeping him prisoner for his own safety. Fuck.

But the worst part? Seth couldn't get the time they'd spent together out of his mind. The way Evan tasted, his scent, the feel of his lithe body under Seth's, the sounds he made when he came. Just the thought of it went right to Seth's uncooperative dick. *Bodyguards who fall for the people they protect always lose in the end. I saw that movie. Kevin Costner ended up alone.*

Shit, this was bad. Because as fantastic as the sex had been, as much natural attraction as there had been between them, Seth genuinely liked Evan. Not just because he was handsome, with chestnut hair and hazel eyes, and a slim, strong body that took Seth's breath away. All those things were great. But Seth had felt comfortable with Evan in a way he hadn't felt around anyone for a long time, not since Jesse. He'd been too obsessed with researching Gremory and his followers to spare much thought for even casual hook-ups, and his track record with boyfriends was disappointing, to say the least.

But if he was going to be with someone, he'd always thought it would be someone like Evan. Funny, easy to talk to, someone who liked the same movies, books, and games. He hadn't felt awkward with Evan; instead, it had felt like slipping on a favorite hoodie, warm and comfortable. They just…fit. He'd known when he agreed to go home with Evan that it was just for one night. That he couldn't stay. But he went anyway.

He was so screwed.

Even if Evan didn't hate him, or think he was insane, what happened once it was all over? Provided he could keep Evan alive? Who'd want to be with a fucked-in-the-head guy who lived in an RV and hunted down bogeymen? Not someone like Evan, who had friends and co-workers and a real life.

No, when Gremory's disciple was dead, and Evan was safe, Evan would find another job and another apartment and another lover. And Seth would drive off into the sunset. Alone.

6

EVAN

Like I'd be able to sleep. Evan lay on the bed and stared up at the trailer's ceiling. The comforter smelled of lemon laundry soap and Seth. Fuck.

Evan couldn't even remember the last time he'd brought someone home with him. There'd been a few, rare, quickie hand jobs out behind the bar or in the backseat of someone's car, and one memorable time in the men's room at one of the nicest restaurants in Richmond. But it had been a while since Evan had liked someone enough, felt comfortable enough with someone, to bring them home. Even longer since he'd let someone fuck him. And when he did, look how it turned out.

He sighed. Last night had been fantastic—right up until the moment it all went to hell. As much as he had been terrified by the armed guys breaking into his apartment, watching Seth go Rambo on their asses would have been a real turn-on—if the bullets hadn't been live ammo. As angry and confused as Evan felt, he knew he owed Seth for saving his life.

But did that debt require believing his wild story?

He scrubbed a hand over his eyes. Evan knew he should be exhausted, but his heart had barely stopped thudding in panic. Even worse, his cock throbbed, hard as a rock. Guess it was true what people said about "fighting and fucking," that almost dying brought out a primal urge for sex. And the best lay Evan had in a long time was outside that door—and off limits.

Evan shifted, trying to get comfortable, before giving it up as a lost cause. His mind spun, thoughts almost too fast to let him focus.

Seth had evidently researched Evan and his family in detail, tracked him from Oklahoma to Richmond, something not even stalker-Mike had been able to do. Seth might call it "protective surveillance," but it felt like stalking to Evan. Seth knew a lot about him, and Evan knew fuck-all about Seth, except the little bit shared just minutes ago.

Warlocks and immortal witches and curses, oh my. Did Seth think Evan was stupid? Or was he just expected to share the same delusions because they'd had some great sex? And more to the point, how the hell did his people-sense get so thoroughly screwed up that he'd not just flirted with Seth, but brought him home and let Seth fuck him into the mattress?

He wasn't even going to unpack why, despite everything, he still really liked the guy, and wanted to believe him.

Shit.

A plan. Evan needed a plan, one that didn't include becoming a sacrifice to an undead witch-psychopath. No matter how wild Seth's conspiracy theories might be, it didn't change the facts. Armed men had broken into his apartment looking for him. Someone set his apartment on fire and blew up Treddy's. Surely the cops could help. Then he tried to imagine filing a complaint.

I didn't get killed because the guy I brought home to fuck ended up being a stealth ninja.

Yeah, that would go over well.

All right, Plan B. Evan would call Liam, see if he could crash at his place, and figure out what was going on. He reached for his phone, and groaned, realizing he'd left it behind in his apartment. Where it probably melted in the suspicious fire.

One thing was certain—until he knew more about Seth, he was better off on his own. Hell, he didn't even know Seth's last name. That hadn't been important when he was just a one-night stand. Not like either of them was going to get pregnant. Now it seemed a little awkward to ask. Just more proof that Evan needed to figure this out for himself.

Crap. He couldn't ask his family about what really happened to Uncle Vince since he was persona non grata on account of being gay. The obituary wouldn't be any use. Maybe if he got to a computer, he could at least see if he could validate the twelve-year death cycle. And in the meantime, he'd hole up at Liam's. Liam had a big dog and a shotgun. Evan just needed a little breathing room to figure out what the fuck was going on.

Top of that list was finding out more about Seth. Evan slipped off the bed and started to quietly open drawers, looking for something with Seth's name on it. A Kindle lay on the nightstand. Evan opened it and felt guilty for invading Seth's privacy. The e-reader had a couple hundred titles, mostly adventure and fantasy, but other titles on witchcraft and computer hacking made him uncomfortable.

In the bathroom, he found a bottle for prescription painkillers from a pharmacy in Ohio for "Seth Tanner." Was that his real name, or an alias? Evan thought about the scars he'd seen on Seth's chest and back. Some were old, but others looked newly healed. What made those kinds of wounds? A knife fight? A motorcycle wreck? Neither possibility seemed right. But with a last name, maybe Evan could find out more about Seth Tanner…and the mysterious Rhyfel Gremory.

Three days. Seth said this Gremory guy's "disciples" wanted Evan dead in three days—Halloween. Of course. What kind of good horror movie didn't have the dramatic magic murder happen on Halloween?

Evan kept hoping he would wake up and find himself safe in his own bed, where he could laugh about having had a really bad dream. Maybe Seth would be there with him, in his nice un-burned apartment, and they'd get that fourth round of sex Evan had promised.

What did it say about Evan that even after everything that had happened tonight, he still thought Seth was attractive as hell? God, he needed to get some more often. Blue balls had obviously affected his brain cells.

Evan argued with himself about what to do next. Stay, or walk away? Both were fraught with danger. He could stay, thinking Seth was his protector, only to maybe discover Seth had been behind everything that happened. *He stalked me. And I've only got his word for it that he didn't know who I was when he came to the bar. Psychopaths can be clever—and how many times have people said that they thought a serial killer was a "nice guy"—until they found the bodies?*

No, he had to get away, figure it out for himself. He couldn't, wouldn't let himself get into another situation like Mike. Mike had made him doubt his intuition—hell, he'd made Evan doubt his sanity. By the time Mike had finally pushed Evan to the breaking point, they were long past the gaslighting phase and into physical abuse. Evan rubbed his arm over the long-healed break, remembering. Mike had dominated him, made him constantly afraid. It had taken everything Evan had to break away, to run and keep running, and to hide when Mike followed.

No way in hell would anyone ever do that to him again.

He glanced out the trailer's window. The early morning sunlight had chased away the darkness. Time to go.

He pulled his shoes on and grabbed his coat, then headed down the few steps toward where he'd left his pack by the door.

Seth was already in the kitchen, and the smell of coffee filled the air. Unlike at Treddy's—had it only really been last night—Seth looked like hell. His blond hair was uncombed, he had dark circles under his eyes, and stubble gave him a haggard look. "Coffee?" He offered but didn't glance up, like he might be afraid to see the look on Evan's face.

"No. Thanks. I need to get going."

"I wish you'd stay." Seth raised his head, his expression hard to read. Worry and wariness shadowed his brown eyes.

"I can't." Evan hefted his pack. "Thanks for what you did, but I need to figure this out for myself."

"You want a lift? We're not close to town."

Evan shook his head. "There's a convenience store just down from the turn—I saw it last night. I can get a cab from there."

"Be careful." Seth turned toward him, looking as if it took willpower not to step closer. "Just because something is hard to believe, doesn't mean it isn't true."

Evan didn't know what to say to that, so he just nodded and stepped out of the trailer into the cold October morning.

The chill nipped at his ears and cheeks as Evan hiked up the long drive to the main road. He shoved his hands into his pockets and hunched against the wind. His fingers closed around something odd, and he pulled out his left hand to find a small faceted crystal he didn't recognize.

That's weird. He slipped his hand back into his pocket, along with the strange rock. It reminded him of one of Jackie's necklaces, and he wondered if she'd broken a strand and sent the pieces flying. He figured he'd ask when he saw her again and tried to keep his wits about him. Wherever the crystal had come from, he had bigger things to worry about.

Once Evan reached the highway, he turned left, mindful of the traffic on the road rumbling by just feet away. He started to jog to warm himself up, glad when he reached the parking lot.

The store was a mom-and-pop bait-and-essentials shop with two gas pumps, and it probably did scant business when the nearby camps closed. Still, it was open, and Evan wondered whether he could get a hot cup of coffee while he waited for a cab.

A white panel van pulled in, parking between Evan and the door to the shop. He moved to go around, and the driver's door flew open, blocking his path.

Annoyed, Evan shifted his path, only to hear the rest of the van's doors open. He realized that the vehicle had pulled in at an angle that hid him from both the road and anyone in the store. Worse, the four men coming toward him were big and angry. One of them had his right arm in a sling, favoring his shoulder.

"You've caused enough trouble," the driver said, pulling a gun from beneath his jacket and pointing it at Evan. "It would have been easier if you'd come with us last night."

Evan backed up. "You've got the wrong guy. There's been a mistake."

The driver gave a predatory smile. "No mistake. You're the one. Get in."

Evan threw his bag at the gunman and dove, coming up underneath a metal and wood picnic table. He overturned it, kicked a garbage can to set it rolling and ran for the shop's back door.

A warning shot zinged past his shoulder, and Evan ducked. He could hear the gravel crunching behind him and knew he wouldn't make it to the door in time. Another shot just to the side kicked up dirt.

"The next one doesn't miss," the driver growled.

Three bottles filled with liquid and stuffed with flaming rags sailed through the air, into the gap between Evan and his pursuers. Evan dropped and covered his head with his arms, rolling toward the wall of the building, instinctively knowing to protect himself from something that looked ready to explode.

When the bottles hit, they broke, and the flaming rags lit the gasoline that flowed onto the gravel, igniting. The ground trembled, and suddenly the wheels of Seth's black motorcycle stood between Evan and his attackers. Seth held a handgun aimed at the men from the van, shielding Evan.

Evan braced for a gunfight, but the men ran, and the van took off, sending a spray of gravel in its wake. Seth lowered his gun and tucked it into his waistband, then turned to offer Evan a hand up. "Please, let me protect you," Seth said, waiting for Evan's response.

Evan picked up his bag, which had managed to not be where the gasoline spread. The back of the bait shop had no windows, so anyone inside had heard the bang but seen none of the attack. Should he go inside and hope the cops believed him, or leave with Seth, who had once again pulled his ass out of the fire?

Evan was in no shape for a fight if the guys came back. The police might even think he had been responsible for the fire at his apartment. Evan walked toward Seth and climbed on the motorcycle, hating how badly he was shaking as the reality of his near miss sank in. Seth turned the bike and followed a barely-there trail, cutting down through the woods and around a pond to come up at the rear of the campground. In a few minutes, they were back at the camper.

Evan climbed off the motorcycle, and Seth crowded him up against the trailer, his face still flushed from the fight, brown eyes sparking with anger and desire.

"You almost got killed. Again." He raised a hand to brush his fingertips across Evan's shoulder, where a bullet had torn the fabric. "Are you hurt?"

Witchbane

Evan shook his head, feeling his pulse pound. He could feel the heat of Seth's strong body against him, and Seth's leg pressed between his, rubbing against Evan's erection and making Seth's hard cock evident through his jeans. "They missed me," he murmured.

"Do you believe me now?" Seth's voice was a low, protective growl, and the sound went right to Evan's dick. "Because I'm not going to let them take you. I came here to keep you safe."

Seth's face was so close to his; his lips parted, pupils dilated. Evan leaned forward, closing the gap, brushing his lips against Seth's. Seth stepped into him, settling his hands on Evan's hips, pulling them together so that their stiff cocks rubbed against each other.

"Please," Evan murmured, pulling back from the desperate kiss just far enough to speak. "Please, Seth."

Seth slid one hand to the bulge in Evan's jeans, and the other moved to cup his ass. "This?"

Evan nodded, then pressed another kiss to Seth's mouth, slipping his tongue between those plush lips, grinding against Seth's thigh.

Seth flicked open the buttons on Evan's jeans and pushed down his briefs far enough to free his stiff, trapped cock, brushing his fingers over the head to catch the slick bead of pre-cum. Evan moaned and leaned into him, exploring Seth's mouth with his tongue as Seth kissed back with equal passion.

Seth had pulled down his jeans and took both their cocks in hand, jacking them against each other in the sheath of his calloused palm. He nipped and sucked at Evan's lower lip, then trailed kisses down Evan's neck as Evan arched against him, rutting into Seth's fist, cocks sliding against each other, exquisitely sensitive.

"Fuck," Evan breathed as Seth kissed and bit at the juncture where his neck and shoulder met, drawing up the skin to mark him and then laving it with his tongue to soothe the sting. Evan felt Seth's weight around him, blanketing him, felt strong fingers sliding against his cock, and buried his face in Seth's hair as the taller man continued to lick and kiss Evan's neck. "Seth, I'm—"

"Come on," Seth murmured, his voice frayed with the tension of the fight and rescue. "Come for me, Evan. Let go."

Evan groaned Seth's name as his release barreled through him, gushing over Seth's fist, slicking the channel of his hand as Seth gasped and stiffened, adding his spill. A few more thrusts for each of them and the friction became too much. Seth leaned against him, and Evan wrapped his arms around Seth, wondering if he would have a mark from Seth's tight grip on his ass, and finding the idea insanely hot.

Evan kissed Seth and noticed that worry had begun to cloud Seth's eyes. "I'm sorry. I shouldn't—" Seth began.

"You saved me. Again."

"Doesn't mean you owe me…this."

"Is that what you think?" Despite the bliss of their shared release, the implication nettled Evan. "That I'm repaying you with favors?"

"No. Shit. I'm…bad at this," Seth said, stepping back. Evan immediately missed his warmth and the press of Seth's hard body against his. "I just want to keep you safe," Seth said, searching Evan's gaze as he wiped his hand on his t-shirt and tucked himself away. "I didn't mean to get involved—"

"Are you? Involved?" Evan challenged, zipping up and lifting his chin in challenge.

"More than I ever expected." Seth reached out and ran the tips of his fingers against Evan's cheek. "I don't know if I can protect you if I'm distracted, and God, you are a distraction," he confessed.

"You…distract…me, too," Evan said with a wry smile. "Even when I'm angry with you. This is probably a terrible idea—"

"It really is—"

"Because either you're right and I'm in mortal danger, or you're crazy, and I'm still in mortal danger."

Seth drew back and met his gaze. "Which do you believe?"

Evan didn't look away. "I believe I'm in danger. I want to believe in you. And I'd be lying if I said I wasn't scared."

"Then you're a smart man," Seth said. "Because you should be scared. Those goons, they didn't come on their own. And the guy who sent them is bad news."

Evan reached into his pocket and pulled out the strange crystal. "I found this. No idea where it came from."

"Fuck," Seth muttered. "Crystals like that can be used to track

Witchbane

someone. That's how they knew where to find you." He looked back toward the entrance to the campground, then dug a hole and buried the tracking stone. "We need to move. Those men won't give up, and they'll scout this whole area until they catch us."

Seth chewed his lip for a few seconds as if debating what else to say. Evan watched, looking at that kiss-swollen mouth, knowing what those lips tasted like. Shit, he was already half hard again at the thought.

"Come with me? Please? No matter what we do about this…" Seth motioned between them to indicate the attraction, "you're in danger, and I'm here to make sure you're safe—and stop a killer from preying on your family ever again. I can't do it without you."

And there Seth went with "please" again, a glimmer of the Midwest boy showing beneath the toughened soldier. "All right," Evan replied. "And when we get to where we're going, I want you to go over everything again." He reached out and ran a hand up Seth's arm. "As for…this," he said, "Let's go slow. Take a step back, get our breath, see what happens."

Evan's heart plummeted when Seth agreed, a little too quickly. He thought he saw a flash of hurt in Seth's eyes, but just as quickly, the walls went up, and he could read nothing in Seth's gaze.

"I think that's for the best." Seth took another step back from Evan. "Come on. Help me get the trailer hitched and the bike lifted." With that, Seth turned and walked toward the truck, while Evan lingered behind.

Why did you say to "go slow" if you didn't want that? Evan accused himself silently, and the confusion that knotted up his feelings provided the answer. *Because I don't know what's real, and what isn't. He's sexy as hell, and I can't turn off being attracted. But…I can't trust my thinking if all I can think about is fucking him. And I've been wrong about trusting before. Trey. Mike. Hell, my whole family. Lust is easy. Trust just leads to disappointment.*

7

SETH

WITH EVAN'S HELP, HITCHING THE TRAILER TO HIS TRUCK TOOK JUST minutes, and not much longer to secure the Hayabusa onto the lift at the back and disengage the trailer from the campground utility connections. Seth readied the inside of the fifth-wheeler and threw Evan's duffel in the bedroom. His Beretta was in the pocket of his jacket, although he hoped he didn't need to use it.

Evan climbed into the passenger seat, and Seth headed out the rear campground exit, in case the witch-disciple's goons were watching. He'd been damn lucky they hadn't been followed back to camp. What had he been thinking, getting his rocks off out in the open like that?

His focus felt wobbly. His head told him that stopping the disciple was the most important thing. But his heart—or maybe his dick—told him to protect Evan at all costs.

Shit. Seth's hands tightened on the steering wheel, and he avoided looking at Evan riding shotgun. He could hear his old sergeant shouting, telling them to listen to their brains, not their hearts. Reason, not emotion won a battle. Listening to your heart would get you killed and probably take your buddies down with you.

Turning off his emotions had never been a problem, back then. Seth could go into a cold, still place in his head the guys in his unit called "wolf mode," giving him a predator's eye for detail and sharp attention. Now, he felt hyper-aware of Evan, and the protectiveness he felt wasn't the detached, almost-clinical concern for an asset; it felt dangerously close to the possessiveness of a lover.

I've got to start thinking with my upstairs brain. I'm just the bodyguard. I can't do my job and be a "bodyguard with benefits." I've got to put some emotional distance between us, for his safety. What good does it do if my feelings make me sloppy and slow and he dies? Fuck. I've got it bad. This has got to stop.

He couldn't look over at Evan. Evan's hair was still askew from the fight, and his ripped jacket and dirt-streaked clothing reminded Seth just how close a call it had been. He'd heard the gunshots as he rode his bike up the back trail to the store and it made his blood run cold. Seth knew the disciple would need Evan alive for the ritual, but the lore he'd been able to uncover suggested that "not dead" was sufficient. Just thinking about what almost happened had Seth's heart hammering and made his throat tighten.

That's why I have to let go. If caring for him puts him at risk, then I care for him best by pushing him away. He did his best to ignore the ache in his chest. *At the end of this, what matters is that Evan is safe and that the disciple can't hurt him or anyone else in his family ever again.*

And didn't fate just suck sending him a guy like Evan to protect? This time, Seth couldn't resist sneaking a look at Evan, who had turned to gaze out the passenger window. He loved the fire in Evan's hazel eyes when they argued or when Evan gasped his release. The feel of Evan's strong, slim body against his own, the way their heights fit together just right so that Seth's chin could rest on top of Evan's head, the sinewy way Evan walked, and the warmth in his laugh all woke something in Seth he had never felt before.

Colin had been a first crush, and the intensity of those feelings was as much about their age and exploring the newness of their sexuality as it was about them as a pair. He'd cared about Ryan, and at one point, thought maybe that attraction could grow into love. Then Jesse died, and Ryan bolted. Seth had never figured out whether Ryan was afraid he'd be tarred with the suspicions that dogged Seth until the police cleared him, or whether helping a grief-stricken, broken man heal was just beyond Ryan's skills. Either way, Ryan had left Seth when he most needed a friend and partner. And after that, like in the army, the few encounters Seth had were hurried and anonymous, leaving him lonely and empty. There hadn't been anyone in a long while. Until Evan.

Fuck. Gratitude isn't the same as love. When Gremory's disciple is dead, there's nothing to keep us together. And attraction alone won't be enough.

Seth's thoughts had him soundly in a funk as he followed his phone's map to the next site.

"Where are we going?" Evan looked worried and vulnerable, and Seth had to fight his instincts to keep from reaching out and laying a hand on Evan's shoulder.

"Plan B," Seth replied, hoping none of his struggle showed on his face. "I scouted some other locations, in case the campground didn't work out."

He turned off the state highway onto a gravel road, then down a rutted farm lane. A sign on the rusted metal gate said "No Trespassing." Seth parked the truck and got out, using a flicker of magic and a mumbled spell to open the old lock and push the gates open. The hinges squealed in protest and fought his efforts.

When Seth pulled the truck and trailer through, he shut the gates but left the lock undone. A tumble-down farmhouse hunkered behind overgrown bushes, and not far away, a barn in even worse condition looked as if a strong wind might bring it down. Holes pockmarked the barn roof, and several of the windows in the old house were broken.

"Does your uncle own this, too?" Evan asked, raising an eyebrow.

Seth shook his head. "No. We're squatting. This place has been for sale for ten years with no buyers. Owner wants a premium because although it seems like we're in the middle of nowhere, the highway is just two miles that way."

He pulled the truck behind the barn and left the trailer connected for now. Evan climbed down as Seth went around back to lower the bike to the ground. "We won't have the hook-ups that we had at the campground because the utilities stay on there all year, but we'll be okay."

Seth pointed to one of the cargo areas beneath the trailer. "I've got a generator, and I filled up the water tank, so we're good for about a week." He opened the trailer door, let down the steps, and flicked a few switches to turn on the generator and engage the bump-out slides that expanded the trailer's interior.

"We only have to make it three days," Evan said. "Isn't that what you told me? That this witch-disciple wants to kill me on Halloween?"

Seth met Evan's gaze and saw the fear and uncertainty. "You're right. We just have to stay hidden for three days, while I figure out how to stop the disciple."

Evan squared his shoulders. "We. How *we're* going to stop the disciple. My life, my fight."

"Evan—"

"Take it or leave it," Evan said, eyes glinting with that fire that went right to Seth's cock. His dick had obviously not gotten the memo about getting more involved being a bad idea because it twitched in anticipation. Seth shifted his stance.

"It's too dangerous."

"Fuck that," Evan snapped. "I'm not going to wait in the trailer like some wilting Cinderella while you go slay the dragon. Bullshit. I might not be ex-military, but I've got a third-degree black belt. I've learned a thing or three about fights working in bars. I know how to shoot a gun. I can help research. I guess I'm buying into this witch-stuff. So you want my cooperation? Then you let me in on this, all the way."

It went against Seth's better judgment, as well as every protective instinct, but Seth had to admit Evan had a valid point. Getting his help was better than locking him in the trailer to keep him from running off, and maybe if he had a better understanding of the danger, he'd be less likely to fight Seth's help. A voice in the back of his head whispered that if Evan could truly come to believe Seth's story and fully trust in him, maybe he wouldn't be so quick to leave afterward. Seth pushed those unhelpful thoughts away.

"All right."

"What?"

Seth chuckled. Evan had obviously expected more of a fight. "I said, all right. It's your life. You've got a right to know what's going on, and since I need your cooperation, it'd be nice to have your help, too."

"Okay," Evan replied, looking a little off balance when the argument he had braced for didn't materialize. "Good. That's good."

"Come on," Seth said, leading the way inside. "Let's get something for lunch, and I'll fill you in."

Evan looked around the trailer while Seth put together sandwiches in the galley kitchen. "It's pretty cool how the sides expand," he said, eying the sections that slid out to provide a dining area and bigger seating space.

"My parents bought it used, but the couple who owned it didn't put much wear on it," Seth replied, working on his masterpieces of bread, cheese, and lunch meat. "My folks wouldn't have been able to afford the new version, but the sellers gave them a good deal on a trailer that was a lot cheaper because it was a few years old. Mom and Dad broke out the maps and had a whole route across the country picked out, stopping at campgrounds and seeing the sights." Seth told himself that his eyes teared because of the onion he was slicing.

"I'm sorry that they didn't get to do that," Evan said, wandering around as if at a loss for what to do with himself.

"Me too," Seth said with a sigh.

"You left your Kindle in the bedroom," Evan said. "I can bring it out for you."

Seth smiled. "Thanks. When my parents' house burned down, I lost all my books, movies, games—everything. There isn't a whole lot of room in the trailer, so now I read mostly ebooks, stream movies and music, and play games online if there's time and a good connection. Cuts down on clutter," he added with a shrug.

"I don't imagine knick-knacks would stay put on the road anyhow," Evan said.

"Probably not. And as for photos...anything that wasn't on my phone went up with the house."

Seth brought their plates out to the table. Evan grabbed two sodas out of the fridge as well as a bag of chips from the counter.

"All right," Evan said, sitting down across from Seth. "More details. Start at the beginning. And plan to do some 'splainin' when you get to the magic part."

As they ate, Seth told him about the Halloween "prank" that led to him and Jesse being at the Hell Gate tunnel, about the strange things that happened that night, and finding Jesse's mangled corpse in the morning. He mentioned the police investigation, and about Ryan bailing. The only details he skirted were the police's short-lived suspicions about his involvement and the fact that the "hospital" had been a psych ward where he'd been admitted on suicide watch and for "delusions" about magic. Seth realized he needed Evan's trust to fight the witch-disciple, and he didn't want to undermine that fragile belief with details that might just muddy the water.

The police cleared me. It's procedure to look at family first when something like that happens. And the hospital...I'm not crazy. I just was too honest. Once I learned how to lie to the doctor, we all got along just fine.

"And your parents died while you were in the hospital?" Evan asked, pushing his empty plate aside.

"Yeah," Seth replied. "That same night, the house burned down. Luckily, the truck and the trailer were in the barn, along with my bike. When I got released, it was all I had left."

"You think the guy who killed your brother was behind it? Your parents, the house?"

"I didn't, at first. But when I started digging, then yeah, I figured it was all connected. Maybe he realized he got the wrong brother. Maybe they went to the house looking for me. But by that point, Jesse was already dead. The disciple wouldn't need another sacrifice for twelve more years. Me, if he realized he made a mistake. Or the next generation. My cousins' kids, maybe."

"Not yours?" Evan's hazel eyes were unreadable. The question caught Seth unprepared.

"Um, did you miss the part where I'm gay?"

"No, I think I remember that," Evan replied, with a wink and a naughty grin that quickly faded. "But gay couples adopt."

Seth shook his head. "An adopted child wouldn't be a Tanner by blood. There's something about needing a blood descendant of the deputies that killed Gremory that works the spell."

Evan frowned. "You said that the disciple got the wrong brother because you're older. Do you really think he'll come back for you in twelve years?"

"Ten now." Seth shrugged. "Maybe. Not planning to give him that chance. I'll circle back around for him once the other disciples are dead."

"All right," Evan said, leaning back. "About this Rhyfel Gremory person. How did you go from being a regular guy who comes home from the army to a boatload of shit, to this," he said, sweeping his arm to encompass the whole mess.

Seth told him about Toby and how he'd learned the ropes from others who had lost someone to forces they once considered to be unbelievable. "We pieced together names for the original sheriff and deputies and traced their descendants. When we matched unusual deaths to the calendar, we figured out the cycle, and which descendants were next to be targeted. Finding out about Gremory's disciples was the hard part. But we managed to get some old journals and letters that let us figure out their names."

Seth went to get them more sodas and took the dishes with him. He brought out a tub of dip for the chips and handed off one of the drinks to Evan before sitting back in his chair. "Witches believe that names are power, and if someone knows your name, they have power over you. So they guarded their names carefully. Toby and I had to do a hell of a lot of digging."

"So which disciple is after me?"

"Corson Valac," Seth replied. "At least, that's the name he went by back when Gremory was hanged. The problem with being immortal is people notice if you never die. So he's had to keep reinventing himself under different names to stay off the radar. All the disciples have had to do the same thing. Makes it hell to trace them, but that's the point. Toby and I called in some favors, and we figured out the trail all the way up to this last 'reboot.' He's learned some new tricks. We couldn't get his newest identity."

"Do you have a description? Photos? Hell, even drawings?" Evan asked.

Seth got up and opened a locked drawer, pulling out a thick folder. "Yes, there are copies of everything digitally in several locations," he said in answer to the question he could see in Evan's eyes. "I'm not stupid. But sometimes, I think better with paper in front of me."

He brought the folder to the table and spread out several pages of blurry photos and a few old sketches. "Think how much a regular person can alter his appearance by gaining and losing weight, cutting their hair or using wigs, growing a beard or shaving one off, changing hair color. This guy's had over a hundred years to get good at hiding—and that's without using any magic."

"Could he change his looks with magic…assuming it's real?" Evan asked, studying the likenesses.

"I don't know how much he could actually change his face or things like his build or height, but he could certainly make himself forgettable, easy to overlook, the kind of person no one pays attention to," Seth replied. "Look how the photos aren't clear. That could just be bad cameras—some of the shots are pretty old. But energy can also fuck with film or screw up image cards."

"If he's immortal, why isn't he rich and powerful? Maybe a senator or the CEO of some big company?" Evan questioned.

"He's been a big shot more than once. I'm sure he's plenty rich. But rich people can't hide well. People notice them. Nowadays, it's hard to be a recluse. From what I can see, Valac liked to switch things up. He'd be a big shot, then on his next identity a regular Joe. He still kept all his money—probably in a Swiss bank somewhere—but in twelve years, people lose interest in the last identity, and when he pops up again, he's different enough no one makes the connection."

"Fingerprints. Retina scans—how does hiding like that work now?"

"If the CIA and the Witness Protection people can figure out a way around the system, I'm betting an immortal dark witch could do it, too," Seth said. "The hard part is tracking him when we don't have government clout or immortal resources. But I couldn't wait any longer. Time was running out. I knew who the target was—you."

"Can't we just catch a flight to Alaska or England and sit it out until Halloween is over?" Evan asked.

"Maybe," Seth allowed. "And not being able to do the ritual might weaken Valac. Maybe he'd find another victim—not as powerful, but better than nothing. I don't think it would destroy him—so he'd be back for you in twelve years. Do you want to live looking over your shoulder?"

Evan shuddered. "No. And I don't want someone else to die in my place." He was quiet for a while. "Why didn't you go after the witch who killed Jesse first?"

That had been the subject of many fights between Seth and Toby at the beginning. Seth had wanted vengeance while the wounds were still fresh. "There'll be time to find him, and make him pay," Seth said. "But if I went after the others, I could save lives. Disrupt enough of the sacrifices, and it might weaken all of them."

"So I'm the experiment."

Seth winced. "That's not really—"

"You haven't done this before, have you?"

Seth met his gaze. "I haven't fought one of the disciples. But I've fought other kinds of monsters. There are things in the dark that no one wants to believe in, but they're real. Some of us hunt them so that other people can sleep at night."

"Those scars. They weren't all from the army, were they?"

Seth ran a hand self-consciously over his chest and belly, remembering how Evan had traced his scars with his tongue and fingers that night they'd spent together. "I took a bullet in Iraq. Got some shrapnel in Afghanistan. The rest were creatures I hunted that fought back."

Evan slipped his fingers through his thick, chestnut hair. "It's a lot to take in. Kinda hard to believe." He frowned and looked up. "If Gremory was a big-deal warlock and his disciples were also witches, then how can you fight them without magic of your own? Are you a witch, too?"

Are you a good witch, or a bad witch? The line from the old movie came to mind, unbidden. "I'm not a witch. But I have a little magic. It's...complicated."

Evan fixed him with a look. "This," he said, gesturing between them to mean their relationship, "is complicated. If you have magic, you're a witch, right? So where's the complication?"

Seth drank his soda and wished it were something a lot stronger. "You know how some people have a gift—they can just sit down and play music or draw beautiful pictures or dance, and they've never had a lesson? And other people don't have that gift, but if they work hard, they can still be good enough? I don't have the 'gift' for magic—but I've learned how to do small magics, and I've gotten better with practice."

"Is that enough?"

"It'll have to be."

Evan drained his soda and shook his head, pushing back from the table. "I'm going to want to see this magic of yours. But…I need to clear my head. This is all a lot to take in."

Seth told himself that the fact that Evan was still sitting here, had listened to him for over an hour, was a good sign, boding well that he wouldn't run screaming out the door. He was asking Evan to believe the unbelievable, accept the impossible with just a day to process. Hell, it had taken Seth two years to wrap his mind around everything.

"I understand," Seth said, gathering up his papers and returning the file to the locked drawer. "Thank you for hearing me out. I know it's not easy."

"That's an understatement." Evan stood. "I'm going to take a hot shower, and then I'd like to watch a movie, something brainless. Then, later on, you can tell me what the next steps are, because after today, there are only two days until Halloween, and I've got every intention of being alive for Christmas."

Seth cleaned up while Evan showered, trying to keep himself from thinking about what Evan would look like wet and naked, those lean muscles flexing under the running water, that dark hair dripping in his eyes. What it would be like to step in beside him, run soapy hands all over that hot body, go to his knees under the warm water and suck Evan off? Or better yet, push Evan up against the shower stall, spread his legs wide, grab those narrow hips and fuck him senseless?

Shit. Seth stood in the kitchen, lost in his fantasies, rock hard and leaking with no relief in sight. His dick refused to understand that taking things further with Evan was a bad idea. Seth squeezed his cock through his jeans and thought about shredded wheat, old gym socks, emptying the garbage—the most unsexy things as he could think of—but it didn't work. His traitor prick remained ready for action, and his heart seemed intent on joining the resistance against what his mind decreed.

By the time Evan came out of the shower, dressed but toweling his wet hair, Seth had managed to get rid of his "problem." He tried not to stare, but Evan looked damn good in a t-shirt that clung to his chest and a low-slung pair of sweats that seemed to be begging to be tugged down.

"I'm…uh…going to get a shower too," Seth said, pretending that every nerve ending in his body didn't tingle when he brushed against Evan in the trailer's narrow hallway. He closed the door to the bathroom behind him and sagged against it. *Bruce Willis never has days like this.*

He tried taking a cold shower, mindful of their limited supply of water. It didn't help. He jacked off to the memory of Evan's lips wrapped around his cock, of his shaft buried deep in Evan's tight ass. He bit his lip, unwilling to have his rushed climax overheard by the man who fueled his fantasies. A quick rinse hid the evidence, and Seth wondered as he dried off whether Evan had rubbed one out thinking of him as well.

When he came out, dressed in worn sweats and a faded concert t-shirt, Evan had found an old movie on TV and curled up on the couch. Seth didn't pay much attention as he pulled out his laptop and grabbed the file again, settling in at the table. His Beretta was on a shelf near the door, and he had a rifle in the closet, a shotgun under the bed. Seth didn't think Valac's men would find them here, but if they did, he intended to be ready.

As Evan watched his movie, Seth activated the small cameras he'd installed on all four corners of the trailer and minimized the screen with their feeds, guaranteeing that he'd see if anyone approached. He paused for a moment, then changed the settings on the guest profile on his computer to restrict any email, internet browsing, social media, phone, or messaging. He hoped Evan was on board with remaining isolated, but until they knew who they could trust, he couldn't risk an email or call alerting the wrong person to their hiding place. With luck, Evan would never notice.

The strains of a familiar, despised song caught his attention, and he looked up at the TV just in time to see Whitney Houston sing about breaking Kevin Costner's heart.

"I hate that movie," Seth muttered. "I really, really hate that movie."

8

EVAN

The shower hadn't cleared his mind as much as Evan had hoped, and jerking off did only the bare minimum to relieve the attraction he felt when Seth was near. He replayed the quick-and-dirty hand job outside the trailer in his mind, and just thinking about it made him hard.

Evan shifted in his chair, wishing he had a throw to cover his lap and hide the erection tenting his sweatpants. He felt the whole day crash down on him, and right now, all he wanted was to lose himself in a brainless movie.

He flipped channels, surprised at what the little satellite dish on the roof picked up, and stopped on a movie he knew he'd seen before but had mostly forgotten. He didn't care that it was old and already half over; his thoughts were too scattered to pay close attention.

Someone had tried to kill him—again. Sure, he'd fought and run, but he had been losing. If Seth hadn't ridden to the rescue, Evan knew he would have ended up shot and carried off in the back of that panel van. Magic or not, that sort of thing never ended well.

Magic. Shit, this kind of Hogwarts stuff did not happen to real people. Certainly not to him. He could understand Seth wanting to hunt down his brother's murderer when the cops abandoned the

Witchbane

search. And chasing the trail of a serial killer was brave, if not suicidal. But Evan still felt unsure about the whole "immortal witch disciple" thing. Much as he enjoyed fantasy books, sci-fi movies, and fantastic role-playing adventures, he'd always prided himself on knowing where the line was between fiction and reality. And now…if Seth was right, that line was less of a rule and more of a guideline.

He'd wanted the shower and movie to buy time. Evan knew he had to ask Seth for proof of magic, and when he did, Seth was going to reveal that he was either a fraud or delusional. On the other hand, if the guys trying to kill him also believed in magic, maybe reality wasn't the point. Evan was in danger because—deluded or not—Valac believed sacrificing him would sustain the witch-disciple's immortality.

Fuck. This problem didn't have a right answer, only bad or worse options.

He shifted in his seat, favoring the bruises where he'd been banged around trying not to get shot. Seth had saved his life twice now. Terrified as he'd been at the time, now that he thought about it, Seth had been damn hot; skidding up to put himself between Evan and his attackers, and the aftermath had been sexy as hell.

So they were back to fighting and fucking. Evan didn't know how to make sense of his jumbled feelings. Terror seemed an appropriate response to the attacks and to the idea that someone wanted to truss him up and slit his throat like something out of a bad horror movie. Having a close call made everything—colors, sounds, emotions—seem twice as intense. *Was that all that this attraction meant between him and Seth, the pent-up release of being glad they hadn't gotten killed?*

And yet, that night in his apartment before things went to shit had been so good. Seth had fit in like he'd been around forever. Finding someone who liked the same things wasn't easy. Evan had only a passing interest in sports, though he knew enough to make conversation with patrons at the bar. But the same books, movies, games—those interests were harder to find. Seth had aced that part.

Evan tried to chase off a growing headache by rubbing his temples, glad his fingers no longer shook. Shit, he was in too deep. He had no business playing secret agent, and he already knew that "taking it slow" when it came to Seth was locking the barn door after the horse was long gone. He hadn't fallen this hard, this fast, in a long time.

And remember what happened when you did, he warned himself. Mike had also been ex-military, and his charming protectiveness turned into an ugly possessive streak and a frightening need to control Evan. That was pretty common for stalkers, Evan had learned later. But Seth had been open about why he had gone looking for Evan, and as much as the thought of being researched made him edgy, he understood the reasons. Kinda hard to argue when he'd seen exactly what would have happened to him if Seth hadn't been around.

Which brought him back to the tangled bunch of yarn his feelings had become. He genuinely liked Seth, and it didn't hurt that Seth was sexy as all hell. Those soulful brown eyes, full lips, and blond hair had Evan from the first glimpse. Now that he'd had a taste of the sculpted body beneath Seth's t-shirt and form-fitting jeans, he wanted more.

So why the fuck did I open my mouth about "going slow?" He sighed. Because inside, he was torn, wanting it both ways. He wanted Seth in bed, warm and hungry, eager to get that missed chance to see if Seth would bottom for him, to find out how good it would feel to fuck into Seth's perfect ass. Then again, he'd enjoyed having Seth fuck him, so there wasn't a wrong choice. And those lips…Evan couldn't decide what was sexier, seeing those plump, pink lips slide down his shaft, or swallowing down Seth's hard, gorgeous cock.

So he wanted to keep going, but he also needed time to figure out what was happening. Because Evan didn't want Seth to be a passing fancy. Seth wasn't just a good lay and a handsome date. He cared about protecting people, and his courage and resolve were just as attractive as his beautiful eyes and hard body. Seth was good in bed, but Evan had the feeling it came less from vast experience than simple empathy, and genuinely wanting to please his partner. Evan knew that kind of lover was uncommon—and precious.

What if the magic part didn't turn out to be true? Stopping a serial killer would still be a good thing, a valuable service. Evan found himself daydreaming, thinking about helping Seth with research and traveling with him in the trailer. Tracking down the witch-disciples was dangerous work. Seth needed someone to have his back. Someone like Evan.

Evan shook himself out of his daydream. Fuck, he needed to get a grip. Next thing, he'd be doodling hearts with both their initials. Seth probably wasn't the settling down type. Evan knew getting his hopes up would only get him hurt. But neither his heart nor his dick seemed to listen.

Intent on shifting away from a dangerous train of thought, Evan forced himself to focus on the movie. Only when he watched Kevin Costner shoot the hitman on stage did he remember the plot, and as the sad reprise played, the words seared through him, far too relevant to his own situation. Was that the only way it could end between him and Seth, walking away from each other to go their separate ways?

"I hate that movie." Seth hadn't seemed to be paying any attention, working on his laptop at the table.

Evan watched the credits roll, feeling his heart pound. Crazy or not, he didn't want to walk away from Seth. Surely if they could just survive the next few days, they could figure out whether what they felt had a chance to be something more than an adrenaline-fueled tryst. Couldn't they?

He flicked off the TV, unable to get the hauntingly sad song out of his mind. Time to get back to the business of outwitting his would-be killer. They'd gotten up early, and a glance at the clock told Evan it was barely mid-morning.

"You want to show me what kind of magic you can do?" Evan asked, then winced at the way that sounded. Seth turned, his expression a combination of amusement and confusion. "I didn't mean that the way it came out...I'm just curious. Do you need a wand or something?" Shit, it just kept getting worse.

"I've already shown you my wand," Seth replied deadpan, and Evan felt his cheeks burn.

"That wasn't what—" Evan just buried his face in his hands. "Forget about it. Just shoot me now."

Seth laughed, low and deep. Evan realized he'd never heard him laugh before, and the sound sent a warm surge to his belly and down to his balls. The light from the window made Seth's hair golden, gorgeously tousled. God, he looked scrumptiously fuckable.

"Come on," Seth said, still chuckling. "Let's go outside. I'll warn you—what I've learned isn't showy or exciting."

Evan and Seth walked to a flat area still within sight of the barn and trailer. Seth's hands were jammed in his pockets, and he looked uncomfortable.

"What's wrong?"

Seth squared his shoulders. "Just a little nervous. Look—I know you don't believe that magic is real, and if you're expecting Gandalf or Harry Potter, you're going to be disappointed. I picked spells to learn that would give me basic skills, like a toolkit. They're not flashy, just useful."

"So spells are really a thing?" Evan had never really thought about magic in the real world.

"They're a memory trick and a way to focus," Seth replied. "They can also store and direct power. Just memorizing the words doesn't mean you can do anything. You've got to either have a natural gift—which I don't—or learn to redirect energy from around you and inside you."

"That sounds dangerous."

Seth grimaced. "It can be. The power isn't limitless for anyone, and it comes at a price." Evan had read enough books and played enough games to understand the idea that magic had a cost. In theory at least, a witch could drain himself to death sinking too much of his energy into a spell. Curiosity vied with concern as he watched Seth gather a few items.

"Watch." Seth took a small rock about the size of a gumball and tossed it. He spoke words Evan didn't quite hear, and the rock stopped in midair. Then Seth thrust out one hand—never touching—and the rock flew, hitting the wooden barn door hard enough to pass through it like a bullet.

"Fuck," Evan murmured. Seth's intense gaze and his determined expression gave him a dangerous, feral handsomeness.

"I popped the lock on the front gate with magic," Seth said, glancing at Evan self-consciously. "Faster than lock picks."

"Useful," Evan agreed. "Can you do other things?"

"I'm still working on this one, but it's coming along nicely." Seth stretched out his hand once more, and a tongue of flame formed above his palm. In the next instant, a stream of fire surged from his hand, shooting nearly ten feet and almost burning down a patch of dry weeds.

"That still needs some fine-tuning," Seth said, running to stamp out the embers. "But I can make the fire go a little farther each time, and I get less of a headache now than when I first started, so there's progress."

Shit. Magic might really be real. Evan stared at Seth, trying to make sense of what he had seen. One part of his mind argued that it had to be a trick, while another part assured him that he'd watched too closely, been near enough to rule out sleight of hand. It felt like the world tilted a bit on its axis, or as if someone pulled back a curtain making him privy to a backstage secret. He'd been a little freaked out when Seth had shot the man in his apartment. What did it say about Evan that the gun still frightened him more than a torrent of flame summoned out of nowhere?

"Say something."

Evan realized that Seth watched him nervously, probably afraid Evan would run screaming for the hills. "That was pretty impressive."

A ghost of a smile quirked at Seth's lips. "You think so?"

"I can see how that would come in handy," Evan allowed, still trying to wrap his head around what he'd seen. Magic. Real magic.

"I'm working on some other spells as well," Seth said. "It still takes a lot out of me, even for simple things, but that will get better as I build up more resilience." He paused. "Now how about letting me see what you can do?"

Evan gave him an incredulous look. "I can't do magic."

"Didn't mean magic," Seth said with a crafty grin. "Sparring. You said you have a black belt. So do I. Show me what you've got. I'll feel better if I know for sure you can hold your own."

"You're on."

The two men circled, wary and watching. A predatory gleam came into Seth's brown eyes, and Evan knew he didn't dare get distracted by the fluid way Seth moved or the wicked smile that promised trouble.

They went at each other almost at the same instant, punches, kicks, and blocks coming fast and furious. Both men stepped back, appraising each other after the first go, determining where to strike next given what they'd learned.

Evan knew he was competition-level good at martial arts, but he'd never had to use his skills to fight for his life, and he'd dared not use them when he helped break up brawls at the bars. He figured Seth was going easy on him, sizing him up. Evan also figured Seth was going to kick his ass.

Evan grinned. "Come on. Bring it."

"You asked for it." This time, Seth attacked for results, rather than testing his opponent's weakness. Evan attempted a few offensive moves, then found himself quickly on the defensive, just trying to fend off the blows that rained down from every direction. Seth drew from karate, Tae Kwon Do, Capoeira, and some traditions Evan didn't recognize. Although they both pulled their punches and kicks, Seth landed more blows than Evan did, and even with the reduced force, Evan felt certain he'd have bruises to show for it.

They were both breathing hard, sweating despite the cool air, and Evan felt a frisson of tension between them, both of them undeniably aware of each other's bodies. Seeing Seth in motion reminded Evan of just how gorgeous—and lethal—the man was, all that harnessed power and hard muscles, in one beautifully masculine package.

Don't get distracted, he warned himself, barely dodging in time to avoid a hit to the side of his head. Evan knew his own capabilities and the limits of his stamina, and he was nearing the end of both. He switched tactics, dropping the rehearsed martial arts moves, and went for the rough and tumble strikes he'd learned in brawls, subduing far too many drunks.

He got in one good hit, but it brought him too close, and with a move Evan barely even had time to register, Seth struck like a viper and had him pinned on the ground.

"What did you do?" Evan gasped, trying to get his breath. Seth straddled him, shifting his weight. Both of them were hard, and seeing

Witchbane

Seth's sweaty, heaving body pressed against him made Evan want to cream his jeans.

"Systema," Seth replied with a grin. "It's what the Russian security forces use. Scary as fuck—and effective."

Evan bucked up, grinding them together. He registered the lust in Seth's eyes as Seth moved in response. Seth's brown eyes were blown dark with lust and exertion, his shirt clung to his body, soaked with sweat, and powerful thighs trapped Evan between them.

"I thought you wanted to go slow," Seth said in a low growl.

"I lied."

Seth pounced, dropping chest-to-chest against Evan, capturing his mouth. Evan groaned and opened his lips, and Seth's tongue slid inside, tasting, exploring, and claiming. Evan brought his arms up around Seth, locking them together, as Seth rolled his hips and Evan arched against him.

"What do you want?" Seth murmured from beside Evan's ear, his breath against the sensitive spot making Evan shiver. Seth licked a stripe down Evan's glistening skin from his ear to his shoulder, and Evan tightened his grip, letting his hands slide down to cup Seth's ass.

"I want you to fuck me," Evan growled. "I want to feel you inside me. Please, Seth. Fuck me now."

Seth got to his feet in one fluid movement, pulling Evan with him, and for a second, Evan almost thought Seth intended to sweep him off his feet and carry him to the trailer. Part of him was horrified at the thought, but from the way his balls tightened and his hole clenched in anticipation, obviously, another part of himself was completely onboard with the idea.

"Come on," Seth said, not letting go of Evan as they stumbled their way back, kissing and groping. Inside the trailer, Seth pushed Evan up against the door and kissed him hard even as he reached around to secure the lock.

"So damned sexy," Seth growled, turning Evan around to face the wall. "I want to fuck you right here, just like this."

"Do it."

Seth pulled down Evan's sweats and briefs, and Evan kicked them away, bracing himself against the wall and widening his stance. He slid down the wall a bit, making the angle just right. Seth chucked off his own jeans and reached for the drawer under the cubby where he kept his wallet, grabbing a condom and lube packets. "Fuck. You look so good like this."

Evan's breath caught as he heard one foil packet tear and then the other. Seth's finger slipped down between his ass cheeks and circled his hole. He arched his back, but Seth gave a low chuckle. "Not until you're ready."

"I'm ready. Very ready."

Seth pushed a lubed finger into Evan's tight hole as he folded himself over Evan's back, licking and mouthing his way down Evan's spine. Evan shimmied his hips impatiently, and Seth wriggled his finger deeper, up to the knuckle. A second slick finger joined the first, sliding in and out of him, stretching him. Evan pushed back, fucking himself on Seth's fingers, and he heard Seth's groan of appreciation. Seth's fingers disappeared, leaving Evan feeling empty and unsatisfied, and then strong hands gripped Evan's hips, pulling his ass cheeks apart as the hard knob of Seth's stiff cock pressed against his hole.

Evan breathed through the burn, wanting to feel Seth inside him. Seth's hands gripped his hip bones, keeping him still as Seth pressed in slowly until his whole length filled Evan.

"Move, dammit."

Seth pulled out and pushed back into the root, then began to thrust in earnest, a hard, fast fuck as fraught as their sparring had been. He changed his angle and made Evan see sparks as his cock hit Evan's prostate with each stroke.

"Not going to last," Evan breathed. Their first coupling had been slow, almost tender. This time, all the tension and adrenaline found a primal outlet. Seth fucked into him hard enough Evan wasn't sure he could support himself against the wall, although his own cock ached and demanded attention. Just as he went to take his release in hand, Seth slipped long fingers across his hip, down his hard belly, and wrapped them around Evan's cock, jacking him in rhythm to Seth's thrusts.

"Yes. More. Yes, oh God—" Evan came hard, overflowing Seth's grip, and his knees nearly buckled. Seth steadied him with a hand clenching Evan's hip, his rhythm stuttering as Seth chased his own climax, his hot come filling the condom. Seth bent over once more to kiss Evan's back before pulling out gently, then tying off the condom and tossing it into the garbage.

"Wait here," Seth said quietly, returning in a moment with a wet washcloth to wipe them both off. His hands were gentle as he cleaned Evan, an intimacy Evan did not expect. Seth turned him around and brushed a kiss to his lips.

"As bad ideas go, this is a good one," Seth murmured.

Evan swallowed. "I was thinking the same thing." If they couldn't stop Valac, Evan would be dead in three days. At least he wouldn't feel alone while the minutes ticked away. And if they succeeded, if they could save his life and stop the witch-disciple's murder spree, then he and Seth could figure out what came next.

"We've got work to do if we're going to stop Valac," Seth said. "Shower first?"

"Is that an invitation?" Evan replied, and his spent dick twitched at the chance to live out his morning fantasy.

"I'm all for multitasking," Seth replied.

The trailer shower barely fit two large men, which limited their options. They took turns soaping each other, hands sliding and exploring, trading kisses as they changed places under the spray. Evan slipped his hard cock against Seth's cleft, settling his hands on Seth's narrow waist.

"I haven't forgotten that fourth go we didn't get to have," he murmured, lips brushing against Seth's ear. "Something to look forward to." He slid his fingers lower, into the tangle of curls at the base of Seth's erect prick, but Seth turned him so that his larger hand could jack both of them at once.

"Efficient," Seth said with a teasing smile as he rubbed their sensitive dicks together. He kept one arm around Evan's waist, holding them together chest to chest and Evan could feel Seth trembling as they both crested at the same time. Evan had one hand on Seth's hip, and the other groped his ass, drawing them close. When they caught their breath, they rinsed off quickly and grabbed their towels.

"I'll take a rain check on that fourth go," Seth said with a sinful grin.

"I'll hold you to that, but technically I think it's now a 'fifth.'" Evan replied, knowing he was smiling like a loon. He cleared his throat and swallowed hard.

"What's the next step?" Evan asked as Seth pulled a clean pair of jeans and a t-shirt from a drawer in the bedroom. Evan dug in his duffel for fresh clothes.

"Toby and I were able to trace some real estate transactions over the years that we think were Valac changing identities. I want to visit the sites and see if we can get a better idea about where to find Valac now. And I want to see if we can find that panel van. I got a partial on it before they drove away."

"Isn't all that stuff online?" Evan asked, toweling off his wet hair.

Seth shook his head. "Yes—and no. I gave Toby the license plate info, and he's looking into it. He'll call me when he finds something—he has a few favors he can pull in. As for the real estate, the information is online, but it's gotten a lot easier to hide who's actually buying and selling with shell companies and the like. Valac's had several lifetimes to figure out the game."

"What do you think we'll find? I can't imagine he's just sitting home watching TV until it's time to kill me." Evan kept his tone offhanded, but he saw Seth's eyes darken at his words.

"I'm sure Valac's gone into hiding. But he's going to have to perform the ritual somewhere, and if we know the site, we're better prepared to stop him."

Seth ran a comb through his hair and grabbed a jacket against the cool fall air. "We also need to find his anchor."

"Anchor?" Evan asked, grabbing his coat and hurrying to follow Seth.

"Everything Toby and I found about this kind of magic says that a witch who is sustaining a spell over a long period—like a century—needs to ground the power to an energy focus," Seth explained as they walked to where he had parked the Hayabusa. "We think we're looking for two things—an amulet, and a spelled container with something very personal to the witch, like a lock of hair or nail clippings.

He's probably wearing the amulet. The amulet would be soaked in the blood of the sacrifice, and the container with the element would be hidden someplace safe."

"The guy's had a hundred years to hide it," Evan replied. "How are we going to find it in three days?"

Seth's smile faded, and his eyes took on a hard glint, a shadow of the soldier beneath the hunter. "I don't know yet. But we will. We're just getting started."

9

SETH

"This is...comprehensive." Evan paged through a list of names when they got to the first stop, a lovely brick Federal-style home in a good neighborhood off Monument Avenue. "And you think these were all Valac, reinventing himself?"

Seth nodded. "Death dates from each prior identity match up very closely with first recorded interactions with each new ID. I think Valac would rig his death or departure, wait, then come back as a new person."

"And no one ever figured it out?" Evan glanced up at the old house, then back at the list.

"If he avoided having his picture taken—or assured photos didn't turn out well—he could just laugh comments off as a remarkable resemblance," Seth said. "I suspect that's also why he alternated between being a big shot and a nobody. Gave people more time to forget. This house is the last one I could specifically tie Valac to owning. That was twelve years ago, right before the last reinvention."

"We know he doesn't live here anymore, so what are you hoping to find?"

"Breadcrumbs. A clue. Something to point us in the right direction." Seth tucked the list back into his jacket pocket and squared his shoulders. "Let's see what we can find."

He couldn't dwell on what would happen if he failed. Evan would die, gruesomely, like Jesse, and once again, it would be Seth's fault. Worse, because Seth let Evan become more than a client. He could no longer be completely detached when it came to Evan's safety, and Seth knew that posed a danger on so many levels.

Seth knocked at the door. "Excuse me," he said with an aw-shucks smile as Frida Mason, the homeowner, came to the door. She looked to be in her early sixties, with a short brown bob haircut. Her trim, athletic figure suggested that the yoga pants and workout shirt were not just a fashion statement. "We're from the Historical Association, and I was wondering if you'd have a moment to talk with me about anything you might know about the previous owner of this house."

Mrs. Mason pushed a lock of brown hair behind her ear. She looked like she'd hurried from the other end of the house, or maybe downstairs, to get the door. "Why? Is he in some kind of trouble?"

Seth's grin widened. "No, no. Not at all. He's been recognized as a historically significant individual, and we're compiling information for an upcoming exhibit."

"I'm afraid I can't be much help," she replied. "We never dealt with the man directly. It all went through our real estate agent. Never met him in person. If I recall correctly, he was out of the country or something. Had to do everything by FedEx."

"Do you have the name of the agent you dealt with?" Seth pressed. "Maybe he or she would know more about what Mr. Larkin's plans were after the sale. We have a few gaps in his history we'd like to fill in, for the exhibit."

"And you can't ask Mr. Larkin directly?" Mrs. Mason replied, eyes narrowing.

"I'm afraid he passed away later that same year," Seth replied. *And again twelve years before that.*

Mrs. Mason shook her head. "Sally, my real estate agent, died not long after the sale went through. Terrible thing. Massive allergic reaction," she said, lifting a hand to her heart in horror. "Bee sting or something."

"I'm sorry to hear that," Seth replied. "I apologize for taking up your time."

"No trouble," Mrs. Mason replied. Seth and Evan turned to go. "There is one thing—"

"Yes?"

"Now that you ask, I do remember something odd. Stuck with me all this time. A name. We didn't actually buy the house from Mr. Larkin himself. The real seller was some kind of real estate trust. I made Sally explain it twice because I had never heard of such a thing and I didn't want to get mixed up in any funny business. CoVal," she said, and spelled it for them, noting the odd capitalization. "Just thought it was odd, which is why I remembered it." She shrugged. "Don't imagine that does you any good—"

"You have no idea," Seth said, shaking her hand. "That was just the piece we were missing. Thank you so much."

"Glad I could help," Mrs. Mason replied, looking surprised that something so trivial seemed to matter. "Good luck with your exhibit."

Evan didn't say anything until they were back at the motorcycle. "The historical association? What if she goes looking for that exhibit?"

"I didn't say *which* historical association. And besides, funding for those kinds of things get cut all the time. We're chasing an immortal serial killer. I think that beats full disclosure."

"You're frighteningly good at lying your ass off."

"We didn't have time to explain the whole thing to Mrs. Mason," Seth retorted, stung a bit by Evan's judgment. While their physical attraction had already convinced their dicks that being together was a good thing, Seth knew that Evan's upstairs brain was still weighing evidence.

He couldn't blame Evan for being skeptical. He'd asked him to believe a lot, and Evan's trust was still shaky. The fact that Seth hadn't told Evan everything gnawed at him, but he pushed the worries aside. *He knows the parts that matter. The police's suspicions about me were unfounded, and the psych ward wasn't one of my greatest hits, but I wasn't crazy. There's too much going on to explain it and have to win his confidence again. I'll tell him later. After I save his life. If it still matters.*

He forced his thoughts away from "after," and remembered that stupid movie Evan had watched in the trailer. If what they had between them was more than just a convenient way to let off steam, they'd know that once the pressure ended. Seth refused to get his hopes up, but a part of his heart didn't listen.

Evan opened his mouth to say something, and Seth's phone buzzed. He saw Toby's number and answered. "What did you find?" Evan's eyebrows raised in silent question as Seth listened, and then nodded. "It's a start. I'll take what we can get. And I've got something else to check into. See what you can find about CoVal. Might or might not be some kind of real estate trust. If you find it, I need the addresses of any Richmond property they've bought in the last twenty-four years. Thanks, man."

Seth put his phone away. "Toby thinks he's got a hit on the partial license plate for the van. He gave me an address. He'll look into CoVal. If anyone can track that, it'll be Toby or someone he knows."

"So CoVal—Corson Valac?"

Seth nodded. "Pretty obvious once you know what you're looking for, like hiding in plain sight."

"What do you think you're going to find?"

Seth rolled his head to relieve the tension in his neck. "I can tell you what I'm hoping to find. A current address. A recent address that might give us a clue about who Valac is now. Something he owned that he left behind."

"Why do you need something of his?"

Seth got on the bike. Evan did the same, waiting for an answer before he put on his helmet. "I found something in the spell books about a locating spell," Seth said. "It requires something owned by the person to be tracked. It looked like a simple bit of magic, but I need something that belonged to Valac."

"Would a house do, if you could find one he still owned?"

Seth shrugged. "Maybe. We just need to find the bastard, and the clock is ticking."

The address Toby gave him led them to the industrial end of the city, filled with drab one-story office plazas and large, anonymous warehouses and shipping centers.

"This place looks deserted," Evan said, as Seth idled the bike in front of an abandoned storefront. The sign over the door said *"Top Granite,"* but plywood covered the large display windows. Next to the side entrance sat a burned-out white panel van, its license plate scorched but legible.

"Fuck!" Seth gunned the motor and took off, fearing a trap. A shot hit the cracked pavement inches from the bike, and Seth veered, zigzagging to present a difficult target until he could make it around a corner. Two bikes revved to life and came squealing out of side streets on their tail, and Seth pushed for speed. Another shot rang out, just missing the rear wheel.

Seth knew that if the gunman wanted to kill them, he could take his shot and probably succeed. But Valac wanted Evan, so shooting into his exposed back wouldn't do if he needed his sacrifice alive. And shooting Seth would send the bike into a high-speed crash, with no guarantee Evan would survive. Betting everything on Valac's men being unwilling to shoot to kill, Seth opened the throttle and hunched low, hoping to outrun their pursuers.

Evan clung tight, his arms wrapped around Seth's waist as they cornered sharply, and the added weight of a rider nearly threw off Seth's balance. He recognized the sound of the motors as the bikes behind him tried to close the distance, and he hoped the Hayabusa was faster. But rider skill and the terrain could even the odds when Seth desperately needed the advantage.

Their pursuers edged closer, one on each side. Seth refused to allow them to flank him, veering and curving unpredictably, counting on their orders to require that he and Evan—or at least Evan—be brought in alive. Every time one closed, Seth maneuvered a tight cut around parked vehicles, road debris, or uneven pavement. The bikes dropped back, then surged forward, trying to narrow Seth's lead.

Up ahead the road widened, making it harder for Seth to keep the other bikes from narrowing the gap between them. Along one side, vehicles parked in a solid line, next to scaffolding for repairs on the building fronts. Seth jumped the curb and sped up, keeping a lead on his pursuers while they could do nothing to cut him off. He burst out of the scaffolding and careened down a side street, heading straight for downtown Richmond.

Once he knew the men on the other motorcycles weren't going to shoot, Seth didn't have to fear civilians getting hit in the crossfire. More people meant more witnesses, cell phones to record an attempted kidnapping, and congestion to slow his pursuers or have them risk being pulled over by the cops. Traffic provided plenty of camouflage, and Seth changed lanes frequently, hiding behind city buses, minivans, and delivery trucks.

By the time they reached the heart of downtown, the other riders had given up. Seth spotted a bunch of food trucks serving the lunch crowd and found a nearby place to park. Evan's arms still gripped him as if his life depended on it.

"You can let go now. We've stopped," Seth said, the humor in his voice masking his relief at their near miss.

Evan released his hold reluctantly and removed his helmet. "You think it was a trap?"

"As in, did they know we were coming? I doubt it. But I do think it proves Valac has his goons watching for us. He might have figured that I'd find the truck, and if he's got enough muscle, maybe he had his men staked out, just in case." He sighed. "It means we'll have to be extra careful because he'll be on the lookout."

Evan looked shaken, and Seth elbowed him. "Hey, cheer up. We're safe, they're gone, and we've got some leads. It'll be okay."

The look in Evan's hazel eyes let him know that he recognized the falsehood. "What now?"

"Until we hear back from Toby on the CoVal lead, let's check out another site that had a connection to Valac—the Pump House at Byrd Park."

Evan raised an eyebrow. "Seriously? Then again, I guess he's been around for a while. That's one of the most haunted places in Richmond."

"Never let it be said that I don't know how to show a guy a good time," Seth replied with a laugh.

After the bike chase, they needed a break, and the bustling park offered distraction and protection. They had their pick of food trucks, and the mix of aromas made Seth's stomach rumble. Greek food sounded good to both of them out of the many options. Seth chose gyros that nearly overflowed their pitas and dripped with tzatziki, while Evan returned with a plate full of pastitsio, dolmas, and spanakopita, as well as a huge piece of fresh baklava big enough to share. They savored their lunch and lounged beneath the tree, letting the meal settle and catching their breath after a close call.

Evan pushed on with a practical determination Seth admired. The more Seth got to know Evan, the more he liked him, beyond their undeniable attraction in bed. The past two years had been lonely since Jesse's death and Ryan's betrayal. He'd stayed busy, often lost in his focus to uncover Gremory's disciples, but that busyness hadn't kept him from feeling more isolated than ever before.

It was nice not to be alone. Seth smiled as Evan un-self-consciously took his hand as they people-watched. Did this thing between them have to end once they stopped Valac? Seth had been so certain he would leave as soon as the witch-disciple had been defeated, but now he wondered if there might not be another option. Maybe he and Evan could work together since Evan knew what Seth was trying to do. Or if Evan didn't want to go on the road, perhaps Richmond could become Seth's home base between missions. His heart leaped at the possibility, surprising him at just how much he didn't want to leave Evan behind. Maybe he didn't have to.

When they finally caught their breath, they got back on the motorcycle, and Seth let Evan guide him to Byrd Park, where they wound around the scenic green space and down toward the James River. There, along what had once been a canal, loomed a Gothic granite castle.

"That looks like a church. Are you sure we're in the right place?" Seth stopped and stared. A slate roof, arched windows, stained glass windows and steep gables gave the large building a stately grandeur Seth associated more with a chapel than a utility building.

"That's it," Evan assured him. "Quite the destination back in its day. Has a ballroom on the second floor with a great view. From what I've heard, a lot of parties were held here, before it started having expensive maintenance problems. It's been closed for a long time, but I saw something on the news that it's been bought. Maybe the new owners will fix it up, and it'll make a comeback." He paused. "How is Valac connected?"

Seth parked the bike, and they walked closer. No one was in sight, and the open space left no room for anyone to hide. "The man who hanged himself inside was a good friend of one of your ancestors. Jacob Malone, your cousin several generations back, was Valac's sacrifice that cycle. Best I can figure, his friend blamed himself for not stopping the murder, and committed suicide."

"Maybe he couldn't live with what he saw," Evan said quietly, staring at the imposing gothic building. "What you lived through, it's more than many people would be able to come back from."

Seth blinked as his eyes suddenly filled, unwilling to shed tears that could change nothing. "I couldn't save Jesse. I'm going to save you."

They headed for the doorway and found it locked, as expected. Since the Pump House hadn't been in use for decades and was at best being slowly renovated, it wasn't open to the public and had no on-site staff. Seth put his hand over the lock, willed a flicker of magic and murmured the spell. He felt the mechanism shift, and with a *click*, the door opened.

"Handy," Evan observed. His flippant tone seemed at odds with the perplexed look in his eyes as if he were trying to figure out how a magician's trick was done.

The solid granite building attested to the money and craftsmanship of a long-ago era. Seth paused inside the door.

"Any idea where the suicide happened?"

"The second floor has offices, restrooms, and the ballroom," Evan replied. "The first floor is the mechanical room. I'd say we start there."

The sheer size of the pump room impressed Seth. A cavernous chamber once housed huge iron pumps that controlled the flow of the canal outside. The iron equipment had been sold off before World War II, but its footprint remained, big square holes half-full with stagnant water. The pipe fittings jutted out from the walls like open maws, some as wide across as the span of a man's outstretched arms. Water seeped into the stone walkway and wide steps around the pump stations, attesting to the need for renovations and improvement. Overhead, rusted iron trusses and a latticework of smaller pipes criss-crossed the ceiling.

Seth shivered. It might have been the aftereffects of tension, or perhaps a primal reaction to the presence of the pump house's ghosts.

"There are supposed to be at least three ghosts, maybe more," Evan said. "The man who hanged himself, and two women. One of the women may have a cluster of ghosts around her, depending on who's telling the story. The ghost hunters love this place."

Seth found a mostly dry spot on the walkway and pulled what he needed from his bag. He set out a candle and lighter, a container of salt, a shallow silver bowl the size of his hand, and a piece of charcoal.

"Come stand next to me," he said, and Evan walked over. "I'm going to draw a circle with salt for protection. You need to stay inside it. If I can connect with the spirits, we don't know whether they'll be friendly."

Evan's skepticism showed in his eyes, but he stood still while Seth laid down the salt lines and then carefully stepped inside. Seth knelt and lit the candle. Then he pulled a knife and a bandage from the sheath on his belt and cut his left palm enough to ooze droplets of blood into the silver bowl.

"What are you doing?" Evan hissed, eyes wide.

"What has to be done if we want answers." Seth wiped off his blade and replaced the knife, and put a bandage over his cut. He took a deep breath to prepare himself. "Whatever happens, whatever you see or hear, stay where you are. Don't leave the circle, and don't touch me. If you stay inside the salt lines, energies on the outside can't harm you."

Seth bent over the bowl, holding his injured hand against his chest. He had only tried this spell a couple of times before, and never with ghosts as strong as the spectral residents of the pump house, if the rumors about the spirits were true.

Two deep breaths helped to center his energy and calm his nerves. This working required a spell that was a bit longer than the usual cantrip. Perhaps it would be easier for a true medium; Seth did not delude himself into thinking he possessed those skills. Then again, a natural clairvoyant would have no need of the spells, which served as a tool for those without such a gift.

The temperature in the mechanical room plummeted, and despite the closed door and latched windows, a wind stirred, rippling the greenish water in the pump bays. Evan's gasp made Seth raise his head to find a figure in the uniform of a workman standing not far outside the protected circle.

"Daniel?" Seth asked.

The apparition nodded. He looked to be in his early thirties, of average height but with a strong build, with broad hands and muscled forearms from a lifetime of hard work. Daniel had fair hair and regular features with a strong jaw, a rugged handsomeness, and a solid masculinity. He stared at Evan as if he were the one seeing a ghost.

"How is this possible?" Daniel said, his voice like a whisper carrying across a great distance. "You died."

Evan had gone pale, and the spirit's words sent a shiver down Seth's spine. "I'm not Jacob. I'm a cousin, long removed," Evan answered. "But I'll be dead just like Jacob unless you can help us."

Seth didn't know how long the spell would last, holding open the Veil so that Daniel's spirit could make himself heard. Evan's matter-of-fact declaration chilled Seth, the acknowledgment that he could be dead in days squeezed Seth's heart. He pushed past his feelings, forcing himself into the cold detachment of battle.

"The man who killed Jacob. What can you tell us about him, or about what happened that night?" Evan pressed.

Daniel's spirit had grown more opaque, and if Seth had only glimpsed him and not known the truth, he might have mistaken him for a living man. "Colin Voorhis," Daniel replied, making the name a curse. "Pretended to be a friend. Managed the night shift for the pump team. Then one night he told Jacob he had a job for him to do, make some extra money. I didn't like it, warned him not to go. We argued. I didn't follow him. Next day, they found him dead—all cut up and Voorhis gone without a trace."

"When?" Seth asked.

"In the year of our Lord nineteen twelve," Daniel replied. "I couldn't live with not stopping Jacob. Cared for him like a brother, and

I didn't protect him. So I ended it, here. Thought I'd move on, heaven or hell, and look what happened."

"I have a friend who's a priest. He might be able to help," Seth said, understanding Daniel's pain. He'd considered doing the same thing after Jesse died. Toby sometimes thought he might still have that intent, just taking the long road to get there. "But first, we've got to save Evan. Did Voorhis leave anything behind, maybe hidden somewhere?"

"Nothing's left here but ghosts and memories," Daniel replied. "I'm sorry."

"Seth…we've got trouble."

Only when Evan spoke did Seth realize the temperature had become icy, enough to send a thin frost over the damp stone and form a skin on the water in the pump footings. The emergency lights began to blink and stutter, and the breeze that shouldn't exist grew stronger.

"Who is that?" Evan asked, pointing to a figure descending the long stairs from the main entrance on the other side of the pump room. A woman in a Victorian-era dress glowed brightly, appearing nearly solid. Even without any psychic powers, Seth felt the malevolence radiating from the ghostly figure.

"Run!" Daniel warned, and vanished.

"She's between us and the door!" Evan stayed inside the salt circle, but Seth could hear the fear in his voice. The woman in white couldn't harm them inside the warding, but Seth had no intention of remaining trapped in the pump house. He grabbed the bowl, shoved a rag from his pack into it to sop up the blood, snuffed out the candle and smudged the soot marking. Shoving all his tools back into the pack, Seth held the canister of salt.

"We have to leave the circle, or be stuck here. See those stairs?" he said, and Evan's eyes traveled to the far wall where an iron spiral staircase wound up to the second floor. "Ghosts can't cross iron. She can't go through the ceiling because of the iron supports, and she can't follow us up the steps. On my word, head for the iron stairs."

Seth threw the canister of salt ahead of them and muttered a word of power. The canister burst apart, spewing salt across the walkway. "Now!"

The woman's ghost moved quickly. Energy crackled around her, a nimbus of lightning that sparked from her hands and traveled up and down her body like a Tesla coil.

Evan sprinted ahead, and Seth hung back to cover him. He bent down to pick up a handful of old bolts and thick iron screws and put them in his pocket, just in case. Salt crunched beneath their feet, scattered nearly the entire way toward the rusted old iron staircase. Behind them, the ghost shrieked, her cries echoing from the solid stone walls, a deafening, shrill cry that raised the hair on the back of Seth's neck.

"Up the steps. Go! Go!"

Evan charged up the steps and got to the first turn when his foot nearly broke through the brittle old iron.

"Keep going!" Seth urged.

"What if it won't hold? Or what if I break it and you can't follow?" Evan hesitated, torn between the fearsome apparition that blocked their only other exit and the questionable safety of the crumbling staircase.

"I'll find a way. Go!"

Evan chose his steps carefully, putting his feet close to the outer supports instead of the middle of the tread. The iron creaked ominously, and the railing rattled, but Evan kept climbing. As he neared the top, the whole structure groaned and listed to the left.

"Watch out!" Seth cautioned. Evan gripped the railing, but it appeared no more steady than the rest of the frame. He reached the top and vanished from view.

"I'm up. Come on!"

Seth started up the rickety stairs. The breeze had grown stronger, and his heart sank as he realized that the glowing ghostly woman had gained control of the wind, and was using it to blow the salt off the platform, steadily advancing on their position.

"Seth, hurry!"

Seth took the steps in the first turn of the stairs two at a time, careful not to press on the weakened center of the treads. The old iron groaned again as its moorings strained, rusty metal made brittle with age and neglect. He moved up the second set of steps with a dancer's grace, catlike and cautious, doing his best to distribute his weight evenly and be as light on his feet as possible.

"She's coming! Get out of there, Seth!"

Six steps separated Seth from the top of the stairs. Down below, the glowing woman was only a half dozen paces from the base of the metal spiral. Iron might keep the ghost from following him, but the energy that crackled and sparked around her form could electrocute Seth if she sent it up the rusted staircase.

Seth sprinted up the last few steps, and the bolts that held the steps popped with a crack like a rifle shot. The whole fragile structure shuddered and tilted, supported by two worn bolts that looked as if they would give way at any second.

Seth shifted his weight, taking the next step carefully, and heard the fasteners shear off with the groan of strained metal. He lunged forward, trying to run up the stairs as the structure fell away beneath him.

"Grab my hand!" Evan lay flat on the upper floor, his arm extended. Seth caught his wrist with his right hand, as a section of the iron railing came away from the rest of the steps in his left, and the whole staircase crashed down to the stone floor.

Evan grunted as he pulled back, trying to haul Seth over the edge and not be drawn forward himself. Seth shoved the length of iron railing onto the floor above and grabbed the opening with his left hand, using all the strength in his shoulders and upper arms to get himself up and over. Evan pulled and tugged, and Seth crawled to safety.

"We're in the ballroom," Evan said as Seth got to his feet. Just in case, Seth grabbed the piece of iron railing. "It's either go over the balcony or down the other set of steps—on her end." Then Seth noticed they were not alone. A blue-white orb bobbed several feet away, but made no move to come closer. "And I think we found the third ghost."

"Think it's friendly?"

Seth regarded the orb. "Seems to be. Much friendlier than the lady downstairs."

While Seth disliked the idea of tangling with the lightning-wielding ghost on the first floor that he'd dubbed "Electra," the idea of dropping into a refuse-filled canal or a two-story fall onto a thin strip of land strewn with all kinds of discarded junk and garbage seemed worse. The orb moved a few feet away then returned to its original spot, like a dog trying to get its master's attention.

"I think it's trying to guide us," Evan said.

"Take this," Seth said, digging out a second canister of salt from his pack and handing it to Evan. "If the ghost downstairs comes close, throw a handful right at her. Keep going, no matter what happens."

They crossed the wide ballroom without a problem, thanks to the underlying iron supports. The glowing orb bobbed ahead of them, helping them to avoid spots where the flooring had weakened.

"Thank you," Seth said to the orb when they reached the top of the wooden stairs. The ball of light rose and fell, then blinked out.

Seth stepped in front to lead the way. As they started down the wooden steps, he saw Electra heading back down the stone walkway.

"Stay behind me," Seth warned, holding the iron rod like a sword.

One second, Electra was halfway across the pump room; the next she loomed at the bottom of the stairs, crackling and sparking like a downed power line. Evan threw a handful of salt in the apparition's face, and she faltered. Seth reached into his pocket and pulled out one of the rusted iron bolts and pelted it through the ghost's torso. Electra shrieked and blinked out.

Seth and Evan scrambled down the steps, nearly reaching the bottom before the ghost materialized once more, blocking their path.

"I'll hold her off, and you go around me," Seth said. "Sweep the salt back and forth and lay down a path for me. I'll bring up the rear."

Evan glowered, but he held his arguments for later. "Don't get dead," Evan muttered, sliding between Seth and the rough stone wall, scattering the salt in a thin, wide fan before him to create a safe path to the door.

Electra appeared out of nowhere in between Seth and Evan, closer than she'd been before, blocking Seth's escape route. Seth threw more iron bolts at the ghost, and the energy arced when the iron passed through her, breaking up her form like a bad TV signal. Seth went around her and cried out as he brushed against the sizzling power, feeling as if he'd touched an electric fence.

"Come on!" Evan urged from just inside the exit door.

Electra screamed and lashed out, hitting Seth with a tendril of blue-white power. It burned where it snaked around his calf, and he jolted with the energy that surged through him.

"Seth!"

Seth threw the iron rod like a javelin, aiming for the specter's head. The ghost vanished once more, and Seth staggered toward the door, his leg numb and useless, and his heart jittery. *One more like that, and I might not make it.*

Evan ran to help him, getting under his shoulder to support his weight. "I'm not leaving without you." He slung an arm around Seth's waist and steadied him as they headed for the door.

Electra manifested again, using the wind to blow the salt away and putting herself between them and the only way out. Whatever effect the iron had on her must have hurt, because the light that limned her form had shifted from bright white to blood red.

"Go," Seth said, twisting loose from Evan's grip and shoving him toward the door.

"The fuck I will." Evan stood shoulder to shoulder with Seth, facing down the vengeful ghost.

A guttural scream rose above the hiss and crackle of Electra's energy. Daniel's ghost solidified behind her. "Run!" Daniel shouted, an instant before he plunged into her charged form and both ghosts shrieked with pain and rage.

Evan and Seth hobbled past, Evan pulling him along as Seth willed his numb leg to carry him forward. They did not look back. Evan threw the door open, and both men stumbled out into the sun, collapsing on the ground a safe distance away.

Before Seth could catch his breath, Evan grabbed a fistful of Seth's t-shirt and pulled him forward. Anger and fear blazed in Evan's hazel eyes. "You scared the hell out of me back there. I thought you were going to die."

"So did I," Seth admitted.

"You die, and I'm fucked. You can't be a hero if you're dead."

Evan's face was so close Seth could feel his breath. One of them was trembling; Seth couldn't tell whether the after-effects of the jolt of energy still thrummed through him, or whether the adrenaline of the narrow escape made Evan practically vibrate. He didn't have time to ponder, when Evan pushed forward and kissed him, hard.

"We're both going to live through his," Evan growled when he came up for breath. Seth's head spun, from the near miss, from the tingling in his leg as feeling returned, and from the swirl of emotions just touching Evan sent coursing through him. "Both of us, dammit. Promise me."

"I can't—"

"Promise me!" Evan tightened his grip on Seth's shirt, and the look in his eyes was fierce and wild.

"I promise—" Seth said before Evan's lips muffled the rest of his words. *I promise to make sure you're safe. If only one of us survives, it's going to be you.*

10

EVAN

Since they had come on Seth's motorcycle, they were stuck at Byrd Park until Seth got the feeling back in his leg. Evan helped him to a bench beneath a tree, and they both sat in silence for several minutes, recovering from the near miss at the pump house.

"I will never doubt another story about a haunting again," Evan said when his heartbeat finally slowed.

"I'll admit, that's more than I bargained for," Seth replied. He bent over and pulled up his jeans to reveal an angry red welt on one calf. "Hurts like a mofo."

Before Evan could respond, Seth's phone buzzed. "Hey, Toby! You got something for me?" Seth answered when he recognized the incoming number. He listened for a few minutes, jotting down information in an app on his phone before he thanked Toby and promised him a beer. When he ended the call, he turned to Evan.

"Toby found three Richmond properties recently owned by CoVal. Two houses and a shopping plaza. The plaza is abandoned and slated to be demolished. One of the houses was sold, but Toby couldn't find any records of the second house being sold or leased," Seth reported. "So I think we need to take a look."

"What are we looking for?" Evan asked. If Seth was right about

Valac, then they only had two days after today to track him down. Evan tried not to dwell on the threat, or he knew he'd spiral. "We can try the tracking spell on the house. If we could find a personal possession, that would be better, but I'm not going to waste the opportunity," Seth replied. "I doubt that a tracking spell would work on something like a shopping plaza—too big and impersonal, too many people."

"What happens when you find Valac?"

"Then I stop him." Seth's voice took on a cold, hard note that sent a chill down Evan's spine. Sometimes Evan glimpsed the warrior beneath the laid-back exterior, and that edge of danger turned him on and frightened him in equal measure.

"What about the anchor?"

Seth sighed. "If it's at the house, that could be a reason Valac hasn't sold the place yet. Doubtful it's somewhere as public as the shopping plaza. He'd want to make sure he hid it where it wouldn't be disturbed, and that's the wild card because all of the houses his previous alter-egos have owned were all sold multiple times." If Noah and Luis hadn't been injured on their last hunt, Seth would have gladly taken them up on the offer to help, but they weren't in any shape for a battle, Toby and Milo were too far away, and he didn't know any of the other hunters well enough to entrust them with Evan's life.

"But not their graves." Evan looked up. "Do you know where Valac's been 'buried?' Because a gravesite wouldn't be disturbed."

Seth leaned forward and kissed him. "You're beautiful *and* brilliant." Evan felt his cheeks heat and kissed Seth back, savoring the moment and slipping his tongue between Seth's lips, tasting and exploring. Seth deepened the kiss, cupping Evan's face with one large hand, stroking his cheekbone with his thumb. Evan's cock decided that the best way to celebrate surviving a near miss was a quick fuck, and from the bulge in Seth's crotch, it seemed his body agreed. Reluctantly, Seth drew back.

"If we weren't in the middle of a park, I'd show you just how glad I am that we got out of that pump house in one piece," Seth said, his voice a low growl that made Evan's already hard prick throb. "Hang on to that thought until tonight, okay? I'll make it worth your while."

Evan shivered at the promise in Seth's deep voice and the lust he saw in Seth's dark eyes. He reached up to tangle his fingers in Seth's hair, and stole another kiss, pausing long enough to breathe in his scent. "I'll hold you to that," he murmured, winning a sinful smile in return.

Evan hovered nearby as Seth walked off the last of the numbness in his leg, proving he had full use of his muscles back by running a short distance and doing a few jumps. When Seth's leg did not go out on him, Evan agreed to get on the bike.

The house was a modest frame home in the Church Hill neighborhood, neat but with the feel of an empty dwelling. Seth drove by once to take the measure of the place and get a look at the surrounding homes, then came back and parked, pulling the bike up the driveway and behind a hedge where it wouldn't be easily noticed.

Evan kept lookout while Seth approached the back door. His pulse quickened and sweat beaded on his forehead. They were breaking and entering, as well as trespassing. Other than a few pranks as a teenager, Evan had avoided lawbreaking. He'd seen the cops take away a neighbor on a drug bust when he was in middle school, and the ordeal had terrified him. "Scared straight" wasn't exactly accurate, but close enough. If Evan had ever thought about tempting fate, the memory of the sirens, lights, and SWAT teams loading his neighbor into a police van quashed the urge for adventure.

The quiet neighborhood suggested residents were busy at work during the middle of the day. Evan remained alert for little old ladies peering through windows or random dog walkers, but none appeared in the few minutes it took Seth to walk up the back steps, place his hand on the rickety lock, and murmur the spell. The door swung open, and Seth jerked his head toward the dim interior for Evan to follow.

"Not much left," Seth murmured as they stepped into the kitchen and closed the back door behind them.

"Can you try the tracking spell?"

Seth nodded. "I'd like to do that upstairs, in the master bedroom. It's a bit more personal. The spell may not work at all. But it's worth a try."

Evan still wasn't sure how Seth planned to face down an immortal warlock once they found Valac. Running for Alaska or the Caribbean still seemed like a good option, until he remembered that Valac might still come after him in another dozen years, and if not, someone else would be the sacrifice. With a sigh, he followed Seth farther into the house, trying to come up with a plausible excuse should they be caught by the cops.

"Doesn't look like anyone's been here in a while," Evan observed. The house had a middle class, post-war vibe to it, solid but unremarkable.

"Didn't leave anything behind," Seth replied. Furniture, curtains, appliances, and rugs were all gone, even a few of the light fixtures. Nothing had been vandalized, so Evan figured the previous owner had cleared the place out. Their steps echoed on the hardwood floors, and the temperature inside felt colder than the autumn air outdoors. The house smelled of dust and disuse.

He followed Seth upstairs, trying not to get distracted by the firm ass in tight jeans ahead of him. Somehow, his cock did not fully appreciate the urgency of their situation, or else his libido decided to make the most of the life he had remaining by going out in a last hurrah of desperate sex. Then again, wondering whether Seth would bottom for him and what it would be like sinking into that tight, hot passage beat the hell out of brooding over an impending horrible death.

The only thing worse than getting caught breaking, entering, and trespassing would be being in the middle of sweaty sex when the cops arrived.

That thought worked as well as a douse of cold water, and Evan hurried to catch up, keeping his eyes on the stair tread instead of Seth's perfect ass.

Seth made a quick recon down the hall to assure that the other rooms were empty and motioned for Evan to follow him into the one he guessed to be the master bedroom.

"Are you going to have to bleed again? That's got to make it difficult to do many spells." Evan glanced out the window, happy to see that the neighbors still had not taken any notice of their arrival.

"No. Different spell, different materials. Although it would work exceptionally well if we had some of Valac's blood," Seth replied, distracted as he rooted in his pack for what he needed. "I'm using a tracking spell." He pulled out a piece of chalk, a map, a candle, and a faceted crystal on a slender silver chain. Seth knelt and drew a sigil on the floorboards, then spread out the map of Richmond and lit the candle on the other side. He held the crystal in his hands and closed his eyes, murmuring the spell. The sigil glowed, and the candle flame flickered as he carefully let the pendant down over the middle of the map.

Evan held his breath. The crystal shimmered, and after a few seconds, the gem began to swing back and forth, though Seth's hand remained still. He didn't know what to expect, whether the stone would circle a spot on the map or pull down to point to a location. For a moment, his heart leaped as the crystal seemed to choose a direction. Just as suddenly, the shimmer vanished, the sigil dimmed, and the crystal hung loosely, pointing straight down.

"Fuck," Seth muttered, sitting back on his heels and staring at the map in disgust.

"What happened?" Evan edged closer, but whatever glow he had glimpsed before was gone.

"Nothing happened," Seth grumbled. He blew out the candle, gathered up his materials and stuffed them back in the bag. A few brushes with a rag erased the chalk marking. He chewed his lip, staring at the spot on the floor in disgust.

"You weren't sure that the house would work the same as a possession," Evan ventured, trying to hide his disappointment and apprehension. Seth's expression had darkened with clear frustration, and Evan hung back, uncertain how to handle his angry companion.

"It was worth a try," Seth said, obviously pissed but trying to put a good face on the failure. "I think we need something more personal to try the spell again. And the house is a bust for any objects, too."

"If Valac has been doing this for a hundred years, he's probably gotten very careful, even OCD about not leaving anything behind," Evan ventured. "I saw a movie once where a witch used hair clippings to kill a rival. Never thought that might be real."

Seth shrugged. "It's real. And you're right—Valac's not an amateur, or he wouldn't have survived this long. So maybe we need to look for something old, from one of his previous lives. Same guy, different name. Maybe he's missed a few loose ends."

He slung the bag over his shoulder. "Let's get out of here. The cemetery sounds like a good next step."

∽

HOLLYWOOD CEMETERY IN RICHMOND WAS A HUGE TOURIST ATTRACTION, a beautiful final resting place for generals, war casualties, presidents, and legislators, as well as movie stars and celebrities. Landscaped, manicured, and filled with amazing monuments, the cemetery was a poignant reminder of how far grieving families would go to immortalize their lost loved ones.

"So we're back to another super-haunted site," Even said when Seth turned off the bike out of respect just inside the cemetery gates. They got off and walked with the Hayabusa, removing their helmets and heading toward the center of the cemetery.

"So the big pyramid over there?" Evan said, pointing to an unmistakable landmark. "People say they hear moans from inside and feel cold spots near it. And over that way," he said, pointing in another direction, "there's an iron figure of a dog next to the grave of a little girl and legend has it that the dog moves around the cemetery."

Seth kept them heading for the first of Valac's burial plots as Evan continued his trivia tour. "And the Pool mausoleum ahead of us is one of the most famous hauntings. It's supposedly the home of the Richmond Vampire."

Seth stopped in front of the large rectangular mausoleum. "Richmond Vampire?"

"Remember that Church Hill Tunnel collapse I told you about?" Evan said, and Seth gave an ambiguous shrug. "So there was a famous railroad accident back in 1925. The tunnel collapsed onto a train, and some of the passengers didn't make it out. A few of the workers escaped, but the cave-in was too big to try to rescue the others. Witnesses said they saw a hideous man who didn't look human leaving the tunnel and that he hid in the Pool mausoleum. They said he was a vampire. The legend stuck."

Seth parked the bike and moved up to look inside the mausoleum's wrought iron grate. "It turned out that the man people saw was a railroad worker who was badly burned," Evan said. "He died. People say the ghosts of the dead passengers are still trapped in the tunnel."

"Huh. That's interesting," Seth replied, taking a last peek inside the tomb before walking back to the bike. He opened the cemetery "find a grave" site on his phone and typed in a name. "Valac's first grave should be that way," he said, pointing to an older section of the grounds.

They walked the bike back to the rows of old, weathered stones. "There it is," Seth said, parking the bike and walking across the lush grass to a dark headstone in the shade of an old oak. He read the inscription aloud. "*Corson Valac, 1872-1912*. Looks like this is it."

Evan stared at the gravesite and the unbroken carpet of grass that covered it. "Doesn't seem like it's been disturbed in a long time." He looked beyond the graves, out across the carefully tended lawn and the collection of angels, urns, pillars, and obelisks that marked the burial spots of Richmonders across the years.

On prior visits, Evan had been impressed with the sense of peace and tranquility he felt from the beautiful grounds and the quiet atmosphere. It seemed a world away from traffic and city noise, wrapped in silence broken only by birdsong and the rustle of wind in the trees. Now, Evan felt jumpy, and although a glance around told him they were alone, he could not shake the feeling they were being watched.

"He might not need to move it, as long as he stays within a certain distance," Seth replied. "Maybe that's why he keeps coming back to Richmond."

"But you said Gremory was hanged in Brazil, Indiana. So Valac wasn't always in Richmond."

Seth laid his hand on the tombstone and murmured a few arcane words. Evan wondered whether he would try the tracking spell again, and how he could cover them to avoid being hauled to the police station for desecrating a grave if Seth decided to dig. To his relief, Seth raised his head and drew his hand back as if burned. "I tried to read for the presence of magic," he said, eying the dark carved granite warily. "I couldn't pick up a sense of anything, but maybe I wouldn't if it were buried under six feet of dirt." Unconsciously, he wiped his hand on his pants. "But the stone feels wrong. Tainted." He shuddered.

"You're right about Gremory," he answered Evan's earlier question. "From everything Toby and I could find, after Gremory died, the witch-disciples scattered to different cities. Probably following the sheriff's deputies, who also moved away. The disciples seem to stay put, and the cities are all large enough that the disciples can reinvent themselves and not get caught. Killing on a twelve-year cycle should help hide the connection between the murders."

"So my dad moved us to Oklahoma for his job, and I came back because I grew up here," Evan mused. "Do you think Valac would have followed me if I'd stayed out West?"

"Probably," Seth replied. "Maybe even kidnapped you and brought you back to Richmond, if his power is anchored here."

Evan watched as Seth straightened and scanned the horizon as if also sensing another presence, his eyes narrowed and body tense. After a moment, he relaxed a bit when he saw nothing to confirm a threat. "Let's check out the other graves," Seth said, turning to the map on his phone once more.

It took more than an hour to find the other nine headstones. The names matched those on Seth's list; birth dates altered to show the death of a man in his late thirties to early forties. "He doesn't age much," Evan observed. "And the dates aren't exactly twelve years."

"I don't know whether remaining the same age forever is part of the immortality, or if he'll just age more slowly. As for the death dates, you're right. Some gaps are thirteen years, but it probably depends on when in the year he pulls his disappearing act, so the interval is likely the same. Although maybe he has a little wiggle room. It's not like Toby and I had perfect resources. We had to piece a lot together."

A low growl made Evan's hackles rise. "What was that?"

Seth reached behind him to pull his gun from the waistband of his jeans. He kept the weapon against his leg, turning in a slow circle as he looked for threat. "Get behind me." His voice was deep and rough. The whole way he carried himself had changed as his military training returned to the forefront, and despite the fear rising in his gut, Evan thought Seth looked sexy as fuck.

Evan moved slowly to stand between Seth and the bike. "Don't make any quick moves," Seth warned. "Get on the bike and put on your helmet. I'll be right behind you."

Evan's eyes widened as he saw three large, shaggy black dogs slink over a rise, headed right for Seth. He didn't recognize the breed, neither wolf nor regular dog. Dark, thick, coarse hair covered heavily muscular bodies, and each of the creatures was easily the size of a large man on all fours. Lips pulled back from long muzzles revealing sharp teeth, and gleaming red eyes made Evan's blood run cold.

Just as he reached the bike, the creatures charged.

"Seth, watch out!" Evan shouted in warning.

The wolf-thing on the right launched itself at Seth, springing into the air and leaping easily across a gap of several feet. Seth fired, the shot echoing across the cemetery, breaking the calm. The creature dropped, still and bloody, but its two companions attacked in tandem, lunging and snapping, forcing Seth back. He fired again, hitting one of the beasts in its broad chest, but as he swung around to shoot again, the second wolf-thing sprang, taking him down to the ground.

Evan climbed onto the bike and revved the engine, trying not to think about how long it had been since the last time he had driven a motorcycle. He shot forward, up the shallow rise and across the slick grass, slewing as he went. Evan hung on to the grips white-knuckled, roaring straight for Seth and the huge black creature that rolled and tumbled across the grass. Seth had dropped his gun in the scuffle, and now had his hands full keeping clear of the sharp claws and the snap of sharp teeth.

"Get off him!" Evan shouted as he steered the bike at the creature and let the engine roar.

The noise broke the beast's concentration, and Seth twisted, getting his knees up beneath the wolf-thing's belly. He threw the creature off and crawled toward his gun as the beast got to its feet and hunched, ready for another attack.

Before Seth could reach his gun, the creature lunged, and Evan drove the bike right for him, turning at the last moment to take the impact on his shoulder and helmet, knocking the wolf-thing aside. The bike skidded, throwing Evan, who tumbled across the turf and lay winded and sore, his momentum stopped by a large headstone.

A shot silenced the beast's angry growls. "Evan!" Seth's panicked voice rang out. Evan wanted to respond, but the fall had knocked the breath out of him, and his head spun from the impact.

Seth fell to his knees beside him, turning him gently. "Evan?" His left hand skimmed down Evan's body searching for damage, his right held the gun. Evan gave a low groan.

"Of all the stupid, reckless, idiotic stunts," Seth ranted, but the fear in his voice outweighed the anger. "What the hell did you think you were doing?"

"Saving your ass."

"Did you get clawed? Can you move? Are you seeing double? Let me check." Seth stared down into Evan's eyes, looking to see if Evan's pupils indicated a concussion, and Evan felt a warm glow from the concern he saw in Seth's gaze.

With a muttered curse, Evan sat up, and Seth slipped an arm behind his shoulders, supporting him.

"I didn't get clawed," Evan said, taking inventory of his injuries. A torn sleeve was due to the fall from the bike, and while his shoulder hurt from the impact with the heavy creature, he hadn't been cut. "I'm going to have some amazing bruises, but I can move everything. And I only see you," Evan said, too rattled to worry about how cheesy that sounded.

"Come on," Seth said, helping him to his feet. "Someone will have called in those shots. We need to get out of here before the cops arrive."

"You're bleeding." Evan felt a little loopy, but he had his shit together enough to recognize blood.

"It's not bad," Seth assured him, guiding him toward the bike. Seth winced as he righted the Hayabusa, but other than some mud, the bike looked no worse for the wear. "I'll patch you up back at the trailer."

"We can patch each other up," Evan corrected. "I'll take care of you. Take your mind off what hurts."

Seth shook his head fondly. "You're cute when you're a little concussed. Proposition me when your eyes can focus."

Sirens sounded in the distance. "That's our cue," he said, helping Evan mount the bike before getting on in front of him. Evan slouched forward, wrapping his arms around Seth's waist and hanging on tight. Evan could feel Seth's gun against his belly where the weapon was shoved into the waistband of Seth's jeans. He glanced behind him as the bike roared out of the cemetery. Three dark shapes lay still on the grass, but as he watched, they shimmered and vanished.

What the fuck? Those were solid. The one I hit threw me off the bike. Where did they go?

Seth headed for the back of the cemetery, following a gravel service road down the far side, finding a rear exit used for delivering landscaping supplies. To Evan's relief, no one challenged them, and Seth maneuvered them back to the main road, where they blended into traffic.

Evan swore he could feel every flaw in the pavement as Seth drove back to the old farm, and he gritted his teeth on the bumpy ride down the rutted driveway that jostled his bones and strained sore muscles. He stumbled as he got off the bike, surprised at how much he had stiffened up. Seth caught him, slipping an arm around Evan's waist and walking side by side to the trailer.

"A hot shower is going to make everything feel better," Seth said, guiding Evan toward the bathroom.

"Need to save water," Evan mumbled.

"We'll shower together," Seth promised. "It'll be good. I promise."

Evan managed to get out of his torn and grass-stained clothing. His shoulder and hip had taken the brunt of the hit with the creature and the fall from the bike, and while the helmet had protected his head, hitting the ground hard left him with a dull headache.

"What were those things? How did they disappear? It was solid when I rammed it."

Seth stripped off his clothing and stepped into the shower stall, reaching out to draw Evan to him. Evan stepped into his arms, and Seth pulled the door shut, folding Evan against his chest. The only way they both fit into the trailer's small shower was by embracing.

"You scared me," Seth confessed quietly, turning Evan's back to the hot water and letting it stream down his skin. "I thought the black dog was going to kill you. And then when you got thrown—"

"I couldn't let it get you," Evan replied, reaching for the soap and running it up and down the muscles of Seth's broad back. He looked at the fresh gashes in Seth's shoulder. "How bad?"

Seth shook his head. "Not too deep. A little holy water and some special salve, and it will heal up just fine."

"What were those things?" Evan asked again.

"There are lots of names, but the most common is a '*grim*.'"

Evan frowned. "*Grim*?"

"It's a supernatural creature, a big black dog that can be a death omen," Seth replied.

"Is that why they disappeared when you killed them? Because they were supernatural creatures?"

Seth nodded, never stopping the slow caresses that washed the dirt from Evan's skin and raised his cock to attention. "Yeah. We either got close to something Valac didn't want us to see, or he's watching us. He's stepped up his game from human henchman. I'm going to take that as a good sign. We're on the right track."

Evan slipped a hand between them to soap down the flat planes of Seth's chest and abs. He handed off the soap to Seth, then returned his slippery hand to stroke Seth's stiff cock and fondle his balls. Seth's broad hands caressed him, slippery and tender as he washed away the sweat and grime.

"Not here," Seth murmured, bending to whisper in Evan's ear. His tone and the rustle of his breath sent a shiver through Evan, straight to his prick. "Bed."

They toweled each other off gently, and Evan tended the shallow cuts in Seth's arm, then Seth led Evan to the bedroom. Evan crawled onto the big queen bed, and Seth followed, closing the distance between them on his hands and knees until he stretched out over Evan, bracketing him between his legs.

"What do you want?" Seth breathed, shifting so their stiff cocks rubbed together and eliciting a moan from Evan.

"Anything. Everything. I want to hold you, fuck you, suck you—"

"Sounds like a good place to start," Seth replied with a chuckle.

"Can I fuck you? We never got our 'fourth round' in the morning," Evan asked, eager but a little hesitant. He didn't mind switching, but he wasn't sure how Seth felt about it.

Seth was quiet for so long Evan felt sure he'd pushed too far. He tried to interpret the look in Seth's eyes, and the expression that told him Seth was caught in an internal argument.

"We don't have to—"

"Shh," Seth coaxed, coming back to the moment and sliding a hand down Evan's cheek. He leaned forward and kissed Evan, then began to leave a trail of gentle nips down Evan's jaw. Evan arched, baring his neck and sliding their cocks together, and Seth lapped and kissed down the tendon from ear to shoulder, then around to Evan's throat. "I'd like that. It's just been a long time."

"We can go slow," Evan promised, feeling his heart leap at Seth's acceptance. "That's part of the fun."

"There's lube and condoms in the drawer," Seth said, with a nod toward the built-in nightstand beside the bed.

"We'll get there," Evan promised, drawing Seth into his arms. He kissed him slowly and carefully, trying to say with his body what he wasn't sure either of them were ready to speak aloud. Seth Tanner had gotten under his skin, plowed through his defenses, and gone straight to his heart. As crazy as the past few days had been, the attraction between them was real and undeniable, like nothing Evan had ever felt before, and he knew he'd fallen hard. Evan had no idea whether or not Seth felt the same, although the concern in Seth's eyes back in the cemetery gave him hope.

Evan took the lead, rolling Seth onto his back. He expected resistance, but Seth went willingly, letting his legs sprawl apart, a clear invitation. Evan kissed him soundly, then peppered his jaw and throat with licks and light kisses, moving down to stroke and lick at his nipples until they were hard buds. He moved farther down, taking his time, hoping that Seth understood that the careful lovemaking spoke for Evan's growing feelings.

Seth groaned and shifted, hungry for more contact, and Evan chuckled, reaching down to stroke Seth's weeping cock a few times before giving the base a squeeze to stave off his release. "In time," he promised, following the dark blond trail to Seth's groin.

He licked at the pearl of pre-come that beaded at the dusky head of Seth's stiff cock, then swirled his tongue around the knob, earning another moan. Seth tangled his hands in Evan's hair but let him lead, and Evan bobbed up and down, sucking and licking until Seth bucked beneath him.

Alternating between licking at Seth's cock and sucking on his balls, Evan enjoyed the shivers and hot sounds he wrung from Seth's arousal. He knew Seth's patience was waning when the lube and a condom packet landed next to his elbow. In response, he let his fingers slide backward on Seth's spit-slicked taint until they reached his tight furl. Evan's fingers traced Seth's hole, teasing, and then he withdrew long enough to squeeze lube into his hand and slick up his fingers.

"Gonna take good care of you," Evan promised, thrilled at the sight of Seth's lust-blown eyes and tousled hair, knowing that he'd put that look on Seth's face. His lover's cheeks were flushed, and Seth's breathing was fast and heavy.

Evan returned to licking and teasing Seth's cock, loving the taste of the bitter, salty fluid and the scent of soap and musk that was uniquely Seth. He slid one lubed finger into Seth's pucker, easing in up to the knuckle. Damn, he was tight. He hadn't been kidding about not having done this in a while. Evan wondered how long, and who had been lucky enough to have the chance before him. That sent a strange bolt of jealousy through Evan, and he quickly shifted his thoughts away, not liking the idea of Seth with anyone else.

Seth bucked again, and Evan eased in a second finger as Seth began to fuck himself.

"Please, Evan. I can't take much more—"

"Gotta get you ready," Evan murmured. "Don't want to hurt you. Gonna make this good for you. God, I want you."

"Want you too. So much."

Evan warned his heart not to read too much into Seth's breathy words, that they only applied to the moment and his building release. He tried not to think of what might happen once they defeated Valac, but Evan already knew he wanted more than just a brief affair.

Scissoring two fingers made it easy to add a third. Finally, Evan moved up on his knees and stroked a hand up over Seth's flank. "Turn over," he urged.

"I want to see you," Seth protested.

"Next time," Evan promised. "You're really tight, babe. Don't want to hurt you."

Seth rolled over and pushed a pillow under his hips, then spread his knees wide and arched his back, offering himself to Evan with a brashness that took Evan's breath away. Evan paused just long enough to roll on a condom, then he took hold of Seth's hips, fitting his fingers around the bone and into the cleft that made a perfect grip, and pushed slowly against the tight ring of muscle. Seth's body quivered with the burn, and Evan paused, giving him time to adjust.

"More." Seth's voice was low and strangled, thick with desire. He turned his head enough to glimpse Evan behind him, pressing inside, and his groan nearly made Evan come right then.

Evan meant to go slowly, but Seth thrust back, impaling himself on Evan's swollen cock until Evan was buried to the hilt in Seth's tight, velvet channel.

"Feels so good. So tight. Not gonna last long." Evan began to move, slowly at first, then encouraged by Seth's moans, faster and harder until he was certain he would leave finger-shaped bruises on his lover's hips. Evan loved the sounds Seth made, the way he bucked back against him, the taste of his sweat as they both climbed toward release. He reached beneath Seth and wrapped his fingers around Seth's hot, leaking prick.

"Fuck yourself on me," Evan breathed. "Show me what you want."

With a cry, Seth complied, fucking himself backward onto Evan's prick and forward into the tunnel of his hand. Seth held on tight to the sheets as the motion of their union forced his body up the bed and rocked the trailer, filling the small room with the sound of flesh slapping against flesh.

Evan wanted this to last forever, but all too soon he felt his balls tighten. He swept his palm over the head of Seth's cock. "Come for me, Seth," he urged. The pillow muffled Seth's hoarse cry, and his whole body trembled with the force of his release. Only a few strokes later,

Evan's climax shuddered up through his body, and he came shouting Seth's name.

They collapsed together, and Evan slid to one side, not yet ready to pull out. He hadn't blacked out, but it had been a near thing, better than anything he could remember except for the last time he had been with Seth.

"That was...amazing," Seth said, his voice sated and lazy. Evan pressed a kiss between his shoulders, wrapping his arms around his lover, unwilling to end the moment. He finally pulled out and slipped the condom from his softening cock, tying it off and tossing it into the bedside waste can.

"Thank you for letting me top," Evan murmured, toying with Seth's hair. Part of him wanted to look in Seth's eyes, and another part feared that he might not see the same feelings returned. *Please be who you say you are. Please be the real thing. Don't make a fool of me.*

"I haven't let anyone do that in a long time," Seth said quietly. "But it felt right with you."

Evan knew he grinned like an idiot at those words, and he ducked behind Seth's shoulder, embarrassed. "Even better," he said quietly, kissing Seth's back.

He reached over to grab a discarded t-shirt and wipe Seth off, doing his best to mop up the wet spot on the sheet and the leaking come between his lover's thighs, before tossing the shirt on the floor. Being tender with Seth came easily, and he found himself wanting to take away the pain he saw in Seth's eyes, lift the burden of guilt and responsibility from his shoulders, let him know he wasn't so terribly alone. Evan had no idea whether Seth would accept that from him, but God, he wanted to try.

"Why did you leave Oklahoma?" Seth said quietly. Evan looked up, surprised. Of all the things Seth might have asked, he hadn't expected that question.

Evan hesitated. He remembered that Seth had researched "Jackson Malone," and his old fears of being stalked resurfaced, breaking the post-sex haze of contentment. But this was Seth asking, not digging on his own, and in the dim light of the trailer's bedroom, Evan felt safe enough to answer.

"My family is very conservative, very religious," Evan said in a voice not much above a whisper. "The church I grew up in didn't tolerate gays. Said we were...well, you've heard it before," he added as Seth nodded. "And there I was, queer as a three dollar bill. Another boy, Trey, went to the same church. He was a little older, and he came on to me. Trey was an athlete, and always getting named to lead activities with the youth group. He was my first," Evan admitted, surprised that after all this time, the memories still hurt.

Seth stayed quiet, but Evan knew from how still his lover remained that Seth was listening intently.

"We talked about running away together, to a city where no one knew us or our parents and people didn't think we were going to hell for loving each other," Evan remembered, unable to keep a trace of bitterness out of his voice. "We made plans for after graduation. And then we went to that damned camp."

Evan fell silent, trying to find words amid the old anger that still simmered deep inside. "It was one of those teen revival weekends that plays up emotions—lots of singing and candlelight vigils and everything's engineered to break down your walls and make you feel like you can confide in people, like they care about you." He swallowed hard.

"We talked about it before we went. Neither of us wanted to go, but our parents really pushed and everyone else was going, so we promised each other we wouldn't let them get to us. It's all so fake. They know how to manipulate your feelings, and we were just a bunch of dumb kids."

Evan wiped a stubborn tear away, glad Seth faced the other direction. "We stuck together as much as we could, but they intentionally split up friends to make us more vulnerable. We had to do these 'trust circles' where you open up your soul to the people in your group and they swear to keep your secrets. That was a bunch of bullshit."

This time, his breath was ragged. "I came up with a bunch of crap about being nervous about going off to college, played it up like I was really afraid, and they swallowed it. But then when we got back with the big group, the youth leader said that one of us had something to share with the whole section. And the next thing I knew, Trey was up front tearfully confessing that I had led him into 'sexual immorality' and he wanted to repent."

"Rat bastard," Seth growled. "I hope his balls fall off."

"Yeah, I'm with you on that," Evan replied. "So there I was, outed in front of everyone. The youth leader called my parents and told them to come get me. I got thrown out of the church, and when I overheard my dad on the phone arranging to send me to one of those 'conversion therapy' programs, I packed my bag and lit out of town on the next bus. Since my parents never tried to find me, I figure they didn't want me back. Been on my own ever since."

Seth turned in his arms and pulled him close, stroking his hair and kissing his forehead and temples. "Stupid, small-minded, backward idiots," he murmured. "Crazy not to see what a great guy you are." His hands ran up and down Evan's back, soothing and consoling, and Evan let his head rest on Seth's broad chest. For the first time in a very long while, Evan felt safe and protected, wrapped around Seth's body, cradled next to his heart as he fell asleep.

When Evan woke, the angle of the light told him he had slept for a few hours. Seth had disentangled himself, and his side of the bed was cold. Evan remembered the intensity of their coupling, and the intimate confession he had made afterward. He felt vulnerable and exposed, wondering what Seth had really thought of his weakness. Then he remembered how gently Seth had held him and kissed away his tears, and Evan forced himself to relax.

Maybe things happen for a reason, he thought. *I liked working at Treddy's, but I didn't want to spend the rest of my life slinging drinks in a bar.* Evan remembered the fight in the cemetery. *I was almost badass*, he remembered with a smile. *Seth and I make a good team. He needs someone to watch his back. And if we work together, we could make a difference, stop a bunch of serial killers, do something that matters. It would do me good to get out of Richmond and see more of the country, go on the road together.*

With a sigh, he pushed the daydream aside and searched for his clothes. His imagination, like his heart, was getting ahead of him. Not only did he need to survive the next two and a half days, but once the danger was over, he and Seth would have to sort out how much of the spark between them was real, and how much just adrenaline. Evan reminded himself that despite Seth's gentleness, he had no way to know whether Seth shared any of his feelings, or would even consider taking a partner on the road.

When Evan padded down to the trailer's living room, he found Seth at the table on his laptop and a stack of files on the couch.

"How are you feeling?" Seth asked, with a shy smile that stole Evan's heart all over again.

Evan grinned. "Sore, but that goes with getting bowled over by a big vanishing black dog." He stepped up behind Seth and rested his hands on his shoulders. "What are you working on?" Evan didn't miss the fact that Seth minimized his screen immediately, hiding the browser he had been using.

"Going over Valac's identities. Cross-checking death records, property titles, driver's licenses. I think I found a link between the company that owned the panel van the guys who attacked you drove and the real estate agent that was Valac's last cover."

"All that's online?"

Seth shrugged. "If you know where to look. You can find out just about anything about anybody if you poke around enough." Seth worked remotely for an online security company owned by Toby and Milo, giving him a steady paycheck—which beat depending on poker games to pay for gas and bullets.

Evan drew back at the words. Seth was too involved in his scavenger hunt to notice. *Find out just about anything about anybody.* Memories of Mike and how he had always seemed to know where Evan was going to be and how to "accidentally" cross his path came back, making bile rise in his throat.

"Okay," Evan said, stepping away. Part of him needed space, while the rest wanted Seth to notice his mood shift and reach out to him. When Seth remained glued to his screen, Evan couldn't help feeling a little hurt. "What now?"

Seth didn't look up. "Time's running out, and we need a break. Do you want to go through those files and see if you can find a connection we've missed? We've still got to find the anchor, and it would sure as hell help to know who Valac is this time around. We've only got two days left, and I am not letting Valac win." The fierceness in Seth's voice sounded cold and hard, obsessed.

"Sure. I can do that," Evan said, taking a seat and opening a folder. He knew his life was at stake, and that besting Valac meant he got to go on living. Still, the unrelenting focus he glimpsed in Seth set off old red flags, especially coupled with how easily Seth ferreted out information that was supposed to be secret, breaking into online databases without remorse. Part of him felt glad that he had an implacable champion on his side. But as he settled in to read, a tiny voice inside reminded him that all too often, trust led to betrayal.

11

SETH

When Evan fell asleep on Seth's shoulder after his tearful story about the asshole bastard that got him thrown out of his home, Seth's heart ached for him. All Seth could do was listen and then hold Evan and stroke his hair as he wept. He murmured reassurance and endearments until Evan finally drifted off to sleep.

Seth remained awake, listening to the cadence of Evan's breathing, feeling the warmth of his lover as Evan pressed against his side. He thought about their lovemaking, and how vulnerable he felt allowing Evan to top. Few of his previous lovers had stayed the night, and only with Ryan had Seth trusted enough to bottom, just to have his heart broken when his world fell apart.

Evan wouldn't do that to him, would he? Seth realized how much he enjoyed the intimacy of sleeping next to his lover, how much he wanted that from Evan, wanted a future. He'd fallen hard for Evan, and it scared him.

In two and a half days, Seth had to either best Valac, or lose the man in his arms to a bloody death. His grip on Evan tightened, as he swore he would not fail. Just the thought of Evan dead like Jesse made Seth's heart stutter. Seth knew he might not be able to keep Evan with him, that Evan might not return his feelings, but he would not survive burying his lover.

A week ago, he hadn't even met Evan; now, he dreaded the idea of leaving him behind when Valac was defeated. Seth knew he had it bad, and although he hesitated to put a name to his feelings, it didn't make them any less real.

He shifted and winced at the sting of the *grim's* cuts on his shoulder. Evan had roared to his rescue, handling the bike like a pro, a modern knight riding into battle. He had Seth's back, and even if magic and the supernatural still seemed unbelievable to him, Evan was sticking with Seth, and gaining a growing understanding of what kind of forces they were up against.

Speaking of which...Seth turned to leave a gentle kiss on Evan's temple, then carefully disentangled himself from his sleeping lover and dressed. Seth made a cup of coffee and fired up his laptop, reminding him that the best way to have a chance at a future with Evan was to get the jump on Valac.

Seth had learned a few hacking tricks from Toby and some of his friends in the hunting community. He picked up a lot more working for Toby's company as a 'white hat' hacker, showing clients where their systems were vulnerable. Breaking into official databases was illegal as fuck, but when the police and Feds were no help against an enemy like Valac, Seth had no qualms about using every asset at his disposal to stop a killer and save lives.

He went back over the trail of names and identities, but still found nothing to link Valac to his current disguise. Then he switched tactics and began looking for clues to personal possessions from Valac's earlier personas, feeling the thrill of victory when he uncovered a few possibilities.

I'm going to find Valac and destroy him and his anchor so he can't hurt Evan or anyone else ever again, Seth swore, surprising even himself on how ferociously protective he felt about the man he had left sleeping in the bedroom. *I don't care what it takes, or what rules I have to break, or what price I need to pay; I'm going to save Evan and stop the madness.*

"What are you working on?" Evan came up behind him so quietly Seth hadn't realized he was there. Knowing how uncomfortable his sleuthing could make Evan because of the old stalker boyfriend, Seth shut down his browser with a guilty pang. He didn't want to give Evan a reason to distrust him. Seth couldn't keep a shy smile from his face at the sight of Evan looking beautifully disheveled and the fact that he had been the one to leave him sated and debauched.

He gave Evan a safe answer and mentioned the link between one of Valac's old identities and the get-away van. Seth couldn't keep a bit of pride out of his voice at making the difficult connections.

"All that's online?" Evan asked. He sounded worried and a little off, but since Evan was behind Seth, Seth couldn't see the other man's face.

Seth shrugged. "You'd be amazed at what's online. I handled computer security in the army. I know the tricks."

"Okay." Evan had been standing with his hands on Seth's shoulders, but he stepped back and removed his touch. Seth felt the absence immediately, but Evan didn't meet his gaze. "What now?"

Seth had already weeded out the most important files and set them aside for Evan to help him review. Just the thought of how quickly time was running out and what would happen if they failed brought out the soldier in Seth, focused and strong, with the obsessive attention to detail that it took to best an enemy in war.

"...two days left, and I am not letting Valac win," Seth promised. He hoped Evan would take comfort from his resolve, that it would ease the fear his lover had to be covering up. Evan had been an equal partner thus far, but as the clock ticked down, Seth had to rely on his military training and take the lead, protecting the civilian in his care. Evan had proved his bravery, but Seth was trained and battle-tested. Not only did he have more experience with a fight to the death, but the growing feelings he could not deny for Evan brought out a protectiveness that frightened Seth in its intensity.

Evan asked a few more questions, then settled down with the files. Hours passed, and Seth began to worry when Evan remained quiet, immersed in the reports. The questions Seth asked received answers that were short, almost curt, and Evan did not meet his eyes when he spoke.

Is he pulling back? Does he regret getting close? Maybe he's afraid I think differently about him since he told me what happened back home. I don't, but he doesn't know that. Or maybe he knows that when Valac is gone, we'll have choices to make. What if this thing between us isn't as important to him as it is to me? After all, who would want to stay with a crazy man in a camper chasing killer witches no one else believes in?

"Are you okay?" Seth finally ventured, when the silence grew too thick.

Evan sighed and closed his eyes, dropping his head back. "No. I mean, how could I be? Someone is trying to kill me, and we're running out of time." He blinked as if trying to dispel a headache. "Maybe we should just turn this over to the FBI. I mean, these witch-disciples are serial killers, right? Even if the Feds wouldn't believe the part about magic and living forever, there've been enough murders just in the last few decades to put them all behind bars. Can't we just send them the leads anonymously and get the hell out of Dodge?"

"I wish we could," Seth answered carefully, stung by the realization that after all they had experienced, Evan still doubted that magic was real. "But they'd just dismiss it as a prank. I'm not going to risk your life waiting for the Feds to catch on."

A stubborn look crossed Evan's face, and for a moment, Seth expected him to argue, but then he just slumped and looked down at the stack of files. "It's creepy seeing all the Malone names in these folders. I recognize the most recent ones from hearing the family talk about the deaths when they happened—my dad's older brother, and my grandpa's brother before that. But the rest of the names, I don't know anything about, and I can't exactly call home and ask."

Seth heard the bitterness and longing in Evan's voice; and it stirred anger deep inside him. He wanted to fold his arms around Evan and protect him, keep him safe from harm and shield him from anyone who would hurt him. Yet he held back, unsure whether Evan would accept that kind of commitment, now—or maybe, ever.

Get through the crisis. Save his life. Sort the rest out later. If I can't save him, there isn't a "later."

In the army, under fire, Seth never had difficulty putting other concerns behind him and keeping his attention trained, laser-focused, on the objective. His unit had relied on him for intel, and being able to break into computer systems and dig out secrets saved lives. He'd been as good at hacking as he was in combat because he didn't get distracted. Now, he couldn't compartmentalize for shit. *Is this what it feels like to be in love? How does anyone get anything done—other than fucking like bunnies?*

They had two and a half days left to catch a killer and save Evan's life. To be the soldier he needed to be, Seth knew he had to pull back, close off. He didn't want to hurt Evan, but patching up dented feelings was a lot better than burying a man he'd started to care about.

"That's why we've got to stop Valac, to keep you safe—and the next Malone and the one after that," Seth replied.

"Bang up job we're doing," Evan said, standing up and beginning to pace. "We've been shot at, chased, nearly kidnapped, attacked by dogs that weren't even real, and terrorized by ghosts—and we don't know any more than we did when we started. At this rate, I'll be dead by the weekend." He strode past Seth and into the bedroom, closing the door behind him and clicking the lock.

Seth stared after him, stunned and hurt. He had thought Evan had begun to trust him. Maybe not. Seth walked over and looked at the folders scattered from Evan's abrupt exit. Despite his reservations, Evan had obviously paged through all the files. Seth opened the top folio and glanced through it. *"Samuel Malone,"* the name on the tab read. The dates suggested the dead man had been Evan's uncle, the most recent of Valac's murders.

A crime scene photo of the mauled and bloody body seemed no less gruesome for being in black and white. Seth swallowed, remembering Jesse's death and fearing that the same fate awaited Evan. He scanned the dossier, noting the police findings, or rather, the lack thereof. *"Family members, work colleagues and acquaintances all check out for alibis. Add to the watch list for individuals fitting a violent transient profile."* Fed-speak for "unknown serial killer."

Seth tossed the folder back on the chair and rubbed his eyes. No wonder Evan's mood soured, and his anger most likely covered very reasonable mortal fear. It also made sense that if the police wanted to involve the Feds, Evan would think that was a rational choice. *And it* would be, if the killer wasn't an immortal warlock. But the Feds don't have a woo-woo division, so it's up to us.

He gave Evan fifteen minutes to cool down, then approached the locked bedroom door and knocked. "Evan?"

"What do you want?" Evan still sounded pissed off.

"I've got leads on a couple of personal items," Seth said through the door. "Plus I need to see if we can get into the rare book room at the library before it closes."

"You don't need me to do that."

Seth pinched the bridge of his nose, staving off a headache and trying to keep his patience. "Two heads are better than one, remember? Plus we're safer together. Please?"

After a moment, the lock clicked open and then Evan stood in the doorway. Unlike the joking, confident bartender Seth had met on his first night in town, Evan looked haggard, worried, and disheveled.

"All right. Let me get my shoes." He narrowed his gaze. "We aren't going to have to break in anywhere or dig up any graves, are we?"

"Not that I know of," Seth replied.

"I don't look good in a jumpsuit, and I've got no intention of making new friends in a cell block," Evan said, but the humor didn't reach his eyes. "So I'm counting on you to keep me alive and out of jail. Lawyers are expensive in this town."

The first stop took them to the Historical Association downtown. Evan feigned interest in the displays while Seth sweet-talked the elderly woman at the desk into letting him into the archives. She led the way down the steps to a temperature-controlled basement lined with shelves and glass-front cases.

"We keep pieces from our collections down here when they aren't on exhibit," Mrs. Stinson told them as she consulted a folder for the whereabouts of the item Seth requested. Seth eyed a tray full of Civil War swords and sabers, while Evan stared at taxidermied songbirds beneath glass domes.

"I can't tell you how much I appreciate your help," Seth gushed, turning on the charm. He kept up a patter of conversation as Mrs. Stinson bustled around the narrow shelves, looking for just the right box.

"Here it is!" She said, taking down a drab container marked with code numbers. "Now the name Caleb Vander doesn't come up often anymore, but a century ago he was a respected leader of the City Parks Commission, right after the First World War." She carried the box to a large wooden table.

"We wouldn't normally have the personal papers of a man like that, but he died suddenly—probably a stroke—and didn't have any family. Everything just got boxed up and stored at the Old City Hall—well, it was the new City Hall back then—and they didn't give the place a good cleaning out until they needed to remodel." She lifted the lid and stared into the box, brows knitting together.

"That's strange."

Seth moved closer to look over her shoulder. "What?"

"I had to come down and find this same box for a college professor who was working on a project about Richmond's Old City Hall a few weeks ago," Mrs. Stinson replied, looking upset. "Very nice man. Told me all about the book he's writing. Like your article for the newspaper," she added, patting Seth's arm. "I know that Mr. Vander's log books and papers were in here when I let him look through the box." She met Seth's gaze with a horrified expression. "My stars! Do you think he made off with them?"

Seth and Evan helped her take everything out of the box and lay the items on the table, but the log books and Vander papers were nowhere to be found. "I never would have expected him to do such a thing," she said, outraged and aghast. Seth figured she was more angry about the desecration of historic materials than she was worried about losing her job.

"Can you describe the man?" Seth pressed. "Maybe he wasn't who he said he was."

Mrs. Stinson looked stricken. "What is the world coming to when people lie about being college professors?" Seth pointedly did not look at Evan, since they were both pretending to be journalists.

"There are all kinds of folks in the world, I'm afraid," Seth replied, laying a consoling hand on Mrs. Stinson's shoulder. "Do you remember what he looked like? In case we cross paths with him while we're working on the article?"

"Short—about my height. I couldn't really see much of his build because he had a heavy coat on, and a scarf around his neck made it difficult to get a look at his face," she said. "But he gave me a driver's license and was so polite—"

"Do you recall his name?"

Mrs. Stinson bit her lip as she thought, then shook her head. "I'm sorry, I don't. You'd be surprised at how many people we get here in a day, looking for this and that. But it should be in the log book."

Seth helped repack the box and replaced it on the shelf, then he and Evan followed Mrs. Stinson up to the front desk. She pulled the large ledger over and flipped back through the pages, and Seth and Evan crowded around her. "That's odd," she mused. "I saw him sign in. I always watch to make sure they actually do…oh, here it is. C. Valac."

They thanked Mrs. Stinson, and Seth left a cell phone number for her to call him in case the light-fingered "professor" returned. Evan fell into step beside him as they headed for the bike.

"He's taunting us," Seth fumed.

"Maybe he's just cleaning up loose ends," Evan replied. "Or maybe it isn't him at all, and someone just pulled a name from an old census and used it to pilfer the archive."

Seth glared at Evan. "If someone just needed a fake name to hide a theft, why bother picking one that belonged to a real person? He could just make up a name, and it wouldn't matter."

Evan regarded him for a few seconds before he replied. "You seem to have given that kind of a thing a lot of thought. And the way you were with Mrs. Stinson, I hardly recognized you."

Seth stopped beside the bike, glancing around to make sure none of the passers-by seemed too interested in their exchange. "Yes, I've thought about it, because digging up the kind of information I need to stop Gremory's followers takes a lot of research, and I don't want to leave a trail. And as for Mrs. Stinson, she reminded me of my grandmother. I just used the same tactics that always got me extra dessert," he added with a grin.

Evan still looked troubled. "Would you have stolen it?"

"What?"

"Vander's papers and log book. If it had been there, would you have stolen it?"

Seth started to make a joke, then realized that Evan was serious. "I might have *borrowed* it," he answered. "But I would have brought it back, once Valac's stopped." He moved closer, laying a hand on Evan's arm, and trying to hide the hurt in his expression when Evan flinched away. "Hey, it's your life I'm trying to save here. No harm done if the book gets back to where it came from—and it's not fair being upset with me over something I didn't even do."

Evan's smile didn't reach his eyes. "You're right. Sorry. This is all still new to me." Implied in "this" was magic, skirting the law, living on the lam and fighting off immortal killers.

"Let's hit the rare book room at the library, and grab take-out before we head back for the night," Seth replied, hating the hesitation he sensed from Evan. How had things gone so wrong since their lovemaking this morning?

It didn't take long to get from the Historical Society to the main branch of the public library. Seth and Evan headed for the reference room, and Seth zeroed in on the librarian, breaking out his best smile to win her over. She reminded Seth of his mom, and he felt a pang of loss as she looked up from her computer.

"Can I help you?" The nametag on her twinset sweater read *"Violet."*

"I'd like to see a volume from your rare book collection," Seth said, pulling out his license for ID. Violet looked it over, checking the photo against his face before handing it back to him.

"Have you used our room before?" She asked.

Seth shook his head. "Special project, I'm new at this."

Violet gave him a sympathetic smile. "The rules are pretty simple. Only one person at a time, no backpacks or bags, no pens, pencils, or markers. You stay in the room with the book, and one of our security people will stay by the door. They have the option to pat you down or make you turn out your pockets if they think you might be making off with something from the collection. Any vandalism to the book—marks, ripping pages, etc.—and we call the police." Her smile remained friendly, but with a steel spine beneath the congeniality. "Are we good?"

"Absolutely," Seth replied.

Violet looked up, noticing Evan for the first time. "Your friend will have to wait for you up here. He can keep your bag."

Seth hesitated. He hadn't counted on having to split up, and he worried that Valac would take the chance to snatch Evan. Evan must have guessed his worry, because he laid a hand on Seth's shoulder.

"That's okay. I'll wait up here, in the thick of things," he added, as if he knew what Seth feared.

"You sure?" Seth asked, still trying to get a fix on Evan's mood. But Evan just smiled and nodded.

"It's not a problem. I'll find something to read." Evan picked up Seth's pack and headed for a bank of comfortable armchairs directly in sight of the librarian's desk.

"All right," Seth said, forcing down his worry. He turned back to Violet. "Let's go."

Violet led him into the library basement, to a small glass-walled room with a climate control panel on the outside to monitor temperature and humidity. A security guard followed them from the lobby and waited silently to one side of the door. Violet shielded the keypad from view as she entered the code, then motioned for Seth to enter first.

"You can have access for half an hour at a time without an appointment," Violet said. In the center of the glass room sat a plain table and a chair. "Give me the name of the book please."

"It's not a book so much as a collection of papers," Seth explained. "They belonged to Vincent Connor, the investor from back in the 1930s."

Violet nodded. "I know who you mean. Yes, we do have some of his papers. Very rare—I believe he was a bit of a recluse."

"So I've heard."

Seth waited by the desk while Violet looked for the documents, and returned with a thin, leather-bound tome and a pair of cotton gloves. She handed the gloves to Seth. "We require these to handle the old books. Keeps oil and dirt off the pages."

"This is all we have from Mr. Connor," Violet said, apology clear in her voice. "He funded a number of research expeditions to remote areas around the globe when money was tight during the Great Depression, but he wasn't one for personal fame. Can you believe we have no photos of the man, despite the fact that he spent millions on archeological digs?"

"Maybe he was just shy," Seth replied, although he knew exactly why "Mr. Connor" had dodged photographers.

Violet shook her head. "Such a shame. I hate it when the historical record has a gap like that." She sighed. "Ah well. Here are your documents. Careful with the binding; it's old, and the paper is fragile. Turn the pages slowly, don't crack the spine, and handle with care." She motioned toward the door. "If you want to leave before the half hour is up, you'll need to buzz the guard to let you out."

"Thank you, Violet," Seth replied, anxious to get started so he could get back upstairs to protect Evan. He was almost certain Evan wouldn't pull a runner, but the fact that Valac was on the loose made him nervous, especially since they still didn't know the witch-disciple's current identity.

"I'll leave you to it then," Violet said and headed out the door.

Seth settled in at the desk and spread out the bound tome in front of him. He pushed his worries aside and tried to clear his mind. Sitting with his back to the door, Seth took off the gloves, pulled out his cell phone and called up a map of Richmond; then he took the crystal from his pocket. He'd have to do without the candle.

Seth wondered what Valac—aka Vincent Connor—had really wanted from the archeological expeditions he funded. Was he searching for arcane relics to amplify his power? Seeking old spell books or supernatural amulets to enhance his magic? Whatever treasures had been uncovered, Seth had not been able to find collections at any museum in the country. Then again, back in the 1930s, laws about protecting such things were lax, and many artifacts ended up in the hands of private collectors, hoarded and hidden. If Seth had to bet, his money was on Valac keeping anything of value for himself.

One of the yellowed pages was a handwritten letter from Vincent Connor to the antiquities department of a major university requesting the involvement of several noted professors on an expedition he intended to fund. It might not be the same sort of personal possession as a watch or a hairbrush, but given that Valac had left so little behind, it would have to do.

Seth glanced over his shoulder at the security guard, who appeared to be staring intently at the wall. Assured that the guard posed no threat, Seth set his phone next to the letter and dangled the crystal over the map. He closed his eyes and recited the locator spell.

The crystal trembled, then began to turn. He stared at the slightly glowing gem, watching as it slowly swung back and forth, first in a wide circle, then in narrowing spirals until it vibrated and pointed straight down, tugging at his fingers.

It worked! At least, I think it worked.

Seth looked down at the location the crystal pointed to on the map, and then expanded the image to show more detail. The crystal repeated its performance. Seth stared at the icon beneath the gem and felt a chill in his blood. It hovered right over the box marked "Richmond Public Library."

12

EVAN

Evan took Seth's pack and went to sit in the center cluster of comfortable chairs, where he could see anyone approaching and where the librarians at the front desk could see him. He knew part of Seth's hesitation to leave was a fear Evan would run off, but he'd learned his lesson. *Someone* was after him, that was certain, and regardless of who it was, Evan wasn't about to make it easy on them by wandering among the stacks or hiding in a remote corner.

He picked up a magazine off the periodicals rack, flipped through a few pages, and found his thoughts too jumbled to concentrate. Two days ago he had an apartment, a job, and a normal life. And if they couldn't figure out how to stop Valac, two days from now, he'd be dead. *This happens to people on TV. It doesn't happen to real people. Not to guys like me.* But it had, and now Evan found himself trapped in something that seemed like the plot of a monster-of-the-week drama.

Witches. Ghosts. Black dog *grims*. Curses and hauntings and spells, oh my. He hadn't believed in any of them before Seth pulled him away from a hail of gunfire, but in less than seventy-two hours, he'd been shot at, almost kidnapped, attacked by ghosts and monsters, seen his apartment blown up, and his bar burned out. And then there was Seth.

Evan knew he'd started to fall for Seth the first time he'd seen him in Treddy's. Seth rocked the rugged ex-soldier vibe, but with a vulnerability that took Evan's breath away. He could be a total badass in a fight, and the most tender lover Evan ever had. Now Evan had to decide whether Seth was right about Valac—or batshit crazy.

Either way, Evan was screwed, and not in a good way. He couldn't forget how amazing the sex had been just that morning before he'd let his suspicions get the best of him and make him pull back. Mike had done a real number on his head, and while he knew that skewed his reactions, the knowledge didn't seem to be enough to keep him from overreacting.

If Seth was right about Valac, then his tendency to be slightly overprotective was entirely reasonable. And if he was wrong about the magic, he'd still saved Evan's life several times. Evan didn't know how to make sense of the tangle of feelings in his heart. He'd started to care for Seth, maybe even love him, and if it all turned out to be a lie, more than his trust would be broken.

Then again, if it was all true, once Valac was dead, Seth planned to drive off into the sunset to hunt the next witch-disciple. Unless Evan could convince him that they were better together.

Shit, I'm so turned around I don't know which way is up. I think I love the guy, but he also scares the crap out of me. I'm in way over my head.

Evan shifted in his chair and wished the library sold coffee. He could use a cup of hot black java to help clear his mind. Then his gaze fell on the rows of computers, and he set the magazine aside. They'd been in such constant motion since escaping his apartment, Evan had no chance to check in with anyone on Seth's laptop, and his phone had been a casualty of the fire.

Making up his mind, Evan shot a glance back toward the front desk and the door through which Seth had vanished. He felt vaguely guilty, like he was cheating on Seth, although Seth had never asked him not to contact anyone, or tried to tell him he couldn't.

Evan took Seth's bag and found a seat at one of the computers, paying the fee for a half hour of access. He checked his email and found mostly reminders to pay bills for an apartment that no longer existed. His friends from work would have texted him, but he had no way to retrieve those messages easily. Instead, he logged into Sonny's social media and found a slew of worried direct messages.

Izzy: Sonny, are you ok? Where are you? I'm worried about your skinny ass, so answer me.

Jackie: Hey Sonny, you heard about Treddy's? Liam said the house that burned was where you lived, and we're worried. Call me.

Liam: Sonny—bar's closed for repairs. I'll let you know about reopening when I get dates. You can file for unemployment. Hope you're okay.

The messages felt like they belonged to another man in another life. He appreciated his co-workers' concern, but it reminded Evan that he had no friends outside of work. Before he met Seth, he thought he was happy. Now, the thought of going back to Treddy's and that life made him feel restless and dissatisfied.

I'm okay, staying with a friend, he texted in reply to each message. *Lost my phone, so message me here. See you soon.*

He sighed and sat back, staring at the screen. A few other posts were from acquaintances he'd stayed in touch within all the cities where he'd worked since Oklahoma. The fact that half of them only knew him as "Sonny" also made him sad. What did it say about him that he had so few sort-of friends and that even they didn't know him well enough to know his real name?

He'd been more open with Seth than he had dared to be with anyone, even Mike. In the dark, wrapped in Seth's arms, Evan felt safe for the first time since he fled Oklahoma. Odd that, since he'd drawn the ire of a serial killer and was running for his life. He wondered if Seth had anyone he missed from his home in Indiana, any friends left since his parents and brother were gone.

Evan sat up suddenly, remembering that Jackie said she had lived in the Midwest—the Indianapolis area if he recalled. On impulse, he looked her up, saw she was online, and jotted off a message.

Hey, I've got a weird question for you. You're from around Indianapolis, right? Know anyone from a place called Brazil?

He was surprised when a reply came back almost immediately. *Sonny? Great to hear from you! Yeah, I'm from Indy, and yeah, I actually know someone who grew up in Brazil. Why?*

Evan stilled, thinking about his reply. Was he doubting Seth's story? Checking up on him? Maybe, he admitted. But then again, he'd gone off in the middle of the night with a total stranger. It wouldn't hurt to do a little due diligence, just for peace of mind.

Can you ask your friend if he remembers a news story from a couple of years ago—two brothers, Seth and Jesse Tanner, attacked on a camping trip. Jesse got killed. Did your friend know them? What did he think about the whole thing?

He sat back and waited. A chime seconds later came with the reply. *I remember that. It was all over the news. Called it the 'witch murder.' I'll ask Jimmy. Any reason you're so interested?*

Evan thought for a moment. *Someone I know might want to hire the older brother as a security guard.* That was close enough to the truth.

I'll ask. Hang on; I think Jimmy might be online.

While Evan waited, he did a little digging on his own. A search pulled up headlines, news articles, and pictures of the "hell gate" where Jesse had died. Evan scanned the articles, disturbed to see that in the early coverage the police had detained Seth as a "person of interest." Evan knew the cops always looked first at family and close associates, but it bothered him that Seth hadn't mentioned that. Later articles suggested that Seth had been cleared, but it didn't look like anyone had been charged.

He scanned the comments, and most were the usual online trash. One, however, stood out. "I went to high school with both the Tanner boys. Always thought there was something off about Seth. Kept to himself, and he was into those weird role-playing games and all that fantasy-magic crap. Maybe one of those games went a little too far."

Evan caught his breath. The comment was anonymous and mean-spirited, and he knew that there'd been a long history of people blaming gamers for everything from satanic cults to cattle mutilations. Even after he clicked away, the words bothered him. A ping brought his mind back to the message window.

Jimmy says he knew the older brother a little from school. Quiet, kind of a loner, didn't have a lot of friends besides his little brother. Went into the army and had just gotten back when everything happened. Said people wondered if he'd had some kind of battle flashback and killed Jesse, but the cops didn't look at him for long. Is that what you wanted to know?

Evan found himself breathing quickly, his heart racing. *Yeah, that's what I needed. Thanks, Jackie. Take care.* He logged out and sat staring at the computer, trying to sort through what he'd learned.

On one hand, the hard information mostly tracked with what Seth had told him and what he'd seen in the articles. The rest was rumors and gossip, which always fed on the worst assumptions. Still, on top of his other fears, Evan couldn't quite shake off the negatives.

A sane person would run. Go stay with Liam or Jackie. But the people after me are real, whether or not they're magic. So I'd just put Liam and Jackie in danger. Seth's been protecting me from the bad guys. But what if I need someone to protect me from him?

"Are you all right?"

The voice at his elbow made Evan jump. He looked up to see the cop who'd become a recent regular at Treddy's looking down at him with concern. Evan managed an anemic smile. "Sorry, I was deep in thought. Yes, I'm good. Thanks for asking."

"I got called out on the fire at Treddy's," the cop replied. "A real shame, but it would have been a lot worse if it'd happened when people were there. Guess this means you're out of a job for a while."

Evan really wasn't in the mood to make small talk, but he didn't want to be rude. "I'm still a little bit in shock," he replied, which was mostly the truth. For a second, he thought about confiding in the cop and then realized what a heap of crazy that would sound like. He couldn't prove that either the break-in at his apartment or the guys in the van had actually happened, and the part about being the next human sacrifice for an immortal witch-disciple wasn't going to go over well. "Just looking for a new job," he lied, with a wave of his hand to indicate the computer and the internet.

The cop nodded. "Yeah, that sucks." He pulled a card from his pocket. "If I can help, here's my number. I can tell a new employer that you make an awesome Jack and Coke."

Evan took the card and thanked him, feeling a little relieved when the cop left. He didn't like lying, and he couldn't even think about jobs or apartments until he knew whether he'd be alive, and what might happen with Seth.

Seth. Doubting Seth hurt, but Evan had learned the hard way that trusting too much held its own dangers. Staying with Seth made the most sense for now, until they found enough evidence to turn over to the cops or the FBI. And if Valac and the whole witch-thing was really true, then the cops and the Feds couldn't help him, and Seth remained his best shot at staying alive.

*I need to put some space between us, just until Halloween is over. It's only a day and a half at this point. If we're both still alive and everything Seth's told me turns out to be true, I can beg forgiveness. And if not...*He didn't want to think about where that led.

Evan glanced at the clock and realized Seth's half hour was nearly up. He grabbed the bag, and went back to his chair. He'd barely picked up the magazine again when Seth burst from the stairwell looking around frantically, eyes wide with fear.

"He was here!" Seth hissed, whispering loudly enough to earn glares from other library patrons.

"Who?" Evan looked around at the mix of mothers with children, retirees, job hunters, and college students who filled the library.

"Valac. I found a letter he wrote and did the tracking spell. It said he was here, in the library." Seth's face was flushed, and he was breathing hard as if he'd run the stairs.

"Dude, look around. Nobody here fits the profile," Evan said, torn between worry and embarrassment.

Seth glanced in one direction and then the other. Evan scanned the crowd as well, but everyone was too young, too old, or female. From what Seth had told him, Valac might have changed his looks and his identity but hadn't posed as a woman. Even the librarians at the desk were the wrong age. "Maybe he'd been here recently?" Evan suggested, trying to save face for Seth.

Seth frowned as if he couldn't believe his information was mistaken. "I thought..." he rubbed the back of his neck. "I thought he'd followed us here, and that he was going to snatch you. Shit. I'm sorry."

Evan managed a smile. "No harm done. Let's get dinner and go back. It's been a long day."

They agreed on Chinese food and brought bags full of entrees, soups, egg rolls, and dumplings to the trailer. The ride back was awkwardly silent, but Evan couldn't get past the thoughts swirling in his head, and Seth seemed distracted.

"Maybe when this is all over, we can go somewhere and get real Richmond food," Seth said, breaking the silence.

"Hope you like barbecue and Brunswick stew," Evan replied, giving him a sidelong glance.

Seth smiled, but Evan thought he looked nervous. "Really? I'm game."

Evan knew that the possibility of Seth sticking around to see the city should have reassured him, but only partly. "That would be nice," he replied, torn between what he wanted and what he feared. "I'd like that."

By the time they cleared away the paper plates and put leftovers in the fridge, Evan could barely keep his eyes open. Seth wiped off the table and got out his laptop, then put on a pot of coffee.

"You staying up?" Evan asked. He'd debated whether to share a bed tonight. Ducking out early might make the choice easier, for both of them.

Seth gave him a look Evan struggled to interpret. He saw sadness and longing, fear and resolve, guilt and hurt. "I've got to catch a break to keep you safe," he said. "I can rest afterward. Right now…" He let his voice drift off and gestured toward the computer. "There are more important things." He winced when he saw Evan flinch.

"I didn't mean—" Seth huffed out a breath and rolled his eyes. "I didn't mean more important than us, together. That came out wrong. But I promised to protect you, and I've done a damn poor job of it. So go ahead and get some rest. You look beat. I'll work for a while, and watch the door."

Seth leaned forward and gave Evan a light kiss, just brushing his lips across Evan's cheek. Evan smiled, although his heart felt conflicted. "See you in the morning," Evan said, feeling cold settle in his bones as he made his way to bed alone.

13

SETH

Seth watched Evan head to the bedroom. He couldn't deny feeling hurt that Evan hadn't urged him to join him. He tried to shake off his worry, but the cold detachment he'd always found so easy to slip into in his army days now eluded him, at least when it came to Evan.

Cue the music from that stupid movie about the bodyguard, Seth thought irritably, pouring a cup of coffee and sitting down at the laptop. *The kiss-off, where the rock star sends him on his way.* He rested his head in his hands. Evan wasn't a spoiled diva like the character in the movie, but he still had a chance of going back to a regular job and a real life when this was over. He might need some therapy from being stalked by a killer, but even so, he'd be a hell of a lot less scarred than Seth. *Maybe he's figured that out. He's pulling back. Maybe I read too much into it, and he was just blowing off steam. Just because the sex was great doesn't mean he's in love with me or something.*

Then again, Evan might just be scared as fuck about dying bloody in less than thirty-six hours. Mortal terror could definitely dampen even the healthiest sex drive. Seth glanced back at the closed door. At least he hadn't heard the click of a lock. He knew he had more pressing matters to worry about than a days-old attraction, but part of him didn't want to let Evan go, even if he thought that might really be best for both of them. Seth hadn't realized how alone he'd been, before Evan. He didn't want to go back to long days driving, long nights by himself.

Save his life, and worry about hearts and flowers later.

Hours later, long past midnight, Seth rubbed a fist against the stubble on his chin and stared, bleary-eyed, at his screen. He checked in with work, just to make sure there were no new emergency projects to worry about. Working for Toby and Milo paid well and gave him the flexibility he needed—and bosses he didn't have to lie to about how he spent the rest of his time.

Everything led back to the cemetery as being the most likely place to find Valac's anchor. Destroy the spelled box that held the personal element, and he'd weaken Valac's power. Get the amulet away from Valac, and Seth stood a good chance of winning the fight. He went back over his spells and cantrips, knowing that his rote magic against Valac's witchcraft was like a pea shooter against a Howitzer.

Then again, Seth remembered his military history classes. Badly-armed insurgents with a passion for their cause had a track record for fighting the world's largest armies and empires to a stand-still. And Seth had passion. This was vengeance for Jesse and safety for Evan. Losing wasn't an option.

Now if he just knew who the hell he was actually fighting.

If Seth read the pattern right, Valac would have shifted into his current identity twelve years ago, give or take a few months. Using some of the computer tricks he learned from Toby and refined on his own, Seth set up a search to find all the new utility hook-ups and drivers' licenses in an eighteen month period around the time Valac would have shown up. Valac might use a fake ID, but few people could manage long without electricity and running water. He knew it would yield a ton of hits, so he added a filter to find first and last names starting in "V" or "C." That might make the list more manageable, although it was still likely to be long. He got the search running, and closed down his computer.

Seth glanced at the clock and made up his mind. If he intended to see whether Valac had buried his anchor at his first grave, he'd have to do it before daylight. Tomorrow night would be too late.

Seth thought for a moment about how best to keep Evan safe while he was gone. He turned back to his computer and switched on the small cameras on each of the four corners of the trailer's roof. The feeds would record, so he'd be able to see if anyone came prowling around. But that wouldn't help if Evan decided he'd had enough. Seth debated a choice with himself, then sighed and gave in to his more practical side. He dug out two small GPS locator disks from one of his gear packs, then activated the trackers and slipped one into the pocket of Evan's jacket. Seth crept into the bathroom and opened the pass-through door to the bedroom just enough to find Evan's duffel and drop the other tracker into it, making sure it fell to the bottom.

Evan would be angry if he found the devices; Seth knew it would trigger Evan's stalker fears. *Saving his life is more important than anything else, even if he hates me for it,* Seth told himself. He stopped to write a brief note warning Evan to stay inside and promising to be home by dawn, and taped it to the refrigerator, figuring Evan would be sure to see it there. Then he grabbed his coat and gun, pulled a shovel, pick-axe, and flashlight from the storage area beneath the trailer, and walked the bike to the top of the driveway before he roared away.

Desecrating a grave would be easier with help. Still, Seth knew how uncomfortable Evan was just breaking into an abandoned house. Maybe that was a sign things were unlikely to work out. Much as Seth welcomed the idea of help with research and back-up on the hunt, lawbreaking came with the territory. He pushed the gloomy thoughts aside resolutely. Tonight, he had a grave to dig up.

∼

SETH FELT GRATEFUL FOR THE LIGHT FROM A WAXING MOON, ENOUGH TO see by but not a lunar spotlight on his questionable activities. Despite a cold night, Seth worked up a sweat quickly. Vampire hunters on TV made digging up an old grave look easy, but after getting only a foot or so down through the hard dirt, Seth understood why modern-day gravediggers used a backhoe. He wished he had the money for high-end equipment to X-ray the additional feet of packed clay ground and spare him the effort. Then again, Seth had no idea what Valac had used for his anchor, and whether it would show up on equipment. He sighed and put his back into the task, trying not to think about the fact that he'd have to replace the dirt.

Two hours later, Seth changed his mind about trying to fill in the hole. After two more hours, he just wanted a hot shower and a cold beer. Four hours of digging, and when he stood up, he measured the hole against his height. Seth stood six foot three in bare feet, taller in his shitkickers. His eyebrows were level with the top of the hole. He stomped down on the ground beneath this boots and heard only a dull thud, not the resonant thump he expected if a casket or chest lay beneath.

Seth drove the pickaxe into the ground around his feet over and over but met only solid earth. With a string of curses, he pushed his tools over the top, then hauled himself out of the hole.

Not only was Valac's anchor not in the grave, neither was anything else.

Knowing he only had about an hour until dawn, Seth cleaned his shovel and pickaxe as best he could, shook off the dirt from his jeans and boots and left the cemetery by the back road as quietly as possible.

If Valac was watching, Seth figured the witch-disciple had a good laugh at his expense. He didn't even merit having the *grims* sent after him this time. Shit. Evan. Maybe Valac hadn't come after Seth because he'd seen the chance to target Evan with no one to stop him. But when Seth returned to the abandoned farm, he found the trailer just as he had left it. The salt circle he'd drawn around the camper and truck lay undisturbed. Seth doubted it would stop Valac himself, but it might halt his conjured minions in their tracks.

He unlocked the door and slipped inside. The note was still on the fridge where he'd left it, and since the sun wasn't up yet, he guessed that Evan was still sleeping and peeked in to make sure. Bone tired, aching from hours of digging and thoroughly pissed off, Seth stripped out of his dirty clothes, chucked them in the laundry basket and took a hot shower to remove the grime. Once he dried off and dressed, he gave the laptop a quick check and saw the search program was still cranking away. Too tired to care, Seth grabbed a throw blanket and curled up on the couch. Once the sun came up, it would be the day before Halloween. Evan was running out of time, and Seth was running out of ideas.

14

EVAN

Evan woke at the sound of Seth's motorcycle in the lane outside. He sat up and rubbed his eyes, shocked to find it still dark. A glance at the clock surprised him further when he realized it was after one in the morning.

Bleary-eyed, Evan made his way out of the bedroom, thinking he must have been mistaken. A note taped to the refrigerator door caught his attention.

> *Evan—Went back to the cemetery. I'll be home by dawn. Please don't go outside—not safe. Trust me a little longer—Seth.*

Evan left the note where it was and growled a curse under his breath. He dug out a beer from the fridge and walked into the trailer's living area. Evan leaned against the wall, trying to decide what to do. His mind spun, and his stomach clenched, a sure sign that he was still conflicted as fuck when it came to Seth.

Seth left him behind, with a note to stay put, and the assumption Evan would listen. Then again, the last time he stomped out, he nearly got dragged away to God-knows-where. So maybe Seth had a point, although Evan hated to admit it. Part of him rebelled against what felt like Seth being controlling and possessive. Another part warmed at the concern behind the overprotectiveness, although his dented masculinity affirmed his ability to take care of himself.

Evan sighed and dropped into one of the leather armchairs. Seth hadn't even tried to make a move on him when they came back from the library. Then again, Evan hadn't taken the initiative either.

Evan took a long pull from his beer, wishing he didn't feel like he had a tempest inside his chest. He wanted Seth. That kind of attraction didn't happen every day, and Evan knew he'd begun to have feelings for Seth. But every time he started to let down his guard, something else happened to make him wary. He'd seen how easily Seth had charmed his way past the archivist and the librarian. Seth had been a smooth liar and unrepentantly manipulative, albeit in a way that caused no one harm. Still, Evan wondered if he had been on the receiving end of Seth's charm as well, maneuvered into following Seth's lead by his charisma and undeniable attractiveness.

That's what serial killers did, wasn't it? Charmed their victims into vulnerability, built up trust, and then went for the kill. A shiver went down his back. He didn't want to believe the worst of Seth, wanted to keep his image of the wounded warrior and damaged champion intact.

But what if he'd been fooled?

Seth's laptop lay on the table, and Evan decided he might as well do a little research of his own since falling back to sleep wasn't going to happen soon.

He checked to assure the door was locked, turned on a light and sat down at the computer. Evan could navigate the computer at Treddy's just fine, as well as his own laptop that was probably slag in the wreckage of his apartment. Hacking, however, went beyond his skills. So when he flipped up the screen, he knew that trying to guess Seth's password would be futile. Seth's laptop also looked a lot fancier than what Evan expected, high end and expensive. He wondered where Seth got his money. A few seconds of searching revealed that Seth had left a "guest" profile for him without a password, and Evan smiled as he clicked the icon.

Evan opened up a search engine and went looking for more news items about Jesse's death. This time, a trail of clicks led him to autopsy photos, released under a Freedom of Information Act search. He recoiled, catching his breath at the savagery of the wounds. How the coroner had concluded anything surprised Evan, given how badly mutilated the body had been. Could a wild animal tear flesh like that? Yet the notes said nothing about teeth marks or bites. His stomach flipped, and Evan swallowed hard as he read further. The coroner's comments listed *"multiple lacerations from edged weapons of varying types"* as the cause of death. Knives, swords, blades, not vampire teeth or werewolf claws. Just sick, sadistic human beings.

No wonder Seth wanted vengeance. And no surprise that waking up and finding his brother like that left him scarred, maybe damaged. He understood Seth's resolve not to let the killing go on, especially when it involved Evan. He just wasn't quite sure how the pieces fit together.

Another search turned up the Hell Gate of Brazil, Indiana, but those sites belonged to ghost hunters and paranormal investigators and leaned toward the overblown and lurid. He found a historical site about the train derailment and a few pages of an old local history that talked about Gremory's hanging and the deaths of the sheriff and his posse. None of it shed new light on the situation, or told Evan anything he hadn't gleaned from the files Seth had already shared with him.

He went back to the news reports about Jesse's death and frowned as he found the obituary for Seth's parents. It mentioned the car wreck, and that they had been preceded in death by a son, Jesse. A link took him to a memorial page on a mortician's website where friends and family members could leave condolences. Reading through the online guest book, he felt the shock of a small community rocked by so much tragedy. One comment caught his eye. "So sorry Seth couldn't be present for the service. I'm sure he would have wanted to say goodbye."

Where had Seth been that he couldn't attend his parents' funeral? Evan searched his memory, but he couldn't remember Seth saying anything about leaving town so quickly.

Evan had some new questions for his friend Jackie, or maybe for her buddy, Jimmy. He typed in the address to log into Sonny's social media site, and the page refused to load. Frowning, Evan tried again, carefully watching the letters that appeared on the screen to assure he had entered the information correctly. A message popped up.

"Site blocked. Administrator approval required to access."

"Son of a bitch!" Evan swore, staring at the screen. He tried to log into his email and into a few other social media sites, with the same outcome.

"Shit!" He could run searches and surf to any news or information site, but all of the interactive features were blocked. Evan ran down all the messaging and video call sites, and they also refused to load.

Angry, Evan paced the room. Seth could have locked the laptop up, but instead he left it available, with the guest profile set up for his use. Then he'd blocked access to any site Evan could use to communicate with someone on the outside. Out of curiosity, Evan walked over to the door to see if it was locked from outside, but it opened easily.

"Then again, I'm on an abandoned farm in the middle of nowhere," Evan said aloud. "Where am I gonna go?"

He closed the door and locked it, knowing Seth had the key. Then he pitched the beer bottle in the trash and stood in the middle of the trailer, debating what to do next. *If Seth has nothing to hide, why keep me from talking to anyone?*

His mind supplied the answer: *To keep from spilling the beans to the killer, because we don't know who it is yet.* Angry and hurt, Evan didn't want to listen to reason.

This is never going to work if he keeps pulling this high-handed shit on me. I'm not a child, and he's not a Fed. Evan went back to the laptop and erased his browsing history, then logged off but left the laptop running.

He debated waiting up for Seth but doubted he could stay awake. And he knew the conversation would require him to be able to hold his own in an argument. Reluctantly, Evan headed to the bedroom with the hope of getting a little sleep, but this time he locked the door behind him.

15

SETH

THE AWFUL RUN OF SCALES ON A MARIMBA WOULDN'T STOP, AND IT FELT like someone was playing xylophone with the back of Seth's skull. He slapped a hand out, found his phone, and silenced the alarm.

Groggy, Seth realized where he was, curled up on the couch in the trailer. The twinge in his neck suggested he had slept in an awkward position, his head throbbed, and the muscles in his arms, back, glutes, and thighs ached like the first days of Basic Training.

Maybe because I dug up a grave by myself a few hours ago.

With a groan, Seth rolled off the couch, stood up like an octogenarian, and swore under his breath as stiff muscles protested. He shuffled to the kitchen, drank the rest of last night's coffee and started a fresh pot. Then he dry-swallowed several ibuprofen and waited for the caffeine and painkillers to kick in.

He'd spent the night risking arrest and had nothing to show for it. Seth cupped his hands under the faucet and splashed cold water on his face. He knew he ought to shave, but that meant using the bathroom and waking Evan, something he didn't feel ready to face just yet. He leaned against the counter, cradling his second cup of coffee, and tried to figure out how he'd managed to hit a dead end.

Seth hadn't expected Valac's gravesite to actually hold a coffin with a corpse—or at least, not Valac's corpse. He figured all of the witch-disciple's many plots had empty caskets. But he'd thought the first grave was the logical place to hide the element for the anchor, and without it, Seth wasn't sure where to turn next. Tomorrow was Halloween, and unless Seth figured out something soon, Evan would die, and it would all be his fault. Just like Jesse.

"You parental-blocked the laptop."

Seth looked up to see Evan at the end of the counter. He looked bleary-eyed, like he hadn't slept much. But tired as he might be, he radiated anger. "Why did you lock me out of sites?"

Seth blinked a few times, trying to wake up because if they were going to argue, he knew he needed to be coherent. "I'm trying to protect you, remember? We still aren't sure who Valac is, but we know he's got his eye on you. It could be someone you know, or one of your friends might be feeding him information without knowing who Valac is. Evan—"

"You could have told me. We could have talked about it," Evan countered. "Instead, I found out the hard way. It's like you're hiding something—"

Seth lifted his hands in appeasement. "I swear, Evan. I'm not hiding anything."

"Then why haven't you told me everything?" Evan snapped. "I did manage to get online at the library, while you were downstairs. Looked some stuff up for myself. You never mentioned that the police considered you a suspect."

Seth set the coffee cup aside, wide-awake now that adrenaline started to thrum through his veins. "I didn't tell you because it wasn't true and the cops figured that out pretty quickly. Even on TV they always look at family first, but they cleared me. They cleared me because the only thing I was guilty of was stupidity. I was stupid to suggest the camping trip, to tempt fate with the Hell Gate legend. And I have to live with that for the rest of my life."

His confession didn't move Evan. "Why weren't you at your parents' funeral?"

Seth's eyes widened. He hadn't expected that. "How did you—"

"It's amazing what's online, even with the blockers," Evan replied.

"So what happened? Because the story you told me isn't hanging together. There's a piece missing."

Seth's thoughts spun. He could admit that he'd spent weeks in a psych ward under suicide watch for ranting about witches and magic, but then Evan would probably walk right out that door before Seth could explain. Just because the truth sounded crazy didn't make it any less true. Or he could lie, keep Evan from running away and putting himself at risk, and maybe lose his trust forever.

If he's dead, I've lost him for good, and there's no winning him back. I just have to keep him safe one more day. Then I'll beg forgiveness, do whatever I need to do to make him believe in me again. Just one more day.

"The disciple's goons threw me around to get to Jesse," Seth replied carefully, trying to stick as close to the truth as possible. "I put up a fight. Got thrown into a tree, ended up with a concussion. While I was in the hospital, mom and dad were in the wreck, and the house burned. When I got out, all I had left was the truck, trailer, and bike. Just like I told you before."

Evan's eyes narrowed, like he seemed to know Seth had left something out, something important. "I don't like being treated like a child."

"You're not a child! You're a target!" Seth shouted, as his raw nerves and fatigue got the best of him. "Don't you get it? This is worse than hiding you from the Mob. These disciples will stop at nothing to renew their power—and your blood is what Valac needs to do it. Running away didn't help. Your dad ran all the way to Oklahoma, and every twelve years, another Malone still died. The only way to shut this motherfucker down is to destroy Valac once and for all. I'm not going to let you die!"

"This isn't about me," Evan shot back. "This is about your guilt and Jesse's death. You're still so twisted up about what happened back then; you'll do anything for a rematch. And you're going to get both of us killed because tomorrow's the day, and we've still got nothing!"

Seth stepped back as if Evan had slapped him. "You're right," he said, finally finding the cold, emotionless calm he knew from battle. Everything inside shut down, leaving only clear rationality. "I don't have time to fight with you. I'm sorry you don't like my methods, but

Witchbane

I'm trying to keep you safe. Please, Evan, just hang in there one more day. I can do this. We can stop Valac, and then you and everyone else in your family will be safe."

"You're asking a lot," Evan growled. "I don't like how this is playing out."

They were wasting time. Walking out now would leave a rift between them, perhaps one they couldn't heal. But letting the clock run down while they argued until Valac made his move would leave more than a rift. Evan would be dead, and Seth would have failed…again.

"I've got another lead to follow," Seth said, downing the rest of his coffee and grabbing a muffin from the counter before he shouldered into his coat and pulled on his boots. "I'll be back as quickly as I can. You're safest here. Please, Evan, stay in the trailer. I know what I'm doing. Trust me."

"I don't really have a choice, do I?" Evan's hazel eyes glinted with fire. "You've made damn sure of that."

Seth had to get out of there before he said something he would regret. "I'll be back," he muttered, heading for the door. "Just stay put and keep your head down. It's gonna be okay. I got this." He didn't wait to hear Evan's response as he headed out the door.

∼

SETH OPENED UP THE THROTTLE ON THE HAYABUSA AND FELT THE WIND whip past him, tearing at his jacket and sleeves, stinging his face. Hurt and anger roiled in his gut, but more than that, fear thrummed through his veins. Fear for Evan's safety, fear that he wouldn't be able to put the clues together fast enough to matter, that he would fail again, that he would lose Evan for good.

Seth had left a message for Toby in the pre-dawn hours; he felt his phone vibrate in his pocket with what he desperately hoped were answers to help piece together this crazy, lethal puzzle.

He pulled the bike to a stop in the parking lot of a deserted shopping mall. Ash Park had been cutting-edge retail when it opened in the 1980s, a boutique mall convenient to Richmond's well-heeled city-dwellers, boasting high-end shops, trendy eateries, and a live dinner theater instead of a cinema. It had also been owned by CoVal, and Seth guessed that in its heyday, Ash Park had made Valac a pretty penny.

Even Valac's magic didn't seem to be able to counter changing consumer tastes. Fancier, bigger malls opened to the west and south, and Ash Park struggled to catch up. But what really put a crimp in its swagger were the murders.

"Yeah, Toby. Talk to me. I really, really need some good news."

"You been to that shopping mall yet?"

"Just pulled up."

"Watch your back," Toby warned. "Part of the reason the mall closed was a higher-than-average level of violence. Murders, carjackings, armed robbery, parking lot brawls, even a suicide or two. Not something you could completely blame on the neighborhood."

"You think Valac had something to do with it?" Seth asked.

"I wouldn't count it out. None of the Malone deaths happened there, and the deaths that did weren't on the cycle, but we don't know everything about these witch-disciples," Toby cautioned. "Maybe extra murders now and then help him power up. Just…be careful. I doubt you'll run into Valac himself, but don't rule out vengeful spirits."

"Roger that," Seth said, mentally calculating what he needed to take with him to check out the old mall. "What I really need is a break on Valac. Got anything?"

"I've been trying to profile his past identities and what we know of the other witch-disciples to look for trends," Toby told him. "Before 1960, they could claim any credentials, and without computers, it was hard to verify, so they got away with it. Since then, they can't really get away with being doctors or lawyers, but other things are easier to fake. So now they tend to be professors, financial consultants, tech company start-up CEOs when they're going upscale. Downscale hasn't changed. Mechanic, plumber, maintenance, security, law enforcement, real estate —jobs that give them plenty of access, and some power."

"Thanks. That helps. I'm running a records scan, but it's taking forever," Seth replied. "I'll use it to weed out possibilities."

"You're worried."

"Scared shitless," Seth confessed. "I feel like I'm going in blind."

"Stick close to the target, and you'll do it right," Toby said. "You've got this."

"That's what I keep telling myself," Seth replied, removing his helmet and keeping a wary eye on his surroundings. "If you get a flash of brilliance, let me know."

"You'll be the first one I call," Toby promised and hung up.

The parking lot was empty except for a few cars that appeared to be as abandoned as the mall. Grass struggled up through cracks in the crumbling asphalt, and trash tumbled across the lonely expanse, swept toward the sagging chain-link fence by the cold October wind. The marquee beneath the mall's sign was blank, a reminder that the last events went dark long ago.

Seth brought a flashlight, his gun, and a variety of knives secured in sheaths on his hip, forearms, and calves. He couldn't afford to waste time; so the plan was just to get in, see if anything gave him a lead on Valac, and get out. He had one more stop before he went back to the trailer, and by then, the name search should have run its course.

If he couldn't find Valac, his fallback was to fortify a small cement block storage building at the old farm and hunker down for a siege. It wasn't much of a plan, but it would have to do. He hoped to have better information, to take the fight to Valac. *Some bodyguard I turned out to be.*

Seth forced down his self-condemnation and strode toward the back of the mall. His magic popped the lock, proof that practice paid off. The door opened into a service corridor, and the plain cement walls made it clear this had not been a public thoroughfare.

The security lights glowed dimly, and Seth drew a knife, unwilling to trust that the mall was as empty as it appeared. At its peak, the one-story mall had been a social hub for its community; now, Seth's footsteps sounded loud in the eerie quiet.

He opened the double doors into the main mall and froze in the doorway, getting his bearings. The storefronts were dark and locked; their lighted signs stripped off long ago. Planters held brown, withered palm trees, and the large fountains were dry and empty.

Another smell reached Seth, the coppery tang of old blood. He pulled his Beretta from his waistband and advanced warily. Ash Park wasn't a big mall. It had boasted two department stores, one on either end with a big atrium, gathering area and food court in the middle. Seth scanned the interiors of the stores he passed, but they were empty and didn't look as if anyone had been in them since the day the lights went out.

The gathering center raised Seth's hackles. He cleared each shop along the perimeter, but he never turned his back on the large central atrium with its dry fountain and dead palms. Once he assured himself no surprises lurked in the dark storefronts, he turned toward the raised dais in the center.

Long ago, the stage was home to rising pop stars, local dog shows and the annual visit from Santa. Now, Seth feared it had been put to darker uses. Toby had seemed certain that the Malone killings had not been linked to the mall, but the deeper Seth moved into the abandoned facility, the more he sensed the presence of the ghosts of Ash Park.

He'd filled his pockets with salt and iron filings, but he'd left his shotgun with its rock salt rounds back at the trailer, uncertain how he could explain it if he were stopped by a cop, or how he could conceal it on the bike. Now he wished he had the shotgun, an iron crowbar, and maybe a whole arsenal as well.

The smell grew stronger as he neared the atrium, not just blood, but rot. At the same time, Seth realized that the air had grown colder, and that new, odd scents lingered in the air: perfume, aftershave, bubble gum, and cigarette smoke. Here and there, Seth caught the glimmer of what might have been orbs. The ghosts were gathering, watching and waiting. But for what, Seth wasn't sure.

"Aw, shit." Seth wrinkled his nose in revulsion once he climbed the dais steps. Six white brick pillars ringed the stage, like a modern Stonehenge. Four candles, burned down to nubs, marked the quarters of a large circle. Sigils around the circumference drew Seth's attention. Some he recognized; others he didn't. In the center of the circle sat a low bowl with the charred remains of bones. Discarded outside the warded space were the skulls and carcasses of small animals that had already rotted to blackened, shriveled skin stretched tight over yellowed skeletons.

The dead things in the circle weren't human, but Seth sensed an unwilling connection between the sacrifices on the dais and the troubled spirits of the men and women who had met their end in the back hallways or lonely parking lots of Ash Park. Valac may not have killed those people or even ordered their deaths, but Seth doubted that Valac's ownership of the mall where they died was a coincidence. Perhaps the doomed men and women had felt the taint of Valac's power, and it had driven them deeper into the shadows of their minds or drawn their killers to them. As for the animal sacrifices, Valac had been involved—of that, Seth felt certain. The bodies on the stage weren't fresh, but they were recent enough that the smell had not faded. Valac had given himself a power boost in preparation for the main event: killing Evan.

If Valac had been here to preside over the sacrifices, then maybe the ghosts could describe him. Seth had brought the supplies needed to summon spirits. He was just about to set out the bowl and chalk his own circle when a bright blue-white spirit orb zipped toward his head, forcing him to duck.

A shot cracked into the tile floor inches behind him, through the air where his head would have been if he hadn't dodged the orb.

Seth dropped and rolled, coming up behind one of the decorative pillars. The smell of perfume and cigarette smoke grew stronger as the orbs danced in the dim light. Whatever magic Valac had raised called the spirits of the mall's dead. Seth hoped they were on his side.

He edged from cover, and another shot whizzed by, taking a chunk out of the pillar. Seth noted the angle of the shot, and as the orbs rose in a flurry like a supernatural snowstorm, he dove for the shelter of another pillar and fired a shot in return. His attacker hunkered behind the fountain, which was large enough to give him cover and room to move along its arc. Up on the dais, Seth was vulnerable. He dropped off the back of the stage, landed in a crouch, and made his way through the darker shadows to the edge of the dais.

The shooter popped up, looking for his target, and Seth got in a shot, striking the man and knocking him backward. He heard a wet crunch as the man fell hard against the lip of the fountain and did not get up again. Seth heard the rustle of cloth and looked up just in time to see two black-clad men hurtling toward him.

Two shots rang out as Seth and one of the black-clad goons fired at the same time. Seth dove for cover without injury, but the first man staggered, holding a wounded arm. The other man dropped and rolled, vanishing into the shadows, and Seth crouched, waiting for the next attack. The air felt electric, as if the ghosts gathered too, awaiting the excitement of the fight.

"Help me," Seth murmured to the ghosts. "I know you can hear me. Help me stop this, and I'll find a way to set you free."

He didn't have time to work his summoning spell; Valac's goons weren't going to give him the opportunity. Seth watched the shadows, wondering if Valac's men were reacting to his presence, or whether they had followed him here to get rid of Evan's protector. Seth resolved that one way or another, he would be the one leaving.

The goons rushed him from the left and the right. He shot to the right and missed, and the man on the left slammed into him, taking them both to the outdated tile floor. Seth struggled to hold onto his gun, tightening his grip as he grappled with his opponent. He brought his knee up, caught his opponent in the stomach and pushed off, adding a foot in the nuts for good measure.

The attacker struggled to rise and lunged at Seth, grabbing for his legs. Seth pivoted, kicking out for the goon's knee and connecting with a crunch. The man went down screaming, and Seth caught him across the side of the head with the butt of his gun, knocking him unconscious. Two down, one to go.

"Put your hands up!" The last goon ordered, holding the gun steady in his right hand while he cradled his left against his chest, still bleeding where Seth's shot had clipped him. Before Seth could make a move, a shower of orbs descended on the man in a glowing maelstrom, hurtling at his head and face so that he was forced to raise his arms to protect himself. Seth dove for his midsection, taking him to the ground and knocking the gun from his hand. In seconds, he had the remaining man pinned face-down, his hands behind him and Seth's knee in his back as the orbs drew back to watch what happened next.

"Who's your boss?" Seth's voice was low and deep.

"We serve the Eternal One," his prisoner rasped.

Seth dug his knee in, grinding it against the man's spine. "Enough with the hero worship. What's his name?"

"I don't know."

Seth shifted his weight, and the man cried out. "Try again."

"I don't know!" The goon writhed from the pressure of sharp knee against ribs and spine. "I've never seen his face. He texts us when he needs us. Coordinates. If we try to respond, the message goes nowhere. Never heard his name. He paid off my gambling debts. The bookies were going to kill me."

"What about the sacrifices?"

"He told us to round up some stray dogs and cats. We brought them in, and then he sent us away. I don't know anything else."

The panic in the goon's voice had a ring of truth to it; Seth doubted Valac had bothered to take his henchmen into his confidence. Now came the hard part; what to do with him. Seth kept pressure on the man's back with one hand while he unfastened the goon's belt with the other, using it to tie his hands. He kicked the man's gun far out of reach, tied his shoelaces together for good measure, and used a glove from the enforcer's pocket as a gag.

Seth made quick work of securing the other two men and taking away their guns. Once he was far away, he'd make an anonymous call to 911 and let the cops see about getting Valac's henchmen medical attention. Before that, however, he needed answers.

"Help me," Seth said, looking around the darkened atrium at the flickering orbs that hung like glowing soap bubbles in the dusty air. They had dimmed considerably from their brightness during the attack, and now they bobbed with deceptive laziness, keeping vigil.

"I need to know what Corson Valac looks like," Seth beseeched the spirits. "He's going to kill again, kill someone I care about, if I don't stop him. The dark magic he used here," Seth said, gesturing to encompass the bodies on the dais, "binds your spirits to this place. Help me get what I need to destroy him, and you can all go free. You can move on."

One of the orbs pulsed brightly and slowly began to drift toward Seth, floating on eye level through the air. It stopped a few feet in front of him and expanded to become the translucent image of a young

African-American woman with elaborate braids and a kind smile. Seth remembered her from the news articles about the murders at the mall. LaQuisha Anderson, mugged for her purse and her cell phone in the parking lot.

"He's short. Got a round face and gray eyes. Jowly. Bald in the middle, keeps the rest trimmed up short," LaQuisha said. "Late thirties, maybe early forties."

"Anything else you can remember?" Seth begged, grateful for the spirit's help.

LaQuisha frowned, thinking. "Yeah. His nose looked like it had been broken a couple of times."

A connection tingled in the back of Seth's mind, there and gone. Something about the description sounded familiar, a face he'd seen more than once but hadn't really noticed.

"Thank you," he said to LaQuisha, and then looked out at the larger group of orbs. "Thanks for your help in the fight. I'll stop Valac, and your spirits can leave this place," he promised.

"Hurry," LaQuisha urged as the outline of her form dimmed. "Time is running out."

∼

Seth zoomed away from Ash Park Mall, relieved the gunfight had drawn no attention. Then again, no one would expect a shootout inside an abandoned mall. It was early morning, and cars still crowded the highways in waning rush hour. Seth stuck to the side streets, avoiding the worst congestion. He found a pay phone at a convenience store and tipped off the cops to the henchmen at the mall. Then he wound his way back to Hollywood Cemetery.

He kept well away from the section that held Corson Valac's desecrated grave. Instead, he stopped in front of the Pool mausoleum, remembering the local legends Evan had shared.

"The Richmond Vampire," Seth murmured. Legend had it such a creature had taken shelter in the mausoleum. But what if it had been Valac, worse-for-the-wear after a spell gone bad, or covered in blood after the sacrifice of one of Evan's ancestors?

Maybe Seth had it all wrong when it came to Valac's anchor. He'd thought the warlock would have wanted the element and its spelled box hidden somewhere difficult to access. But maybe six feet under was too much of a good thing. Perhaps Valac needed the anchor to be safe but still accessible, in case he needed to cut and run. And it would be far easier to remove something from inside a mausoleum than from a casket at the bottom of a grave.

Seth pushed the bike next to a copse of bushes and glanced around. A groundskeeper worked in the distance, but he was hunched over with his back to Seth. No one else was in view. The Pool mausoleum sank back into a hillside, extending out with an entranceway of carved stone, protected by a waist-high iron fence. A metal grating guarded the solid, inner steel door from vandalism. No doubt once the legend spread, thrill-seekers wanted a glimpse of the "Richmond Vampire."

Seth opened the first gate with a touch and the second with a slightly more powerful flicker of magic. He cringed as the grate squealed on rusty hinges, opening it just far enough to slip inside. The steel door took a stronger spell to release the heavy bolt that was stiff from disuse, but it finally surrendered to the magic, and he pulled it open with effort.

Inside, a high window dimmed with years of dust barely illuminated the crypt. A carved stone urn sat on a ledge directly inside the door. William Pool's mortuary drawer was part of the left wall, while his wife's was on the right. The rest of the stark interior was plain, smooth marble.

Seth's first instinct was to ransack the drawers, but he paused, remembering with every twinge of sore muscles the disappointment of Valac's empty grave. Instead, he looked at the urn, the crypt's only adornment.

"Here goes nothing," he murmured. He thought the urn might be solid since no one would be tending real flowers locked up in a crypt. But when he checked the top, he found an opening. Seth pulled out a small flashlight from his pocket and peered inside. A shadowy object lay at the bottom, and as he angled the light to see better, he could make out a brass cylinder with a ring on the top. Seth dug through his bag for one of the tools he carried with him, selecting an extendable metal rod. Hooking the rod through the ring required some fishing, but he slowly teased the prize up to the urn's wide mouth.

He bit down on his cry of victory as the cylinder tumbled out of the urn and into his hand. Seth wasn't sure whether he imagined a tingle, like a spark of static electricity, shooting through him as his skin touched the metal. Wary, he pulled out one of his leather gloves and wrapped the metal tube in it, tucking it carefully back into his jacket and zipping the pocket shut. He'd examine Valac's anchor later, back in the safety of the trailer. Maybe Toby would know how to destroy it, now that they had the object in hand. As anxious to be rid of Valac as Seth was, he didn't want to botch destroying the element, for fear of what consequences that might bring.

Anxious to be gone, Seth eased out of the steel door and put his shoulder into shoving it closed, locking it with another spell. He had just closed the outer grate when a voice hailed him.

"Looking for someone?"

Seth wheeled, startled, and barely resisted the urge to go for his gun. To his relief, it was only the groundskeeper, giving him a measuring look.

"Doing some genealogy research," Seth replied, thankful he hadn't drawn down on the man. "Since my mom can't get around easily anymore." *Because she's dead. No lie there.*

"You're kin to the Pools?"

"Distantly," Seth replied. "Cousins, several times removed. I thought maybe I could see inside from the grate, but there's a door in the way." He gestured toward the outside iron fence. "The gate was open. I hope it was okay to come in." He left out the part about being the one to open the gate.

"No harm done, I figure," the groundskeeper replied. He had the weathered look of a man who had spent his whole life working outside, with a deep tan and crinkles around his eyes. A head of white hair matched his bushy eyebrows. His dirt-stained jumpsuit and the work gloves shoved into his pockets looked like they had seen hard use.

"I took some pictures, for the project," Seth said, sidling down toward the fence gate, anxious to be gone. He remained wary, wondering if the groundsman would suddenly attack. But the older man just regarded him curiously.

"Didn't think the Pools still had family around here," the man said. "You're the first person I've seen come around, except for that policeman who drops by to check on it now and then."

"Policeman?" Seth asked, now on high alert.

The groundsman nodded. "Not surprised, seeing how with all those crazy vampire stories, there was some vandalism a while back. Don't know what gets into kids these days, bothering someone's final resting place." He shook his head, with a glance toward Seth that invited commiseration.

"I'd like to thank the officer, for taking time to check on the place," Seth said. "For the family's sake. Do you happen to know his name?"

The groundskeeper shook his head. "Never actually spoke to the man, just see him come by every so often. Short, stocky fellow, roundish face, reminded me a bit of a bulldog because his nose looked like he'd gone a time or two in the boxing ring and lost."

Valac. He's a cop. Suddenly, Seth remembered where he had seen an officer that met the description from both the mall ghost and the gardener. *Shit. He was at Treddy's the night I met Evan. And I think I saw him leaving the library—when the spell said Valac was in the building.*

Fuck. He's been here all along, hiding in plain sight. Watching us.

"I've got to go," Seth said, rushing out of the iron gate and past the groundskeeper.

"You want to leave me your card?" The man called after him. "I can give it to the cop if I see him again."

"No thanks," Seth called over his shoulder, sprinting toward his bike. "I think we've met."

Valac was playing cat and mouse with them, staying close and keeping an eye on Evan with them none the wiser. Seth caught the disapproval in the groundskeeper's expression when he roared out of the cemetery, but he had much more urgent matters on his mind.

I've got to get back to Evan. Valac's sure to know I've tampered with his anchor. He'll be desperate to make sure nothing interferes with the ritual. I never should have left Evan alone and unprotected. Please, don't let me be too late.

16

EVAN

Evan gritted his teeth as he watched Seth's bike disappear up the farm lane. He fought the urge to throw something, punch the wall, or scream. The argument with Seth had gone even worse than he'd feared, with Seth retreating into bodyguard mode and completely ignoring Evan's rising discomfort from being overprotected.

Evan paced. He had no phone, no way to use Seth's laptop to contact anyone, and he was stuck on an old farm miles from nowhere. Evan didn't doubt that he was in danger, but despite having witnessed some pretty wild things, he still wasn't entirely sure that he bought into the culprit being a dark witch instead of a run-of-the-mill psycho. Being hunted by a serial killer was bad enough, without magic thrown in.

And then there was Seth. Evan had been so sure the attraction between them might lead to something special. Now, doubt tore at him. Sure, they'd had some hot sex, and being together seemed easy enough to encourage Evan to let down his guard. Yes, Seth had protected him and fought off attackers, but that had more to do with Seth's training as a soldier than it did anything supernatural.

Evan glanced at the stack of files on the couch, and back at Seth's laptop. Seth's story about deaths every twelve years among the descendants of each of the sheriff's deputies seemed to be confirmed by all the research, but in his years of tending bar, he'd also heard enough crazy conspiracy theorists spin outlandish tales on everything from the JFK assassination to UFOs, and in the moment, they could make it all sound reasonable. But a closer look always scattered the "evidence" like a house of cards.

Would that be how this thing between them ended, with Seth exposed as a well-meaning crackpot unhinged by his brother's death, chasing shadows in a hopeless quest for vengeance? The thought hurt deep inside Evan's chest. As angry as he was, he didn't want to find out that everything he'd believed about his lover was a lie.

The crunch of gravel made Evan's head snap up, alert and wary. He edged to the window, surprised that Seth would be back so quickly. But instead of Seth's black Hayabusa, a police car rolled down the farm lane. Evan stayed out of sight, afraid the cop was looking to bust them for trespassing. Then the driver's door opened, and Evan recognized the officer from Treddy's.

Seth would tell him to hide and not answer the door. But Seth was gone, Evan was alone and frightened, and right now, the cop looked like safety and sanity. Before the officer could knock, Evan opened the door, grabbed his jacket, and stepped outside.

"Sonny? I'm glad I found you," the cop said. Evan tried to remember his name, and came up with "Officer Clark." "I've been worried. You're in danger."

Evan had watched enough TV to know not to let the cop into the trailer. He came down the steps, as Clark leaned against Seth's truck. "I know. Some guys broke into my apartment with guns. Then they must have set the place on fire."

"They weren't after you," Clark replied. "They're after someone named Seth Tanner."

"Then why did they yell my name before they started shooting?"

"They could have been warning you to get down," Clark said, studying him. "Or maybe, in the panic of the moment, you only thought you heard them."

That couldn't be right, could it? The memory seemed so clear. But now, he wasn't sure.

"Why would they be after Seth?"

"Is Tanner here?" Clark asked.

Evan shook his head. "He'll be back soon. Seth...went out for something."

"Is there a reason you're squatting here?"

Evan bristled. "Not hurting anything. I think the farm belongs to Seth's uncle." That was a lie, and he knew it, but he didn't intend to 'fess up to breaking the law, and compared to everything else at stake, trespassing didn't seem important right now.

"Witnesses saw you leave Treddy's with him the night your apartment was attacked," Clark said. "Your boss worried when no one heard from you. We got a make on the motorcycle's plates from street cameras and ran them through the system. Seth Tanner has a record."

"What kind of record?"

Clark watched Evan. "His brother, Jesse, died under questionable circumstances two years ago. Pretty grisly. The local police investigated Seth because he was at the scene that night, although Seth claims he got thrown into a tree and knocked out. Whoever killed his brother was a real sick bastard. Serial killer-level sick."

"He told me about what happened." Evan might be angry with Seth, but he wasn't about to throw him under the bus.

"The authorities considered Seth a person of interest for some time, but they couldn't make it stick. That's not the same as being cleared—just means the evidence wasn't there to convict."

"Seth got hurt that night. He was in the hospital. That's why he couldn't go to his parents' funeral."

Clark's eyes seemed to hold pity and understanding. "Is that what he told you? Seth did get hurt—the medical records show a head injury—but that's not why he missed the funerals. He had a psychotic break, raving about demons and magic and witches, and had to be restrained. Seth Tanner spent six weeks in a psych ward on suicide watch being evaluated for delusions and psychosis."

Evan felt like he'd been punched in the gut. Could it be true? Had Seth lied to him, or at best, twisted and withheld the truth?

"But I've seen him do things...things I couldn't explain."

Clark sighed. "Ever been to Vegas? Those stage magicians make you think they can fly and disappear and do all kinds of things, but it's all sleight of hand. Illusion, not real."

Evan had resisted the idea of magic, fought against it, then started to come around when he'd seen the small things Seth had done. But then again, it wasn't like he'd called down lightning or turned someone into a frog.

Maybe it was just misdirection. Tricks. Nothing but tricks.

"The wreck that killed Mr. and Mrs. Tanner was ruled suspicious, but the cops could never get any leads," Clark said. "It's possible that someone forced their car off the road. The evidence supported that, but the police never found the other vehicle. And then the fire…it just seemed like too much of a coincidence."

"Seth was in the hospital," Evan repeated, as his head spun and his heart broke. "How could he have had anything to do with the wreck or the fire?"

"The police think that the Tanner brothers either happened onto a big drug deal or double-crossed the dealers themselves and paid the price."

Evan shook his head. "No. You don't know that." But even as he clung to his defense of Seth, details bothered him. How comfortable Seth seemed with breaking the law, how many weapons he carried, how good he was at staying off the grid. They had all fit with his witch-hunter story, but maybe there was a darker, more mundane explanation.

"Tanner's shown up in the system a few times since his brother's murder," Clark continued. "He's talked his way out of traffic violations and trespassing charges. But he always seems to be around when the shit hits the fan, then vanishes before it can stick to him."

"Circumstantial evidence…" Evan's argument sounded weak, even to his own ears.

"By all accounts, he's a charmer. You wouldn't be the first to fall under his spell," Clark commiserated.

Evan looked up sharply, wondering whether the cop meant to imply a romantic connection, but Clark's expression remained professional.

"Guys like him, they find a target and stalk him, get to know everything about him. Then he invents a story about a threat to make the target trust him, sets himself up to be the hero. But it's all phony. There wasn't enough left after your apartment burned to find evidence of a break-in. But you don't look like the kind to owe a bookie or a dealer. Tanner…let's just say he's good at making enemies."

"I need to think—"

"Since you met Tanner, he's kept you away from everyone you know, right? Told you it was for your safety. Do you have a phone?"

Evan shook his head, feeling shell-shocked. "No. It got left behind when we ran from the apartment."

"Computer?"

Evan remembered the site blocker, and anger warred with a growing sense of complete betrayal. "There hasn't really been time—"

"He knows where you are every minute, keeps you isolated out here with no way to leave and no way to call out. I wouldn't put it past him to have you under surveillance when he isn't here."

"I—"

"Check your pockets."

Evan stared at the cop. "Why?"

"Just do it."

Evan stuck his hands into the pockets of his jacket. He found keys to an apartment that no longer existed and to a burned-out bar, plus a comb, some tissues, loose change, and…an odd disk. Evan pulled out the disk. "I don't know what this is."

Clark gave a pained smile. "It's a GPS tracker. Works with a phone app. Let's him know where you are at all times. Did you give him permission to track you?"

Evan stared at the disk in his hand as if it might bite him. His worst nightmare, his deepest fears, were coming true. "No. I didn't. I wouldn't have—he didn't ask."

Clark held out his hand, and Evan gave him the disk. The cop dropped the tracker onto the driveway and ground his heel into it, cracking the device into pieces.

"I believe that you're in danger, Sonny. But you're in danger because you're with Seth Tanner. I can take you to a safe house, the kind of place we shelter people fleeing abusive partners. He won't be able to find you there, and you'll have police protection."

Evan tried to catch his breath as the enormity of Seth's betrayal sank in. "Yes," he managed through a dry mouth. "Yes. I'll go with you. Just...let me get my bag."

Evan ran back into the trailer numb with shock. Anger warred with heartbreak, but giving in to his rage kept him moving instead of collapsing into a sobbing heap. He jerked open the door to the bedroom. The small space still smelled of sweat and sex, and he resolutely refused to remember their last coupling. He'd been pissed off at Seth, ready to argue to demand respect, and up until Clark's revelations, Evan had thought he and Seth might work things out. But not now. His hopes for their relationship lay in as much wreckage as his home and his job.

Evan grabbed his bag and headed for the door, then paused as he passed the kitchen. He snatched up a pen and the note Seth had left for him, and flipped the paper over.

"You lied. Don't try to find me. I never want to see you again."

He taped it to the fridge and slammed the trailer door behind him.

Officer Clark was already back in the squad car when Evan emerged. He went around to the passenger side, but Clark shook his head, rolling down the window and giving Evan and apologetic smile.

"I spilled my coffee all over the seat on the way here. It's soaked—you'll have to ride in the back. Put your bag in the trunk."

Officer Clark popped the trunk, and Evan threw his duffel inside, then got in behind the cop. He resolutely did not look back at the trailer as the car left the lane and headed for the highway.

Evan sat in the squad car, trying to figure out how his life had crashed and burned again. He raged silently, thinking of all the things he'd say if Seth were in front of him, how he'd confront him and force him to admit his deception. The tracker in his pocket hit a nerve, reviving all his nightmares after stalker-Mike. Worst was the betrayal. Evan had broken up more than his share of bar fights, but he'd never swung a fist in anger. Now though, he didn't trust himself not to punch Seth Tanner in the face for being a dangerous fraud.

He'd trusted Seth, believed his wild stories. Evan had let Seth cut him off from everyone, and he'd spiraled into panic listening to Seth's lies. Worst, he'd fallen in love, despite his skill at keeping his distance. He had insurance for the apartment, and he could draw unemployment compensation until he found a new job, but Evan knew he'd be nursing a broken heart for a long time.

Gradually, Evan pulled out of his thoughts enough to look out the window. He frowned, surprised to find the car heading downtown. He leaned forward. "I thought we were going to a safe house?"

"Don't worry. We'll be there soon."

A tingle of alarm buzzed through Evan. Something in Clark's tone had shifted. "Where are we going?"

"Secret location—that's why it's a safe house. Just relax. It'll be over soon."

Evan had always prided himself on listening to his intuition. His gut had told him to take Seth's hand and run the night of the break-in. Now, his Spidey sense was tingling, rising above his anger and hurt.

He glanced out the window again and recognized Shockoe Slip. Clark pulled into an empty lot where a sign advertised a long-defunct diner and stopped the car. He left the engine running and went around to the trunk. A moment later, he tossed Evan's bag into the weeds at the edge of the lot.

Evan grabbed for the door handle and found nothing. *Of course not. It's the back of a police car. Bulletproof glass. Bars on the windows. And no way to open the door from the inside.* Instead, Evan pounded on the window to get Clark's attention. "What the hell is going on?"

Clark got back into the car, and Evan lunged forward, although the glass divider kept him from getting close to the cop. "What are you doing? Why did you toss out my bag?"

Clark turned partway in his seat. His expression had turned crafty and cunning, with a hard glint in his eyes.

"You won't be needing your bag. Couldn't take the risk your idiot boyfriend had a second tracker. We have preparations to make tonight.

You can watch, of course. Then come midnight, you're the guest of honor."

Evan's words stuck in his throat. "The guest of honor?"

Clark's grin turned chilling. "The man of the hour. The main attraction. My ticket to continued immortality. Or, if you prefer—the blood sacrifice."

17

SETH

Seth gunned the Hayabusa, heading at top speed for the trailer. He had to get back to Evan and warn him about the cop from the bar. The late afternoon sun hung low in the sky, reminding Seth that time was fleeting. He had less than twenty-four hours to stop Valac and save Evan.

Save him, and then see if they could put their fractured relationship back together again.

Seth rumbled down the farm driveway, slewed to a stop, and got off the bike. He froze, looking at the muddy spot to the side of the road. New tire tracks, fresh and clean, left marks in the cold mud. A glint of something among the stones caught his eye, and he bent down to pick up the broken remains of one of the trackers he'd planted.

Fuck. He obviously found it—and he's not happy. Shit. There goes any chance of winning him back.

Seth hesitated for a moment, preparing himself before he squared his shoulders and headed for the trailer. *At least he'll be alive, even if he hates me,* Seth thought. *He'll go find another job in a different bar and a new apartment, and I'll go looking for the next witch-disciple. Probably kidding myself that it could have gone any other way, but it would have been nice to end as friends.*

As soon as he stuck his head into the trailer, Seth's intuition told him something was very wrong. "Evan?" He called out tentatively and got silence in reply.

"Evan!" Seth ran for the bedroom and found Evan's duffel gone. The bed was rumpled, and Seth tried to forget how yesterday had started, with his body tangled around Evan's, entwined in the best possible way. Instead, he let his military training take over. *No sign of a struggle. No blood. Nothing's broken, and the door hadn't been forced.*

A car had been here, and Evan was gone. Had he somehow hitched a ride?

Seth headed for his laptop, to look at the security cameras on the trailer corners when something in the kitchen caught his eye. He walked to the fridge and pulled off the note.

"You lied. Don't look for me. I never want to see you again."

He reeled and put out a hand against the refrigerator to catch himself as the paper crumpled in his grip. Evan hadn't been taken; he left, and he walked out angry.

Oh, God. That meant Evan was in terrible danger, and Seth had no idea how to find him.

Seth stood rooted to the spot, numb. He wasn't okay with Evan walking out on him, now or after the mess with Valac was sorted. Seth knew he was lying to himself to think otherwise. Evan had gotten under his skin, even when they fought and disagreed. He woke something in Seth, feelings Seth didn't think he would ever dare to trust again after Ryan had left. Evan made Seth want a future, want to survive the fight to have something of his own when it was over.

Fuck it all to hell. He was in love with Evan Malone. And if he didn't act fast, Evan would never know.

Seth dropped the note to the floor and sprinted to his laptop. In seconds he had the camera feed onscreen, and he rewound the video, then fast-forwarded from the time he left earlier that morning. All was quiet; then he saw the police car make its way down the lane. He recognized the cop from Treddy's and the library, and knew from the mall ghost's description that it was Valac.

The cameras didn't have sound, but Seth didn't need it. He saw Evan come out to speak with the officer, watched the argument as Valac slowly wore away Evan's defenses, and winced at the look of hurt and betrayal on Evan's face when he found the tracking device in his pocket. He saw the cop break the tracker. Evan ran back for his bag, but as soon as he was out of sight, Valac took something from his jacket and bent down, slipping it under the body of Seth's truck. If Seth had any doubts about the cop's intentions, seeing him maneuver Evan to get into the back seat confirmed the worst.

"Fuck," Seth swore and slammed his hand on the table. The time stamp on the tape told him hours had already passed since Evan's abduction. He forced himself not to think about worst-case scenarios, and opened up the name search that had run all night.

The list scrolled down the screen and Seth murmured more curses. But the program not only returned the first and last name and address, it also included a field for "profession." Only one of the names was for a police officer. Vincent Clark.

Toby answered on the first ring. "I got the element, but Valac's got Evan," Seth rambled without prequel.

"Slow down," Toby urged. "Tell me what happened."

Much as Seth chafed at the delay, he recounted everything that had happened, as Toby listened in silence.

"Do you have any idea where Valac might take him?" Toby asked after Seth had spilled out the whole sorry tale.

Seth raked a hand down over his face. "Not the mall, not after I sent the police there and they found all the bodies. They'll have it locked up for a crime scene, and even Officer 'Vincent Clark' might have trouble sneaking in a prisoner for a ritual killing."

"The house?"

Seth forced himself to breathe more slowly. "Maybe. It just doesn't feel right. There's a tracker in his bag—if he hasn't found it and gotten rid of it already. I'll follow up on it next. But I'm missing something, and I don't know what it is."

"Take it easy—"

"I can't take it easy! By midnight tomorrow, Valac's going to kill Evan if I can't get to him first."

Toby cleared his throat, and Seth felt a cold dread fill him. "You don't have that long, Seth," Toby said. "Halloween starts at midnight tonight. Now that Valac knows you're on to him, he won't wait longer than he has to, and noon would be the next optimal time. Too exposed, too many people around. He'll do it tonight. You've got about seven hours. And Valac will be punctual. The knife will fall on the stroke of midnight. That's how magic works."

Shit. "What do I do with the element? If I destroy it, how much damage does it do to Valac?"

"I'm not completely sure. This is new territory for me," Toby confessed. Seth could visualize his mentor, bright blue eyes crisp in a lined face tanned from years in the sun. Toby would be playing with a pen, twirling it between his fingers, clicking the button, tapping it on the desk, as he always did when he was deep in thought.

"I need something to go on, Toby. We're down to the wire."

"All right. Let's think this through like soldiers," Toby replied. While his war was in the jungles of Vietnam and Seth's service harked to the deserts of Iraq, they both had been on Special Ops teams, both trained to run a quarry to ground. "Does Valac know you have his anchor?"

"I don't think so. I'm pretty sure he expected his goons to take me out at the shopping mall."

"Then you've got surprise on your side, for now," Toby mused. "If you destroy the anchor before you know where Valac has Evan, you might force Valac's hand, and he might rush into the ritual so he can finish before he's too weakened. We've got to time this right."

"I wish 'we' were doing this," Seth grumbled. "I've got boots on the ground, and you're a helluva long way from here."

"Focus."

Seth drew a long breath and blew it out. "Okay. We know he's not at the mausoleum because he was snatching Evan while I was there, and besides, there's not enough room. I don't think that's the site. If he meant to use the mall, I think the police crime scene will force him to go somewhere else. Maybe the house. I'll go over there next, as soon as I see if I can pick up the tracker in Evan's bag."

"Any other possibilities?"

Seth shook his head. "The address the data dump gave me for Valac is an apartment in a high rise down in The Slip. I just looked it up while we were talking. Too many people around, not enough privacy. Assuming he really lives there."

"Keep thinking. He's got to make his move soon, so he'll hole up somewhere close if he can't get to his location this early. That's where he'll have Evan, but you need to pick your battleground," Toby cautioned. "I mean it, Seth. You go in there half-cocked, you'll get yourself and Evan killed, and that's no use to anyone. You've learned strategy. Use it."

"What about the element?"

Across their connection, Seth heard Toby pour himself a drink, although whether it was coffee or whiskey, he had no way of knowing. Maybe a little of both. "Valac's anchor stores some of his power in that container. It's spelled, so don't go trying to open it. You don't need to. Whatever's inside it—hair, nail clippings, blood—links to his essence. You've got to contain the power and obliterate it."

"Contain it how?"

"Short of a bomb silo, I'd recommend concentric circles of salt, holy water, and holy oil," Toby replied. He paused, and Seth could hear a muted voice in the background.

"Milo says that the bomb silo isn't a bad idea. Solid stone walls, preferably banked into the ground—"

"Shit. The Pool mausoleum. It'll make a mess, but that's the best I've got."

"Use it."

"How about the obliterate part?"

"If you could nuke the thing, that would do," Toby replied, and Seth wasn't entirely sure his friend was joking. "But that's messy, and the Feds get their panties in a wad. So use the best explosives you've got, but make it count. That should wipe out Valac's stored energy, and sucker punch him at the same time."

"Got it."

"You have a plan for going in there?" Toby pressed. "Because Valac won't go down without a fight."

"A little magic and a lot of firepower," Seth replied. "I've gotta go."

He ended the call and pulled up another screen, hoping that neither Evan nor Valac had found the second tracker. "There," he breathed, as a red dot pulsed. "Thank God." He zoomed in on the map and made note of the address, then stuffed his laptop into a messenger bag and started to gather what he needed to go to war.

Seth kept most of his extra gear stowed in the cargo compartments beneath the trailer. He'd modified those compartments to have a false back, where he could stash his more unusual tools—silver and iron knives, a gallon of holy water, silver bullets, sharpened wooden stakes. The hidden storage area also held contraband that would get Seth in a lot of trouble if it came to the wrong people's attention—C4, dynamite, fuses, gunpowder, and wiring to make explosives.

The army had taught Seth all kinds of skills—in computer security and otherwise—and while munitions and detonation weren't his specialty, he'd learned plenty about blowing shit up. He considered his options and pulled out what he needed, carefully loading his go bag.

Tonight he needed the truck. He couldn't risk riding the bike with a duffel full of questionable items, and he wanted the power and protection of the truck more than the Hayabusa's speed and maneuverability. It took Seth less than ten minutes to uncouple the truck from the trailer, and all the while, he couldn't keep his thoughts from Evan.

What if he's hurt? What if that bastard is torturing him? What if I don't get there in time? Seth had started this quest as vengeance for Jesse, and that need remained strong. But as much as he still ached over Jesse's loss, as much as he would always have a hole in his soul for his brother, during the past four days, the fight had changed. Now he was fighting for Evan, even if he couldn't keep him, even if Evan meant what he said about never seeing Seth again. None of that changed how Seth felt.

No one had ever gotten under Seth's skin and into his heart like Evan. He had given up hoping that a connection like that was possible. The thought of Evan in pain or dying hurt so much it nearly stole Seth's breath. It didn't matter whether Evan returned the feeling. It made the battle personal, not just to avenge something that was lost, but to fight to keep someone important from being lost. That changed everything.

Deep in thought, Seth almost swung up into the cab of the truck before he remembered Valac's odd movements on the video. He walked over to where Valac had been standing, knowing the man hadn't had much time while Evan ran inside for his bag. Seth dropped to his hands and knees, then lay flat on his back and pushed himself beneath the truck with his heels.

"Son of a bitch."

The IED was small, made from easy-to-find, legal components that when put together in an entirely illegal way, created a hand-sized antipersonnel bomb. Seth had seen explosives like that in Iraq and defused more than his share of them, but since they were one-of-a-kind and jerry-rigged, each device was different. They all had two things in common. They were tricky to defeat and lethal as hell.

No one could "hurry" defusing an IED unless they wanted to get dead fast. Seth swore under his breath. He could leave the truck to worry about later, but if he took the bike, he'd have to leave most of his weapons behind. Given that he couldn't compete with Valac on magic, technology gave him an edge he couldn't do without.

Take the time to defuse the bomb, and the clock ticked down on Evan's life. Go into battle half-assed, and they could both end up dead.

Cursing creatively, Seth slithered out from under the truck and dug out a set of tools he'd assembled from legal and not-so-legal sources, then carefully got himself into position.

Valac didn't have time to do more than place the bomb, so that ruled out any elaborate wiring connected to the motor or the electrical system, Seth mused. The IED probably attached magnetically, but removing it could set it off and engage the detonator. He doubted it was on a timer since Valac would have wanted to make sure Seth was in the truck, not just blow the vehicle up to make a statement. That meant some sort of trigger with motion, or maybe heat.

Seth felt the sweat bead on his forehead as he stared at the bomb in the glare of his small flashlight. He hadn't defused a live explosive since he'd left the army, but he'd had enough practice back in the day, and he hoped that would carry him through.

"Here goes nothing," he thought. Seth narrowed his eyes and gritted his teeth, keeping his hands steady as they gripped the small tools that would determine whether he crawled back out from under the truck in one piece, or died bloody underneath a mangled mass of steel.

Minutes ticked by as Seth probed and prodded, ruling out possibilities and coming up with new alternatives. When he felt certain that he had explored all the options, he held his breath, said a prayer, and gripped a sensitive trigger with the tool in one hand as he gently pried the panel loose with the other.

It nearly wobbled out of his hold, and although the drop between the IED's position and Seth's chest was mere inches, he did not want to test the sensitivity of the bomb by seeing if it exploded on contact. He tightened his grip, then carefully eased out from under the truck and into the sunlight.

"Damn," he murmured as he hunkered down to look at the device. Seth had learned the hard way in the field that a crude weapon could be just as lethal as any high tech alternatives. Now he studied the bomb and tried to figure if he could repurpose it for his needs. The homemade mechanism would do the job, but it was primitive, a beginner's handiwork. Seth reminded himself that he'd lost teammates to explosives that were equally simple, and took his time, although he begrudged every second.

Once he understood the wiring and had guessed at the material used to make the charge, Seth relaxed a bit. The bomb would have been deadly if it had gone off beneath his seat while he was driving, but deactivated, transporting it would be safe. After all, he reminded himself, Valac had gotten it to their campsite.

That gave Seth an idea, and he carefully picked up the explosive, double checked that it had been turned off, and put it gingerly into a padded box in the cargo container at the back of the truck. Experience had taught him to never waste a weapon, and he had plans for Valac's amateur bomb.

The IED gave Seth ideas. He dug back into the trailer's secret compartment and pulled out a few more "toys," thinking about the work that lay ahead of him. Between his rote magic and his weapons, he was as ready to confront Valac as he'd ever be.

Now, he just had to find him.

Armed to the teeth and pissed as fuck, Seth debated whether to destroy Valac's anchor first or go after Evan's tracker. The cemetery lay in the opposite direction of the signal from Evan's bag. Much as he wanted to throw caution to the wind and charge after Evan, doing so with the element in his possession would be stupid. He glanced at the clock and realized that only five hours remained until midnight. The IED had cost him precious time, and while he had saved his own life, he now feared more than ever for Evan.

Hang on, he thought, willing Evan to hear him. *Even if you're through with me, I won't let you down. I'm coming after you.*

18

EVAN

"Get out." Officer Clark...Valac...held a gun pointed at Evan's chest and twitched the barrel to indicate direction.

Evan remained where he sat, glaring at Valac. "Shooting me would ruin your perfect sacrifice. I'm not going anywhere." The cop car sat behind the house Evan had broken into with Seth, and he knew that the sound of a bullet might bring neighbors' attention even if they paid little notice to burglary.

Valac raised the weapon to aim between Evan's eyes. "I need your blood. You don't have to be in good shape; just a beating heart will work when I do the ritual. Plenty of places I can shoot you that will give me the blood I need and take quite a long time for you to die. Your choice."

Evan glowered, but he swung his legs out of the police sedan and walked ahead of Valac up to the small back porch.

"Open the door. You and your boyfriend left it unlocked when you were here snooping."

Evan weighed his chances. He'd taken plenty of martial arts classes, and fought his way out of more bar brawls than he wanted to remember. But he'd never disarmed a man with a gun. Still, getting shot had to be better than whatever Valac had in mind for him. Evan remembered the gruesome police photographs of Jesse Tanner and the other victims. He would much prefer a bullet between the eyes.

Evan led the way into the dark kitchen. A second later, he whirled, striking out with one hand to knock aside Valac's gun hand, while he swung a solid punch for the jaw with his left fist.

A single word, spoken in a language he'd never heard before, froze him in place. Evan could see and hear, feel his heart beating, but he could not move a muscle. Valac chuckled, locked the door, and stepped around him.

"That really wasn't necessary," Valac said to someone just out of Evan's line of sight.

"He could have gotten lucky. I didn't want to take the chance." Jackie stepped into view, standing framed in the doorway to the empty living room. "You think I kept an eye on him all this time, to let him get away now?" She grinned. "Let's see what he has to say."

"Jackie?" Evan felt like he'd been gutted. "I don't—"

"No, you sure didn't," she replied. "You never saw me coming. Poor little gay 'Sonny' with his stalker problem and no friends," she drawled with exaggerated, sarcastic sympathy. "You never worried about me, because you knew I didn't want to get into your pants. That made it so pathetically easy to get close, make sure we knew where to find you when the time came."

"And everything you told me about your 'friend' from Indiana remembering Seth and Jesse?"

Jackie grinned. "Did you like that? All improv—pretty good, I think. Told you what we needed you to hear, what would drive a wedge between you and your hunky champion. Did you argue with him when you got home? Throw a hissy?" Evan's silence clearly gave her all the confirmation she needed. "Damn, I'm good."

"Izzy and Liam, were they in on it, too?" Evan couldn't help asking, as he tasted bile in his throat at the thought of this new betrayal.

"Nope, they actually liked you. It was so cute how they were worried to death about the apartment fire. It was all just little old me." Jackie sauntered closer and bopped him on the nose. "Surprise."

"Is everything ready?" Valac moved into the other room and

stripped out of his police uniform, unconcerned about undressing in front of the two goons who lingered near the front door. He picked up a ceremonial robe from where it lay across the back of a chair, and tied the rope sash, securing the ends so they did not dangle. Evan glimpsed a strange talisman on a strap around Valac's neck and remembered what Seth had said about the witch-disciple's anchor, a spelled container with potent contents, and an amulet tied to that element.

"Where are the others?" Valac demanded.

Jackie gestured with one hand, an outward motion, and unseen power picked Evan up and tossed him into the living room as if he weighed nothing. Another gesture and he hung flattened against one wall, feet off the floor, arms splayed, held in place by an invisible hand.

"Now you're just showing off," Valac chided. "Release him, Jackie."

Jackie spoke a few unfamiliar words, and Evan felt the paralysis fade, though the unseen force still held him against the wall.

"Easier than ropes, don't you think?" She said to Valac, her tone unconcerned. "After all, he really ought to have a good view of what we're doing, since it's the lead-up to the main event." She leveled a cold smile at Evan. "And he's the star of tonight's show."

"Where are the other guards?" Valac looked around, his brow furrowing.

"Tanner showed up at the mall earlier today. Managed to shoot them all," Jackie said, and her voice tightened with anger. "Stupid fucker reported it to the police. I would have thought you'd have heard the call over your scanner in your little toy car."

"Have a care how you speak!" Valac admonished. "As for the chatter on the radio, I had more important issues at hand." He paused. "Are my men dead?"

Jackie's lips twitched in a knowing grin. "They are now. I know how you hate loose ends."

Evan stared at the woman he thought he knew as a co-worker and a friend. At Treddy's Jackie had been sassy but caring, quick with a joke and fun to be around. Clearly it had all been an act, an elaborate con, since this version of Jackie seemed completely different, from the hard glint in her eyes and tight line of her lips to the impatient gestures and intimidating stance. *Valac sent her to keep an eye on me, so he knew where to get me when it came time to kill me. Shit. I've been played—again.*

"Nicely done." Valac turned to look at the living room, which had been rearranged since Evan's last visit. A large circle marked in what looked to be blood took up most of the center of the room. Candles burned at the quarter points, and an assortment of small charms and totems lay between the candles, bits of bone and rag tied in intricate knots or bound together into small bundles.

"You have the sacrifice?"

Jackie nodded. "Bound and gagged in the other room. No need to listen to him beg."

"Good. Fetch him. Fresh blood will ready me nicely for the summoning tonight. Some blood for me, and more for my master," Valac said with a smile. Jackie made a shallow bow and went to make ready, barking orders at the goons who hurried to do her bidding.

Valac walked over toward where Evan strained against the power that held him tightly to the wall. "We redecorated a bit since you were here," he said, and his cold smile sent ice through Evan's veins. "Do you like it? It's just a shadow of what's to come. Now, don't you mind the bit of ritual we're going to do in a moment. You needn't be jealous. Your own ceremony at midnight will be far more elaborate and important. This is just the power boost before the real show."

"You're insane." Evan might not be able to pull free of the force that bound him, but he at least retained control of his speech.

"Maybe. So hard to tell after enough time goes by," Valac mused. "Or maybe I'm just less inhibited since there's no one to pass judgment."

"I thought you said that magic was all just parlor tricks." Evan's low growl suggested that he wanted to tear his tormentor apart, although he had no way to follow up on the threat.

"I lied," Valac said with a shrug. "A good performance, don't you think? And you so earnest and worried, torn between loyalty to your lover and giving in to your fears. I told you everything you needed to hear to make you fall right in line. It was so easy to plant the doubt, suggest darker possibilities, give your imagination some shadows to deal with. And you played your part perfectly, as if you'd already read the script." He leaned closer, unconcerned about Evan posing him a threat. "Bravo."

"Seth will stop you," Evan countered, though fear made his voice rise.

"He's certainly tried, hasn't he?" Valac replied. He twitched one finger, and without laying a hand on Evan's body, a long thin rip started down his shirt as an invisible claw dug into Evan's chest, deep enough for blood to well up in the gash. "Magic," he said as Evan cried out. "Real. Powerful. Such an easy secret to keep when fools like you don't want to believe, even when the evidence is in front of you."

"You sent the men to my apartment. You burned it down and blew up the bar."

Valac tilted his head, with an odd smile as if acknowledging a litany of accomplishments instead of accusations. "Yes to all. Though I did regret the necessity of closing down Treddy's for a while. I'd gotten to like the place. No matter. It will reopen soon although, sadly, without its star bartender."

"So it's true, about Gremory? You were a disciple, and now you're just…what? Going to keep killing someone from my family every dozen years so you can live forever?" Evan's whole body ached from the tension of his muscles against the unyielding force that kept him in place. He might not be as tall or solid as Seth, but Evan's over six-foot frame and one hundred eighty pounds of lean muscle still should not have been as easy to suspend as a rag doll.

Valac chuckled. "Of course I am. A nobody dies, and I remain…it's quite a bargain." He regarded Evan like a specimen pinned for examination. "You don't come from the bravest of stock, boy. After they killed my master, when I caught up with Deputy Malone, he screamed and cried and begged, even offered to give me his son to make me stop, can you believe that?" He leaned in as if he were telling a secret. "As if I weren't going to come for the son in due time anyhow."

Valac paced as Jackie and the others made ready. "You're the first to be smart enough to see the pattern, although I guess *you* didn't—it's Tanner again. Bothersome meddler." Valac regarded him, studying Evan's features. "You take after the one I killed most recently. An uncle, perhaps? He was quite entertaining. Lectured me about God and Satan, as if they had anything to do with it. Tried to pray me away, even tried to exorcise me. Died cursing the God he asked for help because nobody came when he called. Nobody ever does."

"Seth will," Evan replied, raising his chin. "He'll hunt you."

"Seth Tanner is dead," Valac answered as he walked away. "I put a bomb under his truck when you went to get your things. So if that's your last hope, best be saying your prayers while you can, boy."

"You're lying." Evan felt panic rise. Valac had to be wrong. Seth couldn't be dead.

Valac turned partway to look at him. "Sorry, no. I'm good at what I do. He's not coming to save you, assuming he would have even tried after how quickly you gave him up. Pathetic."

Evan wanted to scream and rage, to curse Valac and denounce his lies. But the very thought of Seth, dead, took the breath from his lungs.

Not Seth. Seth isn't dead. Valac is wrong, or he's playing with me, trying to break me. I won't believe him. Seth's smart. He was right...he was right about everything. Oh God, what a fool I've been! Evan had never felt so terrified, or so alone. And Seth...

Evan began to shout and curse. Valac merely smiled. "Scream all you want to. I warded the house. No one will hear you." The goons returned from the other room with a prisoner in tow, dragging an older man between them. From his grimy clothing and dirty hair, Evan guessed the man was a vagrant. The prisoner wriggled and bucked against the ropes that bound his wrists and ankles. The gag in his mouth muffled his shouts and curses. At Jackie's behest, they lifted the stranger up and over the chalked lines of the warded circle, and placed him inside on the floor.

As Valac stepped up to work his magic, Jackie drew back to stand between the two thugs. Valac lifted a hood over his head that partly hid his face. He picked up a curved knife with a wicked blade and began to walk counter-clockwise around the chalked circle. As he passed each candle, the flame flared, and once he completed the circuit, the circle began to glow.

The witch-disciple stepped over the boundary and into the warded space. He stretched out his left hand, and the terrified prisoner began to rise from the floor without being touched. The man kicked and fought, but he continued upward, as the same force rotated his body so he hung perpendicular to the floor, without any tangible support.

Evan watched in horror. Magic. Real magic.

Snippets of conversation came back to him, things Seth tried to tell him about how magic worked; Evan had been too quick to tune it out because he thought he knew better. How arrogant he'd been, dismissing Seth's warnings out of hand, trying to find alternative explanations that enabled Evan to keep on denying the truth of what was right in front of him.

He'd been wrong about magic, and about Seth. Evan thought about the note he'd left, how angry he'd felt and how ready to walk away. Seth deserved so much better. He deserved someone who believed in him and his cause wholeheartedly, someone strong and brave enough to fight beside him to bring the witch-disciples to justice and make them pay for all the murders through the years. And if Seth had lived, he would have come after him anyhow, despite the note, even if no hope remained for their relationship, because Seth wouldn't let Evan down.

None of that mattered because Seth was dead, and in scarcely more than an hour, Evan would be too. Valac would live on, and a dozen years from now, the next Malone would pay with his life, on through the years.

Now, when it was too late, Evan knew for certain that he loved Seth. No one had ever woken that kind of passion in him or made connection so easy and natural. He'd been angry and frightened. Deep inside, he had hoped Seth would come after him, explain it all, make things right. Since he'd met Seth, Evan had begun to let himself think about a future that offered more than bartending and empty nights, the possibility of making a real difference in the world beside the man he loved. Valac's bomb took away that future before it had the chance to become more than a daydream. At least Evan wouldn't have long to mourn Seth before he joined him on the other side.

Evan blinked back his tears and struggled against the tightness in his throat. If Seth couldn't save him, then Evan would take matters into his own hands, fight Valac with everything he had, make the witch's victory as costly as possible. Stop Valac, if he could. Honor Seth's quest and the lost lives of Jesse and all the other sacrifices, and make his own death count for something.

Valac's chant continued, and he bowed to each of the four compass points. As he did so, the candles flared again, their flames changing color to blood-red. The circle still glowed, growing brighter as Valac recited his litany.

Evan tore his gaze away to look at Jackie, still raw from her betrayal. She watched with rapt attention, eyes wide and lips parted, as if aroused by the raw power of the magic. The goons remained stoic, gaze forward, expressionless. Whatever savagery Valac intended did not bother them.

Valac thrust out his right hand, the one holding the curved blade. Although the knife stopped inches above the bound man's chest, a wicked cut slashed through his shirt, baring his chest, and gouged deep into his skin. Valac made a sideways motion with his left hand, fingers drawn up like claws, and four parallel gashes appeared on the prisoner's chest. Blood coursed freely down the man's skin, and his cries grew more panicked and shrill.

Taking a shallow bowl from within the circle, Valac stepped closer to the doomed man and held the lip of the container where blood would flow into it. He never stopped chanting, and his voice rose in a triumphant crescendo as the bowl filled.

Valac swung the curved blade, ripping the razor-sharp point through the prisoner's throat, and lifting the bowl higher to catch the bright red jets of lifeblood. When it was full, Valac raised it overhead like an offering, turning his face upwards as he shouted the last lines of his crazed recitation. He tilted the bowl and let the blood sluice over him, soaking his hood and robe, covering him in crimson. The lines of the circle and its sigils flared so brightly that Evan had to avert his eyes, and the flames from each candle rose like thin towers of fire, dancing impossibly high in an unnatural, blood-red hue. For an instant, lines of glowing power, like a latticework of sparks, radiated from *beneath* Valac's skin, there and gone, but Evan knew what he had seen.

The prisoner hung silent and motionless, suspended but forgotten, his usefulness at an end.

Evan's heart threatened to beat out of his chest as his gut twisted with cold fear. What he had just witnessed was impossible, unbelievable—and true. In that instant, everything he thought he knew about the world turned upside-down and inside-out. Magic was real. Valac was indeed a powerful witch, and very soon, Evan would be the latest in a long string of murders to assure that power continued.

Valac kept on muttering, but whether he spoke the words of a spell or prayed to his long-dead master, Evan could not guess. Finally, Valac let the dead man's body descend to the crimson-stained floor. Gore spattered his face and hands, and blood soaked his robes. With a whisper, Valac extinguished the candles and dulled the brilliance of the chalked circle to plain white pigment once more. He smudged the circle open with the toe of his shoe and strode out.

Valac stood in front of Evan, breathless and flushed from the infusion of stolen energy. "That was only a glimpse of the power that awaits the true sacrifice. Your blood is so much more potent. I will offer you up, and unlock my portion of the master's power and I will live forever."

Any response Evan might have made died in his tight throat and dry mouth. The power holding him against the wall winked out, and he fell with a crash, stunned and bruised. When he tried to get his feet under himself, he found the sharp point of Valac's curved blade beneath his chin. "You're not going anywhere, boy. I have plans for you."

Evan came up from the floor with a roar. He slammed into Valac, and they rolled back over the smudged circle, into the cooling puddle of blood. Evan fought for all he was worth, striking out with fists and feet, but every time he struck, thin air met his blow. Fighting Valac was like wrestling with smoke. In the next instant, Valac had him by the throat, lifting him off the blood-soaked floor effortlessly and nearly strangling him in the process. He tossed Evan away as if he weighed nothing.

Valac turned to Jackie. "Get him in the car. It's time to go to the shrine."

19

SETH

Seth parked the truck a block away from Hollywood Cemetery and walked the rest of the way. The gates were closed, which meant fewer chances for anyone to disturb his work. Seth spoke the opening spell and slipped inside. He knew the way now, even in the dark. If any of the cemetery's famous ghosts walked abroad, they had best leave him the hell alone, Seth thought, his jaw set in a grim expression. He had work to do, and not much time remaining.

The Pool mausoleum looked like a dark maw opening into the hillside. Seth opened the gratings and doors with a muttered word, bringing Valac's element back to its hiding place. This had to work; he told himself as he laid the brass cylinder on the floor in a bed of C4 one of Toby's contacts had supplied before Seth headed to Richmond. If plastic explosives in a contained blast didn't destroy the anchor, then nothing humanly possible would, short of that nuclear blast Toby joked about.

He sank the detonators and ran for cover, making sure to close the solid steel door behind him. A downward slope and dry ditch protected him as he pressed the button. Seconds later, the sound of an explosion echoed across the cemetery grounds, with a flare of light from beneath the door and a growing wreath of smoke surrounding the newly fractured stone entranceway as the ceiling tumbled in, burying the evidence of what he'd done.

Seth didn't wait to find out whether the blast drew attention. He scrambled out of the ditch, ran for the cemetery gates, and in minutes pulled the truck from its hiding place as if nothing had happened. The rapid beating of his heart assured him otherwise, as did the cold sweat on his back and his moist palms.

"Any explosion you can walk away from is a good explosion," he muttered, quoting his sergeant. If the Richmond Vampire really did make his home in the mausoleum, he'd have to find somewhere else to haunt.

The drive to find Evan's duffel seemed to take forever, although only a few miles separated the cemetery and the location of the tracker. Seth slowed as the pulsing circle on the map grew closer, looking from one side to the other for any likely places where Valac might stash a prisoner.

The beeping shrilled, and seconds later, fell off to a dull blip, telling Seth he'd passed the tracker.

"That can't be right." He did a U-turn and moved at nearly idling speed down the same stretch of road. The GPS led him to a warehouse district that had yet to feel the effects of gentrification. Instead, it offered huge featureless box-shaped buildings and acres of parking lots. None of them looked right for Valac's grand ritual.

Once more, the tracker's beep crescendoed and then fell away, forcing Seth to turn around again. This time, he kept his foot off the gas, letting the truck creep forward ever-so-slowly until the squeal reached its ear-splitting apex.

"There's nothing here," Seth argued with the empty passenger seat. "I don't get it."

Then he spotted a dark lump tossed near a rusty pole holding up a sign for a long-defunct diner. Seth got out of the truck warily, gun in hand, advancing. He knew as soon as he saw the duffel up close that it belonged to Evan, from the patch on one side to the odd pattern of stains in the middle. Seth poked it gingerly with the toe of his boot, expecting a booby trap, but when nothing happened, he jerked open the zipper and found only Evan's neatly folded clothing.

"Fuck!" Seth shouted into the night. He stamped his boot and turned in a circle, trying to make sense of the bag's location. It looked like Valac had just dumped it to throw him off the trail, and Seth had to admit that was probably what happened.

"Son of a bloody bastard, I'm going to kill you double for that," Seth growled. He grabbed the bag and tossed it in the back of the pickup, then sat in the driver's seat, trying to figure his next move.

Somewhere out there, Evan was the prisoner of a serial killer. Seth had an hour to find him.

The shopping mall or the old house? Seth debated between the two, and couldn't shake the feeling that whatever Valac's original plan might have been, the shopping mall now came under too much scrutiny. It also felt wrong, from what little Seth had learned of magic. A big public place dispersed energy when a witch would want to concentrate power for a major ritual. No matter who owned the mall, it lacked personal history and resonance.

Betting Evan's life on a hunch, Seth headed for the old house.

He cruised past the darkened building twice before parking his truck down the block and heading back on foot. Seth kept his Beretta in one hand and a knife in the other, and prayed he didn't run into a real cop.

At this time of night, the neighborhood lay silent and dark. Seth kept to the shadows to reach the kitchen door and felt his heart sink when he saw it hanging open.

Moving carefully, Seth sheathed the knife and entered holding his gun and flashlight in front of him as he swept the kitchen, tensed to react to an attack. Nothing but silence met his entrance. When he and Evan had searched the house, the air smelled musty and stale. Now, Seth smelled candle smoke, sweat…and blood.

He pivoted into the doorway to the living room, ready to fire. Nothing moved. His light caught a slumped figure on the floor. Seth stepped closer cautiously, alert for a trap. His heart sped up as he took in the ritual trappings, recently used and abandoned. Valac had been here, not long ago.

In the center of the smudged circle lay a still form, lying in a pool of blood.

Evan? No. God, that can't be. No, please.

Seth crossed to kneel next to the body. The blood beneath it hadn't had time yet to congeal, and the corpse rolled over with a loose-limbed sprawl that told Seth death hadn't yet stiffened the muscles. He held his breath, feeling his heart stutter and his stomach knot as he raised the flashlight to see the dead man's face.

Not Evan.

Seth's rapid breaths sounded loud in the silent room as he reined in both relief and fresh panic.

The bloody body wasn't Evan. Evan could still be alive. Seth still had time to save him. But if Evan wasn't here, then where the hell was he?

Seth stared at the remnants of the dark magic ritual, wracking his brain for ideas. A glance at the blood-soaked corpse raised the fleeting idea that the victim looked like a vampire's leftovers.

The Richmond Vampire.

Seth took one last look around the murder scene for anything he might be able to use against Valac, then headed back to the truck as quickly as stealth allowed. He tried to remember what Evan had told him that first day at Hollywood Cemetery, something about the Pool mausoleum, and a man with his skin hanging off because he'd just come from a deadly train wreck.

Just like the legend of the wreck at the Hell Gate back in Indiana.

Seth did a quick search on his phone, his fingers clumsy with fear as he tried to type. The Church Hill Tunnel wreck. Where the fuck was what remained of that damned tunnel?

"C'mon, load already!" Seth swore as his phone retrieved the website. He scanned down through the information until he found what he wanted. The center of the tunnel collapsed onto the train, trapping several workers. One end of the tunnel had been sealed with heavy wooden doors, and a patio for a trendy apartment building ran right up to that portal to hell. The other end remained open for quite a ways until the tunnel reached the concrete wall erected to shore up the damaged ceiling. That end lay neglected in a gully, overgrown with vegetation, safeguarded only by a broken chain-link fence.

A legendary wreck and a death toll. Bodies never recovered, giving rise to trapped spirits. Stories about strange noises coming from the tunnel on Halloween. A bloodied man seen leaving the scene of the wreck and said to take refuge in the Pool mausoleum.

"Shit. I've got to find the east end of that damned tunnel," Seth muttered. "That's where he's going to kill Evan." He set his map and sped off into the night, praying that this time he wouldn't be too late.

20

EVAN

"Where the hell are we?" Riding in the trunk of Jackie's old Ford Taurus left Evan disoriented and short of breath. His wrists were handcuffed, and rope hobbled his feet. Back at the house, he and Valac had rolled in the vagrant's blood. It streaked his skin, stiffened his clothing and stank like a slaughterhouse. The two goons manhandled him out of the trunk, and Evan fixed them with a deadly glare.

"We're here," Jackie replied. "That's all you need to know." She had parked the car on the side of the road beside a deep ravine. Evan could make out little else since the nearest streetlight wasn't working.

"Come on," one of the goons growled, taking hold of Evan's left arm with an iron grip, while the other guard grabbed his right. He fought them, twisting to break their hold, slamming his body into first one and then the other to push his way clear, shouting at the top of his lungs to attract attention should any cars pass by.

Evan managed to break their grip and went stumbling down the shoulder of the road, yelling for help. The rope trammeled his steps, making his gait short and awkward, and his cuffed wrists kept his arms at his sides, throwing him off balance.

The rebellion ended before he'd gotten more than a few car lengths away. A heavy weight sent Evan crashing to the ground, pinned beneath the bulk of one of Valac's goons. He could barely breathe, and his head slammed against the side of the road. The large man rolled off of him, grinding his knee into the small of Evan's back for good measure, and then he and his partner hauled Evan roughly to his feet and gave him a shove in the direction they'd come from.

"Try that again, and I'll make sure you stay wide awake and completely paralyzed," Jackie hissed. "It's so much more satisfying when you can move and scream, but the ritual only requires consciousness." Evan had never noticed the hard set to Jackie's mouth or the utter coldness in her eyes. *She's a fucking great actress, and she suckered me one hundred percent.*

The two goons frog-marched him down a barely visible trail descending the steep bank, into an urban tangle of trees, scrub plants, brush, and garbage. Evan tried to figure out the location and drew a blank. He heard the rumble of cars going by from nearby streets and the distant whistle of a freight train. Yet this neglected ravine didn't belong to any park Evan knew about, and he suspected they hadn't traveled far enough from the old house to have gone beyond the Richmond city limits.

Jackie led the way with a flashlight that had a green filter over the lens to dim the brightness. The guards had similarly fitted lights to help them find the path. Evan stumbled as his foot caught on vines and branches. His captors jerked him up, dragging him down the muddy trail toward the bottom of the hillside. They struggled along, fighting their way through overgrowth as well as the litter of old tires, plastic grocery bags, discarded boxes, and junked appliances.

Evan's eyes widened as they paused with their destination in sight. A stone arch stood in front of them, an open maw leading into darkness. Water trickled down the floor of the ravine, forming a shallow stream that led into the tunnel. A broken chain-link fence failed to keep out trespassers, twisted and cut by thrill seekers and urban explorers.

Finally Evan realized where he was, though he'd only ever seen it in photographs. He stood in front of the east end of the infamous Church Hill Tunnel, a tomb for the men whose bodies remained unclaimed from the 1925 cave-in, and the rumored hiding place of the Richmond Vampire. He looked from the dark tunnel entrance to Valac in his blood-soaked robe and felt his gut twist as he realized that the legend was more true than not.

How many of his Malone ancestors met their death inside that tunnel? Were the spirits of his uncle and his other murdered relatives still trapped here, or did Valac's ritual steal both life and soul?

The wet ground squelched beneath their feet as they entered the abandoned tunnel. Evan never credited himself with any kind of psychic ability, but the deeper they went into the darkness of the east entrance, the more he swore he could feel the press of spirits. He remembered the nearly fatal battle at the pump house and shivered.

Seth had gotten them out of the pump house with nothing more than bruises to show for it. But Seth wasn't here, and he wasn't coming. Evan felt his heart break all over again at the thought, but he pushed the pain away, trying to stay focused. What would Seth do in this situation? Evan might not have Seth's army training, or his years preparing to fight a supernatural foe, but he'd always prided himself at being quick-witted and fast on his feet. If he could somehow stop Valac, make the ritual fail, maybe he could escape and live to take up the fight in Seth's name, to keep more of the descendants of the long-ago deputies from dying young and bloody.

They kept on walking, and by the time Evan reckoned they had covered nearly half a football field, the filtered glow of the flashlights revealed a cement wall blocking the rest of the tunnel. Behind that barrier, entombed forever beneath a cave-in of rock and dirt, were the unlucky railroad men and the mangled remains of the train that would remain trapped inside the tunnel for eternity.

A slab of concrete sat in the middle of the space like a cement altar. Jackie took candles and other trappings from a bag she'd carried from the car, preparing for the ritual. The concrete barrier was far enough from the fenced entrance, no one would come back here to see them, and the moisture in the air would erase the marks before long, leaving no trace of yet another ritual murder. The two goons kept Evan pinned between them, standing off to one side while Valac began to chant once more. His voice carried in the darkness, echoing from the stone walls.

Though he had no magic of his own, Evan felt power rising, like the shift before a storm or the primitive uneasiness of being near a lightning strike. He had no idea how long remained before midnight, but Valac was preparing to work his magic, summoning energy to him, just as Jackie readied the space that would become the scene for the ritual—and the last place Evan would ever see.

Valac gave a sudden cry of pain and clutched his chest, sinking to his knees. The goons on either side of Evan started to move toward him, but Jackie held up a hand in warning. "Stay where you are!" She ordered. This version of "Jackie" had none of the bar server's college student hesitancy. Every word radiated confidence and control. The Jersey accent was gone, and now that her true nature was revealed, the black Bettie Page bob and red lips looked more vampire than vamp.

Evan wondered if he could be lucky enough to have Valac keel over from a heart attack. He doubted fate would be so kind. From where he stood, he saw Valac trembling, gasping for breath, though he kept Jackie at a distance with a malevolent glare and an outstretched hand. Apparently, Evan thought, Valac didn't trust his second-in-command too close when he was vulnerable.

"Go on with the preparations," Valac insisted. "This is nothing, nothing that matters."

"We can wait—"

"I said, go on!" Valac snapped. "Time is running short."

Whatever had happened it didn't seem to be part of the magic, and Valac didn't intend to share with the class. But despite his protests, it wasn't "nothing." Evan could see that, and he felt certain Jackie could, too. Valac appeared to have aged a decade, suddenly haggard and wan. He rose to his feet, but he moved with the caution of an old man instead of the vigor of the age his magically-preserved body appeared.

Is this what happens the closer he gets to midnight? He starts to show his true age until the ritual gives him back his immortality?

Another possibility occurred to Evan, but he was afraid to let himself believe it. *What if Seth found the anchor and destroyed the element?* He believed that Valac had left a bomb. But they'd been long gone by the time Seth came back to the trailer. Could Valac know for certain that Seth was dead, or did he toss out that barb to break Evan? Part of Evan dared hope, though after the way he took off and the note he left, he'd burned that bridge, no matter how much he regretted it. The idea of Seth still alive gave him a reason to fight, even if he'd given up his chance for a relationship with the damn note he'd written. *Just please, let Seth be alive. Even if I can't keep him, let him live.*

Evan's mind raced, trying to figure out how he might take advantage of Valac's unexpected weakness. He leaned back against the rough rock wall, scraping the lock on his cuffs against a sharp stone.

Jackie had laid out a large circle around the altar, using a long braided rope instead of chalking lines or laying down a stream of salt. The rope held strands of differing colors and materials, and along its length, small charms were tied in with strands of hair and sinew. Next, she arranged candles at the quarter points, but these also looked different from what was used at the old house. The yellowish tallow was laced with darker veins of something that looked like blood. Evan did not dare to wonder what had gone into the making.

Valac chanted once more, but his voice sounded strained and thin, and he had to pause to gasp for breath. At the house, he'd stood straight and tall, his movements powerful and his attitude cocky. Now his steps faltered, and while the look on his face radiated indomitable will, he seemed smaller, weakened, and worried. Valac paused three times as he walked counter-clockwise around the altar to chalk sigils on the walls.

Jackie withdrew small items from a box carved with runes. Evan gasped as he realized what she held. Wristwatches, pocket watches, and wallets—trophies from the Malone men Valac killed down through the years. Jackie murmured her own incantation as she placed the items at the cross-quarters between the candles. Nine stolen trophies—and Evan's wallet would make it ten—souvenirs of lives lost and futures stolen.

The cuffs chafed against Evan's wrists, as he tried to free his hands. Both guards gripped his arms, and with his ankles hobbled, making a run for the far-off tunnel entrance was doomed to fail, let alone trying to scrabble up the embankment and hail a passing car before being caught.

If his hands had been bound in front of him, Evan could have used his joined fists to strike at his captors or grab rocks to throw. Cuffed behind him, he had few options. He shuddered when Valac turned his dark gaze in his direction.

"Bring him. It's time."

Evan had always heard about someone's life flashing in front of their eyes. He had few regrets, not even about severing ties with his family if it meant he could be true to himself. But when Evan thought back to the last time he saw Seth, to their argument and his harsh words, and the note he'd left behind, he felt a weight in his heart. In just four days, Evan had learned Seth was someone special, that the spark between them was rare and to be treasured. Yet he'd let his ego and anger get in the way, and lost everything.

Unbidden, that stupid song from the movie Seth hated came to mind, sad and bittersweet. "I'll always love you, too," Evan murmured. Maybe it wouldn't have worked between them, perhaps Seth's quest or Evan's insecurities would have torn them apart. Still...if he hadn't acted in anger and fallen for Valac's fake cop routine, he might be safe in the trailer right now, and Seth might be alive.

"I'm sorry," he whispered, although he knew Seth couldn't hear him. "I'm so sorry."

The goons hustled Evan toward the warded circle. Jackie watched with hunger in her gaze, and he wondered what Valac had promised her. "He'll betray you, Jackie," Evan said as he resisted the goon's pressure to hurry him forward.

"Shut up."

"Did he tell you you're special? And you believed him?" Evan baited. "He needs an assistant for his magic tricks, but how long do you think you'll last once he's leveled up? You know too much. He's going to ditch his cop ID like a snake sheds skin, and he won't want people around who could blow his cover. You think he's going to leave loose ends?"

"I said, shut up!" She snarled and took a step toward him. Valac raised a hand, and Jackie flew backward against the wall.

"Do not interfere," Valac warned. He turned back to the guards. "Bring him."

"What about it, Vinnie?" Jackie challenged, using Valac/Clark's most recent first name. "I've done everything you said—now I want what you promised me. I want a piece of the power."

"You'll get what you deserve," Valac snapped.

"I don't like the way that sounds," Jackie argued, getting to her feet and squaring her shoulders. "You need me."

"And once the ritual is complete, I will reward you," Valac promised. "You have served me well. Do this last thing, and I will give you everything you desire."

Evan knew that look on Jackie's face; he'd seen it often enough when she argued with Liam at Treddy's over her shift hours.

"How do I know you'll keep your part of the bargain?" Jackie retorted. "I did what you told me. I kept an eye on him. You *owe* me."

Evan saw the look that crossed Valac's face, even if Jackie didn't. Maybe he wasn't going to kill her as soon as Evan's death sealed the twelve-year deal. But now, she'd become a liability, and Evan felt certain that Valac wasn't one to leave bad behavior go unpunished.

"You've done it now," Evan goaded, drawing on what he knew of Jackie's vulnerabilities from working together at the bar. "He's been using you. Gonna toss you aside. They all do, once they get what they want. Thought you'd have learned by now." Normally, he'd never be that cruel. But Jackie was onboard with Evan being mutilated and bled dry, and that pissed him off royally.

"Shut your mouth. You're wrong."

Jackie had always been insecure, covering her lack of confidence with bravado, too easily swayed by men who complimented her looks and intelligence. Maybe it was part of her act, but seeing how she'd fallen in with Valac, Evan suspected that part of her personality was real. A few muttered comments after one drink too many suggested an absent father and a desperate desire for approval. Maybe it was playing dirty pool, but Evan wasn't above exploiting that weakness if it meant stopping a serial killer and saving his life.

"C'mon, Jackie. Can't you see it? He's using you—just like the others did."

"I said, shut up!" Jackie started toward Evan, one hand raised with her fingers curled like claws, ready to rake her nails across his skin.

"That's enough!" Valac roared, in a commanding tone that brought Jackie up short. "Do not forget our bargain."

Jackie paled, and the fight went out of her. "I'm sorry, master. Forgive me."

What hold did Valac have on her? Evan wondered. Maybe the witch had promised to help her get out of her crushing student loans, or find a job in her field when she graduated, or take vengeance on someone who'd hurt her. Evan guessed Jackie had made a desperate bargain, and now she found herself trapped in Valac's web.

"Help me," Evan said, meeting Jackie's gaze. "We were friends at Treddy's. He's going to kill me. Do you want that on your conscience?" Evan dug his heels in, fighting the guards with all his strength, letting his full weight hang in their grip to stall being gutted on that altar. "You know he's going to frame you for killing me."

"You don't know—" Jackie bit off the last of what she started to say, and Evan saw naked fear in her eyes. Just as quickly, her expression shuttered. "That won't work on me. Sorry." Her tone suggested she was anything but.

"I'm sorry too," Evan replied. The guards pushed him to the edge of the warded circle. Even without magic, Evan could sense power thrumming through the braided coil, just like he could feel the watchful gaze of the spirits trapped against their will in the dark tomb of the tunnel.

"You're out of time," Valac said, smiling a rictus grin. Invisible hands seized Evan and hauled him over the edge of the warding as if he weighed nothing, slamming him down on the altar with enough force to make him gasp for breath and send his vision spinning.

"Time to join your relatives," Valac said, drawing the curved blade from the recesses of his blood-soaked robe. "Make your peace. Your time is up."

21

SETH

LESS THAN AN HOUR UNTIL MIDNIGHT.

Seth had to believe that the explosion back at the Pool mausoleum had destroyed the element part of Valac's anchor. But even weakened, Valac would be a formidable enemy. Seth's magic would be no match, so he needed backup.

He parked the truck just beyond the bend on East Franklin Street at 31st, where he found another car nosed off onto the shoulder of the road. Just in case it was Valac's, he let the air out of the tires of the parked car—although he didn't intend for Valac and his helpers to get away. Seth pulled out his gear, including a sniper rifle, night vision goggles, and a few special surprises.

He eyed the ravine his map said led to what remained of the east end of the Church Hill Tunnel. The overgrown slope presented a tangle of brush and a dangerous mix of urban trash. Before he headed into the lair of the witch-disciple, he had to call in the cavalry.

Seth knelt next to the truck, shielded from the view of any passersby. He pulled out the silver bowl and knife he had used at the Boyd Park pump house, made a shallow cut on his arm, and dripped blood into the vessel. He spoke the incantation and projected his will, hoping that the spirits would hear him and answer.

When he opened his eyes, they stood before him, gray shapes against the night. Three men dressed like railroad workers from nearly a century ago, and nine men whose features held an unmistakable resemblance to Evan—the Malone sacrifices.

"I'm here to stop the killing," Seth said quietly to the ghosts. "He's going to murder Evan Malone tonight if we don't stop him." He looked to the ghosts of Valac's victims. "Evan's one of yours. I have to save him. And I need your help."

The ghosts did not vanish, and Seth took that as a good sign. "I'm going to need a distraction," Seth said. "I can't take them all on at once. Anything you can do to keep Valac and his goons busy so they can't finish the ritual or focus on me will help. You'll save Evan—and others," he added, thinking of Valac's casual sacrifices, like the man in the old house and the ghosts at the mall, as well as future generations of Malones. "Please, you're the only chance I've got. Just wait for my word."

One of the spirits stepped forward. He wore clothing from the early 1900s and had the gruff look of a lawman. Seth wondered whether he was the original Malone deputy who had helped to destroy Rhyfel Gremory. The deputy fixed Seth with a piercing gaze, then slowly nodded. He turned back to the others, and the ghosts disappeared. Seth could only hope that meant he'd gotten himself a posse.

Even with the night vision goggles, descending the steep slope was hellish, a tangle of brambles and vines that tugged at Seth's feet and snagged at skin and clothing. Yet he could tell that others had come this way not long before from fresh footprints in the mud and the broken and trampled vegetation. Whoever had followed this path hadn't taken any care for stealth, lumbering through the underbrush and in places cutting the trail clear. That made it possible for Seth to move quickly and quietly, closing in on his quarry.

Was Evan still alive? It wasn't quite midnight, but maybe Valac had rushed the ritual. Seth couldn't help thinking of Jesse, and his mind supplied Evan's face on Jesse's mangled corpse. He pushed the image away, trying to ignore his fear and the pain in his chest at the thought that he might be too late.

Seth knew that with the way they'd left things between them, Evan wasn't likely to want to continue their budding relationship. That hurt, but at least Evan would be alive, able to go on with his life, as Seth returned to his quest. Saving the lives of the other deputies' descendants was a worthwhile purpose, and maybe even suitable atonement, but it no longer felt like enough without Evan beside him.

He couldn't afford to let feelings get in the way, not now, not when the enemy was so close. Seth let himself drop back into soldier-mode, emptying his mind of distractions, seeking clear, cold focus. He readied his rifle and made certain the other weapons he brought were handy. Without any way to be sure of how many goons Valac had with him, Seth didn't know exactly what obstacles awaited. He had a little magic, a lot of bullets, and a rickety plan. Would it be enough?

Seth had spent less than ten minutes scanning through what he could find about the east entrance to the Church Hill Tunnel online. Once he passed the fence, he'd have to trek one hundred and fifty yards inside the tunnel to get to where the passage was sealed, moving through mud or shallow water, with no cover. Seth thought about several distraction spells and illusion cantrips he'd learned, but while they might keep him from being noticed by someone without magic, he worried that the spells themselves might draw Valac's attention.

Seth returned to his Special Ops training. He wore all-black, with a black beanie to cover his hair and charcoal smudged on his cheeks to help him blend into the shadows. Just in case, a Kevlar vest beneath his jacket offered extra protection against everything but magic. The night vision goggles gave his surroundings a greenish hue, and helped him navigate around the debris that littered the tunnel entrance and the stones that had fallen from the ceiling, a reminder that the passageway was not really stable.

As he closed the distance, he made out light toward the back of the tunnel, where it should have been the darkest. Seth moved with a predator's grace, fixed on his quarry. The ground next to the sides of the tunnel was firm and dry, and he could move without the suck and slap of thick mud clinging to his boots.

Finally, shadowy figures came into view. Seth drew his rifle and moved into position. He could see Valac, dressed in a hooded robe like the villain from a late night low-budget horror flick. An unnatural light radiated from the floor of the tunnel near where Valac stood, and Seth spotted a raised platform. A woman who looked vaguely familiar served as acolyte, and two muscular thugs stood guard. He strained to see Evan. The two goons moved in tandem toward Valac, and Seth caught a glimpse of another figure between them.

Shit. He couldn't get a shot at the guards without risking Evan.

"Now," he whispered, hoping the ghosts were listening.

A cold wind swept down the length of the tunnel toward its end, and Seth shrank against the side to avoid notice. The autumn night grew frigid, and the temperature plummeted enough that fingers of frost formed rapidly down the moist tunnel walls. The gust carried dirt and loose papers with it, whipping up a small storm that howled down the dark passageway like a ghost train.

Seth smiled when one of the goons screamed like a little girl.

He sighted the rifle, waiting for his chance.

The spirits took shape as they reached the ritual altar, shrieking and keening, swirling around the dark witch who caused their deaths and fed off their misery. The woman shoved Evan toward Valac, who pulled him inside the glowing circle. Before she could join them, the circle flared, and an iridescent, shimmering curtain of energy rose from the markings, cutting off Valac and Evan from the woman and the guards.

Two shots, and the guards fell dead. Before Seth could get the woman in his sights, she sent an arc of power lancing toward him, lighting up the tunnel like daylight. Seth dove and rolled, narrowly evading the strike that sent up a shower of dirt and mud where it struck.

"Stop her!" Seth murmured to the ghosts. The woman—he recognized her now as Jackie from Treddy's—was a distraction, but Valac had Evan inside the circle and was minutes away from completing the ritual. Seth could not, would not come so far only to fail now.

The spirits gathered around Jackie, a swirling maelstrom of ghostly faces and gray spectral shapes. A thin skin of ice formed over the shallow water and wet mud in the center where the train tracks once ran. Jackie shouted a word of power, and a blast of blue light flared around her, scattering the revenants as she fixed her attention on Seth.

Seth moved into position and aimed. A disembodied force yanked the rifle out of his hands and sent it spinning away into the darkness. Blue lightning arced toward him, and Seth threw himself out of the way, then pulled a homemade flash bang grenade from his pocket, jerked the pin and lobbed it at Jackie before he hit the ground. Seth covered his head with his arms, squeezing his eyes shut. Even so, he glimpsed the flare and heard the deafening boom.

Training won out over instinct as Seth scrambled for his feet and ran straight for Jackie. He tossed a handful of gravel into the air, spoke the spell, and sent a hail of rocks pelting at the witch-disciple's acolyte before she could regroup.

Seth risked a glance into the protected circle. Evan was alive, covered in blood, and struggling against Valac, who held a vicious-looking curved knife. Seth's momentary distraction gave Jackie her chance, and she sprang for him with a blade of her own raised for the kill. The knife hit Seth square in the chest, and momentum took them both to the floor. He felt the strength behind the blow, but the Kevlar kept the point from piercing skin. Jackie screamed in fury when she realized she had not made a killing strike, and clawed at Seth with her nails, scratching his face and drawing blood.

Valac's chant rose above the noise of their struggle. The ghosts tried to cross the shimmering barrier, but its energy repelled them, leaving Evan inside, trapped with a desperate killer.

Seth kept his grip on Jackie and rolled, grabbing for the gun in his waistband as Jackie marshaled her magic for a deadly spell. She spoke the first of the words of power, and Seth brought the gun up between them and fired.

The sound of the shot echoed through the tunnel, as Jackie slumped. Seth scrambled back from her body and turned toward the shimmering curtain of the warded circle.

Valac's chant had reached a crescendo, and as Seth watched in horror, a third shape took form, more shadow than substance, but growing darker and more solid with each word of the litany Valac recited.

Valac called to the wraith of his dead master, and the twisted spirit of Rhyfel Gremory answered, come to share a measure of his power to renew Valac's immortality. Evan's blood would be the conduit, the currency that bought Valac's renewal and sated Gremory's beyond-the-grave bloodlust.

Seth threw himself at the curtain, only to be thrown back, his whole body tingling like he'd touched a live wire. He fired at Valac and fell to the ground to avoid the ricochet as his bullet failed to pierce the barrier. Evan had little room to maneuver, with his hands cuffed and his ankles hobbled, but he fought Valac with everything he had, twisting out of reach, bucking and kicking to keep that deadly blade away.

Seth had one chance left, slim and unlikely. "Be ready," he murmured to the ghosts. "Evan!" He shouted, and in the next breath, spoke the unlocking spell, focusing all his limited magic on the handcuffs and rope.

The bonds fell away, and Evan lurched to his feet. He grabbed the amulet that hung from Valac's neck, pulling hard enough to snap it from its strap.

Valac swung his blade as Evan dove through the coruscating light, kicking at the rope circle. Seth scrambled to catch him before he hit the ground, and pulled him close protectively, tucking him against his left side as he held his Beretta aimed at the two figures inside the warding.

Valac shrieked in fury and started to cross the circle. But Gremory's specter stretched out an impossibly long, thin arm and caught his failed disciple by the throat. As Seth and Evan watched in horror, Gremory's ghostly fingers sank through Valac's neck, until he held the warlock by the spine. With the amulet's protection gone and the circle's warding broken, the ghosts descended on both witches, ready to take their long-overdue vengeance.

"Run!" Seth grabbed Evan's wrist and took off toward the mouth of the tunnel, unwilling to see what happened next between the dark witch and his dead master. He reached into his pocket, pulled out the IED Valac had planted beneath his truck and flung it as hard as he could, aiding its course with a spell. As they reached the tunnel entrance, he set off the trigger with a word of magic.

"Down!" Seth pushed Evan ahead of him, then fell on top to shield him with his body, hoping the Kevlar would protect him from the blast. He wrapped his arms over his head and pressed his face against Evan's neck.

"I love you," he whispered, as the tunnel exploded behind them in a roar like an avalanche, and the improvised bomb finished the job begun by the long-ago collapse.

22

EVAN

Evan and Seth staggered up the muddy slope, slipping and sliding and holding each other up. Evan's ears rang from the explosion, his lungs burned from the cloud of stone dust, and his heart hadn't stopped thudding.

Seth never let go of him. When they reached the top of the ravine, Seth pushed him against the truck and kissed him, hard, leaning against Evan, bodies pressing from lips to toes. Seth's mouth plundered his, desperate and hungry, seeking and affirming. Evan could feel Seth's hard cock through his jeans, rubbing against his own arousal.

"I thought I lost you," Seth murmured, pulling away at the sound of distant sirens. "Come back with me, please."

Evan grabbed the back of Seth's head and pulled him in for another kiss, hoping his lips got across the message he wasn't sure his brain could put into words right now. "Yes. Oh God, yes."

They climbed into the truck and Seth hit the accelerator, making sure they were long gone before the cops arrived. Seth's hand slipped across the seat, seeking Evan's, twining their fingers together, as if he were afraid Evan would disappear if he let go.

Evan's mind rebelled against the enormity of what had just happened back in the tunnel, how close he'd come to death, the unexpected rescue, and the horror of coming face to face with both Valac and Gremory's wraiths within the circle. He knew there'd been more to the fight than he'd seen since his own attention had been focused on keeping clear of Valac's blade. But one thing seared with clarity in his mind; the moment Seth sheltered him with his body and told Evan he loved him.

"I'm sorry," Evan said quietly. Seth did not turn his head, keeping his eyes on the road, but his shoulders tensed, although he did not withdraw his hand. "I'm sorry about the note, about leaving, about not believing. I fucked the whole thing up."

He drew a deep breath and had to look away, staring at the night through the windshield. "I thought you were dead," he added, his voice barely audible above the rumble of the engine. "Valac told me he'd rigged the truck."

"He did. Lucky for me, I found it."

Evan shivered, realizing how close a call they'd had. "I didn't think anyone was coming for me," Evan got out, licking his dry lips, forcing himself to keep talking before he lost his nerve. He'd made such a mess of everything, and if it all went to hell, he needed to say what was on his mind.

"I didn't really believe the whole magic thing until I saw it. Now… yeah, it skews my world, but I get it. And I'm sorry it took me so long. I'm sorry I let you down. You were trying to protect me, and I got in the way." He bit his lip, trying to figure out how to make Seth understand, knowing that words came easier in the confessional darkness of a car at night on the highway. Spoken in bed—assuming Seth still wanted him—words were suspect. Evan had to make sure Seth knew the truth, in case he didn't have another chance to say what was in his heart.

"I realized how I felt, when I thought you were dead," Evan continued in a quiet voice. "And I know this thing between us is new and all sorts of crazy, but…I want to make it work. I want to be with you, help you. Watch your back. I knew that I loved you from how much it hurt to think I'd lost you."

Seth remained a silent statue, one hand tight on the wheel, eyes fixed on the road.

"Umm...say something? Kinda dangling in the wind here," Evan said added nervously.

Seth pulled into the farm lane, slowing as they approached the trailer. Finally, he turned to Evan, his face a contrast in light and dark in the glow of the dashboard.

"We're here. We're alive. Let's get cleaned up, and then I want to confirm that we're both still breathing by fucking you into the mattress. We'll deal with the rest tomorrow."

Seth kept his fingers laced with Evan's as they locked the truck, stowed the weapons, and staggered into the trailer. As soon as the door shut behind them, Seth pushed Evan up against it, reaching around him to throw the bolt, and trapping Evan between his arms as he went in for a deep kiss.

"You scared me," Seth admitted, and the low rumble of his voice went right to Evan's cock. "I was afraid I wasn't going to get there in time. I only figured out where you were at the very last. And I had next to no plan for what to do. But I wasn't going to let that bastard take you away from me."

Evan stretched up for another kiss, tasting ash and blood and Seth. He brought his hands up, cupping Seth's face, and let his fingers slide down to find reassurance in the throb of Seth's pulse and the warmth of his skin. When he finally pulled back, they were both breathless. Seth's brown eyes were dark with desire. Evan took one look at his lips, swollen from kisses, and went painfully hard thinking about that mouth around his cock.

"Shower. You stink like blood, and I smell like cordite," Seth said with a smirk. "Go."

Evan hoped Seth might join him in the shower, but had to admit he needed more than a quick rinse to get all the blood and dirt out of his hair and pores. He yelled out to Seth to let him know when the shower was free and toweled off in the bedroom, then crawled onto the bed and waited.

Minutes later, Seth appeared in the doorway, skin still glistening with droplets, and a towel loosely canted across his hips, doing nothing to hide the erection beneath.

"God, I want you," Evan breathed. "Get over here and fuck me. Don't make me beg."

Seth dropped the towel, and Evan let his eyes roam down the muscles of Seth's broad shoulders and chest, the washboard abs, strong thighs, and thick, hard cock standing proud against his belly. It was the kind of body that came from hard work, not a gym, and it made Evan's mouth water.

"Fuck, you're beautiful," Seth said, eyeing Evan's naked body.

Evan spread his legs, exposing himself, and dropped a hand to languidly stroke up and down his length, smearing the pearl of pre-come at the tip. "Gonna look all night, or do something about it?"

Seth dove onto the bed, crawling up between Evan's legs, and the look in his eyes reminded Evan of a starving animal. His hands seemed to be everywhere, combing through Evan's dark hair, caressing his jaw, sliding a calloused hand across his chest. He pinned Evan beneath his taller, broader body, licking and nipping, diving in for a kiss and exploring Evan's mouth with his tongue, and then tasting his way down over the sensitive skin of his ear, the hollow of his throat, the curve of his shoulder.

Evan ran his hands down Seth's strong back, braced Seth's hips with his own thighs drawn up in an open, wonton invitation. He took in the smell and taste of Seth, reveling in the heat of his body and the strength of his arms. Evan arched his back and bared his throat, offering himself, begging to be claimed.

Seth growled and sucked a mark on the juncture where Evan's neck met his shoulder, leaving a bruise as proof that they were here, together. He laved the bite with his tongue, easing the sting, then moved down Evan's writhing body, sucking his nipples into tight buds, teasing down his stomach to make the muscles tighten, and then lower, drawing moans and pleas from Evan's mouth.

"Please, Seth. I need you in me. I need to feel you, so I know we're both still here." Evan slipped his fingers through Seth's short hair, tugging gently to get his point across as Seth chuckled. His breath ghosted over Evan's inner thigh, making him shiver.

"Need it too. Need you. So much." Seth's whispers were barely loud enough to be heard, but they made Evan's heart clench.

Almost dying heightened every sensation, riding the line between pleasure and pain. Seth's hands ghosted along Evan's body like an act of worship, sliding down his thighs, cupping his ass, wrapping around his cock and giving a couple of slides before his mouth took over, swallowing Evan down to the root.

Evan fought not to fuck Seth's mouth, as those plump lips closed around his prick and his tongue swirled over the sensitive head, lapping up the pre-come and then tracing the veins along the hard shaft. Seth's hand slid down below as Evan spread his thighs in wordless invitation. The scrape of Seth's calloused palm over his sensitive sac had Evan nearly whimpering with sensation. Seth bobbed up and down, taking his time, sucking and teasing, as his hand cupped and rolled, gently tugging. Seth pulled off, and his tongue moved lower, its tip sliding down Evan's taint to his hole.

Seth spread Evan's thighs over his shoulders and began to rim him in earnest, alternating the broad flat of his tongue with the delicious torture of the thin tip, and then finally bringing up a spit-slick finger to press into the tight furl as Evan gave a groan of encouragement.

After a moment, Seth added another finger, and swept them across Evan's core, sending a jolt of pleasure through him and making Evan see stars.

"Not going to last," Evan panted, and Seth repeated the brush over his sweet spot, bringing Evan nearly off the bed.

Seth gave a lascivious chuckle, and withdrew, leaving Evan feeling empty. He reached for the drawer and grabbed the lube and a condom, making a show of wrapping up, rising on his knees so Evan could watch and stroking himself once or twice for good measure as Evan licked his lips appreciatively.

"How do you want it?" Seth asked, his voice low and husky, a growl that went right to Evan's balls.

"Like this," Evan replied, running a hand along Seth's shoulder and up to touch his cheek. "I want to see your face." He grabbed a pillow and lifted his hips, sliding it beneath him. "Come here."

For just a second, Seth hung back, taking in the sight of Evan sprawled and open to him, and Evan glimpsed yearning and vulnerability in his eyes. Then Seth brought Evan's legs up, pressing the slick head of his cock against his tight ring of muscle, and sliding in as Evan gasped against the intrusion.

Despite the prep, it burned. Seth's cock was long and thick, and it stretched Evan and filled him. Evan knew he'd be feeling their coupling tomorrow, wanted that reminder as much as he coveted the marks of Seth's fingers on his hip bones or the bites on his throat. Seth entered him slowly, carefully, but Evan wanted it all, and he thrust his hips forward, fucking himself on Seth's hard shaft.

"Move!"

Seth picked up the pace, sliding in balls deep, then pulled back almost all the way and sank in to the hilt once more.

"Harder. Make me feel it. Make me yours."

Seth set a hard rhythm, and Evan wrapped his legs around Seth's waist, locking them together. Every thrust reminded Evan that they were together, alive, and as close as two people could be. This was real, and if Evan had any say in the matter, he intended to hold on to Seth long beyond this night.

"Close. Not gonna last much longer," Evan gasped, tightening his legs around Seth, grabbing the sheets in his fists.

Seth brushed his lips over Evan's, then dipped down to lick each nipple before drawing back and increasing his speed as they built to a climax. Evan reached between them, stripping his cock as his balls drew up and he felt his pleasure cresting.

"Come for me, Evan. Let me see you come," Seth murmured, angling to strike that perfect spot inside.

Evan cried out Seth's name as his body seized and hot seed pumped over his fist, white ropes that spattered his chest and neck.

"So damn hot," Seth groaned, and his rhythm stuttered with his impending orgasm, taking him a few more deep, hard thrusts until he gasped and his whole body trembled with the power of his release.

Seth collapsed on top of him, then angled to slide off to one side, still joined, legs tangled together. Evan stretched to kiss him, searching for his gaze in the near darkness.

"I meant what I said in the truck," Evan whispered. "Every word of it. I love you, Seth Tanner."

Seth raised a hand and stroked his knuckles against Evan's cheek. "I love you, too." His voice was wistful and tender, quiet as if he feared he might shatter a fragile moment. Evan tried to understand the swirl of emotions he saw in Seth's eyes, wanting to make sure Seth not only heard, but believed. Seth shifted, pulling out carefully, then brushed his lips across Evan's and rolled over, pulling off the condom and dropping it in the waste can. He went to the bathroom and returned with a warm cloth, carefully wiping off Evan's belly and between his legs, gentle and intimate.

A million questions warred in Evan's mind as Seth pulled him against his chest, but he forced them back, knowing that daylight and the aftermath were not far away. Evan settled against his lover, resting his head on Seth's shoulder, safe and warm beneath the blankets. He breathed in Seth's scent, tasted him on his lips, felt the proof of their joining deep inside. Evan slipped one hand over Seth's chest, splaying his fingers over his heart.

"Gonna be right here," he murmured as his body finally succumbed to the events of the day. "With you."

"Go to sleep," Seth replied. "Morning will come soon enough."

EPILOGUE

SETH

Sunlight streamed through the window of the trailer's bedroom, telling Seth they'd slept well into the morning. He lay curled around Evan, protecting him, snuggled up against Evan's back with an arm across his chest and their legs tangled. The press of Evan's naked ass against his morning wood made him harder than usual, but he didn't move to do anything, not wanting to tarnish the memory of the perfect night before.

Even if he knew that, come daylight, all dreams had to end.

Reluctantly, Seth untangled himself, leaving Evan beneath the covers with a gentle kiss to his shoulder. Seth moved silently to get dressed, then headed to the kitchen.

He relived the battle in the tunnel as he started the coffee and set out bacon to cook. Seth could still feel his fear for Evan's life, his fury at Jackie's betrayal, and the cold satisfaction from being the instrument of Valac's destruction. Yet the victory itself felt hollow if all it yielded was Valac's death. Before he'd come to Richmond, seeing the witch-disciples brought to justice was all that mattered to him, the single purpose that kept him from giving in and joining Jesse.

All those things still mattered. But the feelings Evan woke in him meant even more. For the first time, Seth realized how alone he'd been, now that he had something so much better for comparison.

Last night, drunk with the adrenaline of the fight, the high of not dying, they'd made promises, and Seth had put into words what he'd never expected to say out loud. Their lovemaking had been tender and passionate, then hard and unrestrained as terror and relief stripped away inhibitions. He knew without a doubt that he loved Evan Malone more than he'd ever loved any partner, more than he thought it was possible to love someone.

And now that it was daylight and the threat was defeated, Evan would certainly realize that he could do much better than Seth.

He bustled around the kitchen, trying to fight back the heartache he knew was inevitable. Seth braced himself for Evan's change of heart, as the scenario played out in his imagination. Evan would come into the kitchen quiet and subdued, they'd make small talk, and then at some point, Evan would thank him for saving his life, and say once more than he really cared about Seth, but that they were better off going their separate ways.

Seth would be quick to agree—maybe too quick to hide his pain—because of course, Evan would be better off without him. Evan would tell him to stay in touch and stop by when the road brought him through Richmond again, knowing it wouldn't happen. Seth would lie, knowing that he couldn't come back here without breaking his heart again. They'd chat about nothing a few minutes longer, and then Evan would get his bag and Seth would drive him downtown. Seth would come back too gutted for even a bottle of Jack to dull, hitch up the trailer, and head to the next city where there might be a witch-disciple.

"Morning." Evan stood in the doorway, sleep rumpled and handsome. His dark hair was a sex-mussed tangle, stubble shaded his cheeks, and more gold than usual flecked his hazel eyes. Seth's heart clenched. He wasn't ready to live the reality of the scenario he envisioned. *Not yet. Just let me keep him for a little longer.*

"Morning," Seth replied, hoping his voice sounded steady. As much as he wanted to fight for Evan, argue his love, he knew that he had nothing to offer. *If I really love him, I'll do what's best for him, even if it kills me.* He plastered on a smile and looked up from the pan. "Hungry?"

Evan's chuckle was filled with naughty promise. "Very. But a little tender, not that I'm complaining in the least."

Seth looked away, hoping Evan didn't see him swallow hard. "Bacon's almost ready. I'll have eggs in a few minutes—"

"Don't do this."

Seth turned, surprised. "Do what?"

"You're talking yourself out of what happened last night," Evan said, padding closer. In the tight galley kitchen, Seth felt crowded, although Evan remained out of reach. "Telling yourself that it won't work, that I won't stay, that it wasn't real. Please, don't."

"Evan—"

"I love you, Seth. Yes, you infuriate me sometimes. But I think that goes with the deal," he added with a lopsided grin. "You are crazy and brave, kind and strong, and you don't let anything stop you when you put your mind to it. And I can't imagine ever being without you."

Seth put down his spatula and turned off the stove. He forced himself to look at Evan, hoping he could put on a courageous front. "Evan, think about it. I've got nothing to offer you. I'm a drifter who fights bad guys no one else believes in, and the odds of me making it to thirty suck." He sighed and shook his head. "You can go back to a real life, where you're safe—"

"A real life?" Evan challenged. "I've got no home, no job, and one of my co-workers just tried to sacrifice me to an evil warlock. My family isn't even in the picture. I tend bar, Seth, because I'm awful at waiting tables. That's not a life; it's a holding pattern." He closed the gap between them. "We can do this, together. I can help you research, and watch your back. You can teach me about magic, and we'll go after those other sons of bitches—together. Do something that really makes a difference."

Evan brought his hands up to cup Seth's face. "Don't push me away, Seth. Please don't. I want to stay here, with you. I know what I'm doing, how I feel. You don't get to decide for me, unless you didn't mean what you said last night." He stood only inches away, too close for Seth to evade his gaze. "Did you mean it?"

Seth's rehearsed denials crumbled. "You know I did," he murmured, fearing Evan saw far too much in his eyes. "I love you. I just want you to be safe. I thought he'd killed you. I can't lose you again."

"You won't," Evan promised.

"You don't know that."

"And you don't know that I'd be safe without you," Evan countered. "We're stronger together. I'm safer with you than anywhere else, and I'll be here to protect you, too." He stroked a finger down Seth's cheekbone, ghosting the tip over his lips, and Seth trembled.

"I want to do something that matters, Seth, not just spend the rest of my life slinging drinks. And I want to do it with you, *beside* you, partners. Nobody's ever made me feel like this before, and I'm not stupid enough to let a good thing get away." He brushed Seth's mouth with a light kiss. "Please, Seth. Let me stay."

Seth wrapped his arms around Evan, pulling him up tight against his body, answering with a bruising kiss. "I want you to come with me, but I'm so afraid you'll leave."

"And I'm afraid you'll get yourself killed," Evan replied, not trying to hide his tears. "So we'll just have to learn to trust each other, won't we? And if you get all 'noble' and try to leave me behind 'for my own good' I will hunt you down and follow you."

"Oh God, yes." Seth hugged him close, breathing in the smell of his hair, his sweat, and the musk left over from last night's sex. "Yes."

Evan started to chuckle. "If you're not careful, you're going to sit on the bacon."

Seth pulled away from the counter, never loosening his grip on Evan, and looked ruefully at the ruined eggs and the too-close pan of bacon. "I can start over," he said, "if you're still hungry."

"I'm starved," Evan replied, but the look in his eyes made it clear his appetite had nothing to do with food. "Why don't we start with a little sugar, and take it from there?"

Seth leaned in to kiss Evan, and his heart pounded at the warmth and want in Evan's response. Right now, in this moment, Seth had the victory he'd been looking for, and the promise of a future he'd never dared to dream could be his.

"Gimme that sugar," he murmured, cupping the back of Evan's head and drawing him in for another kiss. "Now that I think about it, breakfast can wait."

ACKNOWLEDGMENTS

Thank you so much to my editor, Jean Rabe, to my husband and writing partner Larry N. Martin for all his behind-the-scenes hard work, and my wonderful cover artist, Lou Harper. Thanks also to the Shadow Alliance street team for their support and encouragement, and to my fantastic beta readers: Mindy, Trevor, Andrea, Alexandra, Donald, Chris, Kris, Joelle and Maya, plus the ever-growing legion of ARC readers who help spread the word! Many thanks also to the fabulous Jordan L. Hawk, Rhys Ford, Charlie Cochet, Lucy Lennox, and Mary Calmes for their help, encouragement, and inspiration! And of course, to my "convention gang" of fellow authors for making road trips fun.

ABOUT THE AUTHOR

Morgan Brice is the romance pen name of bestselling author Gail Z. Martin. Morgan writes urban fantasy male/male paranormal romance, with plenty of action, adventure, and supernatural thrills to go with the happily ever after. Gail writes epic fantasy and urban fantasy, and together with co-author hubby Larry N. Martin, steampunk and comedic horror, all of which have less romance, more explosions.

On the rare occasions Morgan isn't writing, she's either reading, cooking, or spoiling two very pampered dogs.

Watch for additional new series from Morgan Brice, and more books in the Witchbane universe coming soon!

Where to find me, and how to stay in touch

Facebook Group—The place for news about upcoming books, convention appearances, special fun like contests and giveaways, plus location photos, fantasy casting, and more! : The Worlds of Morgan Brice

Twitter: @MorganBriceBook

Pinterest (for Morgan and Gail): pinterest.com/Gzmartin

Support Indie Authors

When you support independent authors, you help influence what kind of books you'll see more of and what types of stories will be available, because the authors themselves decide which books to write, not a big publishing conglomerate. Independent authors are local creators, supporting their families with the books they produce. Thank you for supporting independent authors and small press fiction!

Made in the USA
Monee, IL
16 August 2023